Carried on the Wind

By

Tom Nelson

First Edition

Carried on the Wind

By

Tom Nelson

Cover art by Robert Robbins

Copyright 2016

ISBN: 978-1512274509

www.wharhalen.com

Carried on the Wind

1

THE YEARS HAVE TUMBLED unstoppable down the steep and uneven hillside that is the span of my existence, so I hope that I can faithfully relate to you these events long past. Time is not only a thief of memories but also a great deceiver. It alters and distorts and conspires with those twin demons guilt and regret to create confusion in those things that we once knew for certain. I sometimes need to escape to a place of familiar serenity to view my years with sufficient clarity. There is a location high on the mountain that has given me comfort for much of my life and will continue to as long as I can still get there. Of course, now it takes nearly all day to reach that promontory, spend a couple of hours there and then make my way back down. At one time I could run all the way there and back down again before the sun reached its peak. Perhaps one of these days I will get up to that lofty perch and just stay. In time, my body will be found where I have spent so many peaceful hours.

I think men have always sought high places for contemplation. The view allows us to look at the world in a different way, a way that lifts us above our problems and makes them seem smaller. Being on the same level with soaring birds makes us more proud. And I think high elevations make us feel closer to God and heaven.

I remember the first time my father took me there. I was about eight, and poked along the footpath like young boys do, examining each insect that my sharp eyes would spy. I picked up sticks that became swords or spears in my hands, and rocks and trees were transformed into enemies to fight or creatures to be slain. Sometimes I would stray from the path to chase a butterfly or swing on a vine, and my father would sit patiently waiting for me to catch up.

When we finally broke into the clearing after our long climb and stood where a rock juts out over the steep drop-off, my unsuspecting gaze was arrested by the scene that spread out before me. It is the unison of parts that make a vista of great beauty, thus it is futile to try to construct in words what the eye takes in at a glance. But I will try to describe what my young eyes saw on that occasion, and what I hope my old eyes will yet see again with similar clarity.

After my initial wide-eyed consumption of the view that sprung upon my consciousness like nothing I had ever seen before, I began to examine the elements within it so as to fix them in my memory. In the center were the blue waters of the lake which runs roughly north and south through the valley. Visible at the north end were the roofs of houses clustered around its banks. The buildings are more numerous and cover more area now than on that day when I first saw the town as an eagle might. As my eye followed the course of the lake as it extended to the south, the sun reflecting off its rippled surface created first a white swath in the midst of the blue expanse, and then burst out from it in a thousand gleaming points of silvery light like stars on a winter's night. The southern end of the lake was too distant to make out, but filling the horizon in that direction were towering mountains raising their jagged peaks to the blue sky. The white cloak of snow covering the top of each one had shed its lower portion for summer, leaving ragged streaks of grey cascading down its slope like the tattered tunic of a beggar. Turning my attention to the opposite bank I could see a number of small open spaces in the otherwise continuous sea of dark green. Some were a paler shade of green where there were pastures, and others showed the tans and deep browns of the earth where the fields were cultivated. But most of the hillside that rolled away to the north was blanketed with a myriad of forest hues.

We didn't speak for the time that we sat gazing across that vast valley, each of us transfixed by the beauty before us and immersed in whatever thoughts it propagated within our minds. But as we were leaving to begin our descent back down the mountain I felt the need to express my appreciation to my father for sharing his place of contemplation with me. "It's wonderful," I said simply.

"Yes," he replied.

Walking down the narrow path between the towering trees that fragmented the bright sunlight into areas that were alternately warm or cool, my thoughts were turned more inward than on the ascent. Seeing the world from the broader perspective of the mountaintop had raised many questions in my young mind. "Who is king over all these lands?" I asked.

"Otto is king of all the Germans," my father answered.

"Where does he live?"

"In Saxony."

"He is a Saxon?"

"Yes."

"Have you ever met him, Father?"

"No, Otto just became king a year ago. I knew his father, King Henry, and I imagine I will soon meet Otto."

"Why?"

"The young king faces many difficult challenges. He will need the help of his vassals to stay in power."

"What challenges?" I asked, trying to use the same words as my father so as to sound more grown-up.

"Otto has three ambitious brothers. They may not be willing to let Otto have all the power. There is also the threat of the Magyars from the east. Their raids come deeper into German lands every year. To the west, the young French king faces difficulties of his own from the powerful noble, Hugh. There are disputed lands between East and West Franconia. And it is said that Otto has ambitions to conquer the Kingdom of Italy."

I thought about those things and it all sounded very confusing to me. In my young, simple mind I thought it would be much easier if there was only one all-powerful king in the world.

We lived in the town called Zurich in the Duchy of Swabia. Father received his lands from King Henry and therefore his first loyalty was to Henry's son Otto and secondarily to Herman, who was Duke. At the time of Otto's ascension to the throne, not all the dukes were pleased with Otto as absolute ruler, but Herman pledged his loyalty to the young king.

Father was gone for war service about two months a year and the rest of his time was occupied with administering his lands. All of the various industries of the community fell under his jurisdiction, as well as his duty to maintain a small corps of knights for the king. He particularly involved himself in agriculture. I think he liked that best, and often took me along as he walked the fields checking the soil, supervising the planting, inspecting the crops as they grew, overseeing the harvest, processing the grains, and storing them properly. I believe that he was liked and respected by the serfs for his personal involvement with all phases of their work. He also treated them well, and consequently, they worked hard for him and our community was always a prosperous one.

Of course, I found most of these things out as I grew older. At the time that my father and I first climbed the mountain together to look out over the lake, the valley, and the mountains, I had merely the thoughts of a child. The world was a place of wonders both real and imagined. From snakes that lay coiled under logs to the magnificent red deer that ruled the forests, I was enchanted by all of it. In my imagination both savage warriors and mythical monsters fell to my mighty sword. The world was mine to conquer, and I could see most of it from the top of our mountain.

2

The following year, father was called away for a time to help Otto put down a rebellion by Eberhard, Duke of Bavaria, and the king's half-brother, Thankmar. During his absence, I had a great deal of freedom to explore on my own. My mother, with a kind and gentle nature, had no inclination or will to suppress my boyish wanderings, and I was generally gone from her influence from dawn until dusk.

One of my favorite places to go then was about two miles from our home in the gently rolling hills that emanated out from the river valley. There, enclosed in a wide rim of forest, is a farm where horses are born, raised, and trained for various uses. It is a patchwork of green pastures that spread upward toward the higher elevations, fenced into sections that, almost always are dotted with small groups of the magnificent animals.

The farm is charged with the responsibility of supplying the cavalry horses that carry knights into battle. Although the number of knights kept standing at all times is generally small, it is still necessary to have a reserve of mounts for times in which a large army is needed. The farm also raises many large, versatile draft horses.

I was drawn to the horse farm by a strange attraction that, even now, I don't fully understand. Just being around the regal animals somehow seems both exciting and calming at the same time. My feelings, however contradictory, in a way match the mysterious temperament of the horses themselves. At one moment they can be as calm, timid, and gentle as a flock of spring lambs, and at another be frightening bundles of muscle, speed, and violence. Their explosions of aggressiveness or flight, chords of taut muscle responding with alarming quickness, can, at once, nearly stop my heart from beating but at the same time cause, within me, exquisite exhilaration. These tempests, which race through a herd like a wind-swept fire, can subside in an instant, like that same fire deprived of fuel. And then afterwards, as with a collective consciousness, all the individuals within the group return to a state of complete peace.

Filled with these feelings of wonder I would sit on a fence and watch the horses interact with each other and then drop down into the pasture to mingle with them. Their reaction to me varied. Some individuals were curious about the interloper within their midst and would walk over to me to investigate. Others eyed me warily and would move off in another direction. I wondered if horses, like humans, had different personalities—some more cautious and withdrawn and others more bold and outgoing. As I moved from pasture to pasture climbing fences as I went, I found that I could elicit different responses from the animals by how I presented myself. If I crouched low, for example, like a wolf, the horses would become alarmed and rush off until they had obtained some distance from me. But if I stood upright their reaction bordered on disinterest. If I walked toward a horse facing directly at him, he generally moved away from me. However, if I took a less direct route, never moving straight toward the individual, he would usually hold his position.

As a nine-year-old boy, I was fascinated by the different reactions I could cause in the huge, powerful animals by just the slightest changes in my behavior. I began to experiment with various postures. If I stood small and motionless, the horses would walk around close to me with mild curiosity. But if I puffed up as large as I could make myself and raised my hands in the air to appear even taller, the space between me and the horses would grow wider. In each instance I was the same person, but the horses were very sensitive to the differences in my appearance. I resolved to investigate this further. What I learned from watching and mingling with horses would become very valuable to me later on in my life.

In charge of the farm was an old man named Helmut. He was a large man (of course, everyone seems large to a nine year old), with white hair and mottled skin. Veins coursed red in his nose and forehead and both those features of his face protruded bold and bony. His ice blue eyes pierced and held your gaze like two fish hooks. In spite of a pronounced limp in his walk he still appeared strong and imposing. Adding to his fearsome visage was a jagged scar on the left side of his face and the absence of the last two fingers of his left hand. Helmut had been a knight in King Henry's army and had fought in the campaigns that brought Bavaria and Lorraine under Henry's rule. It was said that his most serious injuries came in a battle against the Magyars before the truce that halted the conflict for a time was negotiated. One of Henry's best riders, but no longer able to fight, Helmut returned home to Swabia where Duke Herman assigned him to a position that would allow the old knight to put his great knowledge of horses to good use.

I had been a frequent visitor to the farm by the time I first met Helmut. The other men who worked there regarded me with indifference as I hopped fence after fence to spend time among the horses. One day, however, as I was coming out of the pasture at the edge of the forest behind the barns, the old stable master was waiting for me. "What are you doing?" He asked; suspicion and accusation mingled in his tone.

"Watching the horses," I answered.

"Just watching?"

I nodded, unable to shake off his gaze.

"I don't want you bothering my horses. Besides, you could get hurt."

"I don't bother them. They think I am one of them if I act like a horse. And they aren't really your horses." I immediately regretted the last statement.

The old man's eyes narrowed. "Then whose horses are they?"

I was in deep now. "My father's."

"Who is your father?" Helmut asked, probably having already guessed the answer.

"Sir Ludwig."

His expression softened a little. "What is your name?"

"Max."

"Well Max, I don't think your father would be very happy with me if you were crushed under the hooves of one of his horses."

"They're careful not to step on me."

"Yes, horses are like that. They notice small things and know when they're not a threat. But if something startles them they could still accidentally hurt you. What did you mean when you said that you act like a horse?"

We were walking now. I shrugged. "You know, kind of shy." I dropped my shoulders, lowered my head, and turned away. When I straightened up and looked back at the old man there was a faint look of amusement on his face. When our eyes met, the look vanished and was replaced with a frown and a snort. He shook his head slightly. "Horses are dangerous. Does your mother know that you hang around here?"

"Yes," I lied.

"Well, stay outside the fences from now on," he said with the conviction of someone who knows that their directive will be ignored.

I continued to visit the horse farm from time to time throughout the summer and my presence was tolerated by the old stable master. Most of the time I was ignored, an attitude that emboldened my actions and allowed for deeper incursions into the operations of the farm. I watched the blacksmith at work as he fashioned shoes out of pieces of crude iron. I stood close by as they were nailed onto the horse's feet. I observed older boys carrying buckets of water, walking horses, and cleaning out stalls. It was an experience not only of sights but of sounds: the clanging of the blacksmith's hammer on his anvil, the voices of the horses as they called out to their companions, and the rhythmic pounding of hooves in the pastures. Add in the sweet aromas of horses, hay, straw, and manure mingling with wood smoke from the blacksmith's oven and all my senses were drawn into an enticing realm from which I had no resistance.

Summer gradually transitioned into fall. Father came home and soon was immersed in his responsibilities. Horses returning from the brief campaign joined the ones already in residence at the farm. Fall brought with it preparations for winter. The last cuttings of the hay crop were brought in. Wagons pulled by the huge draft horses arrived loaded with logs from the surrounding forests. The hunters went out daily to kill game that would help sustain us through the winter months.

As the winds grew colder and frequent storms kept me inside for many days at a time, my visits to the horse farm became fewer. But when the weather calmed at intervals and the snow wasn't too deep in which to walk, I would still wander up the valley to the farm that took on a different appearance in winter. The dark fences stood out starkly against pastures void of their green mantles and now snow covered. The horses were still turned out on most days when I was there and the cold air had an enlivening effect on them. Snow flew high in the air behind them as they raced each other from one end of the pasture to the other. The sprays of white left in their wake would sparkle in the sunlight for an instant before vanishing like stars at dawn. Regardless of their ages, the animals would seem to revert to foals again as they reared and bucked and kicked and got down and rolled in the fresh snow.

Some of the horse's work went on throughout the winter months. Sledges replaced the wheeled wagons to haul loads through snow that was on the ground from November to April. The horses grew heavy winter coats that became wet and matted when the work was hard. Clouds of steam billowed from their wide nostrils and the action of their knees was high as they churned through the deep drifts. Watching horses at work for their human masters was interesting, for

14

surely harnessing the power of these great beasts was one of man's most important achievements, but I still learned the most from watching horses when they weren't under the control of men, but simply interacting with their own kind.

3

The first time I saw Verena she was chasing a goat. I was walking along the stream that runs down to the river on the hillside northwest of the village. About a half-mile from the river, the water is diverted from the stream into a millpond, and then onward from the pond to the mill. On either side of the stream are gently sloping meadows. On that particular day, I saw a girl about my age tending a flock of goats among the red and yellow wildflowers that blanket the verdant hillside. It was a warm, sunny day in May and the girl's flock contained many exuberant kids that kept her busy preventing them from straying too far. One particularly adventuresome kid bounded far from the rest and headed toward the woods that borders the meadow on the upward slope. As the girl chased the misbehaving individual, the full skirts of her plain frock brushed the long spring grasses and made it hard for her to keep up with the kid. She lifted the ankle-length hem of the dress above her knees as she gave chase, and the curls of her long blond hair bounced along on her shoulders. Whenever it looked as if she might end the pursuit by catching the animal, it would change directions quickly and leave the poor girl grasping at the air.

It was a funny, charming scene and one that sticks in my memory, etched there for all time. I finally decided to come to the girl's aid and joined her in the chase. I tried to get ahead of the kid and succeeded in getting him turned back toward the girl. Still it eluded capture for a little longer, making us look foolish by dashing away each time one of us tried to pick it up. At last, when the girl and I were about ten feet apart, with the kid between us, it decided to give up on its escape plans and stood motionless while I scooped it up in my arms.

The little goat's sides heaved in and out following its exertions, but it settled contentedly in my arms. I finally got a good look at my partner in pursuit as the girl and I stood facing each other. Her fair cheeks were infused with color and strands of blond hair clung to her wet forehead. Clear blue eyes that rivaled the intensity of the sky looked out from under long lashes. A faint smile creased the corners of her strawberry lips and she held out her arms. For a moment I was transfixed as if by some enchantment. The spell was broken when the girl tilted her head and wiggled her hands as if to say, "Give me the goat you silly boy." I place the kid into her arms and stepped back. The image of that lovely girl, as fresh as spring itself, holding that equally innocent creature, is a memory that has never faded. Years later I realized that I loved her from that moment on.

That chance encounter ended with me mumbling something unintelligible and then continuing on my way down the path that followed the millrace. A day which had started out like any other had taken a strange turn that left me in high spirits but also more than just a little bit bewildered. We were ten.

The weather turned hot early that summer, and by June my friends and I sought respite from the heat by swimming in the lake. There was a spot not far from the base of our mountain south of the village where there were grassy banks leading up to the water and sheltering willows that kept us concealed. Our mothers didn't approve of our activity but I'm pretty sure they knew we did it anyway. Usually there were three of us, sometimes four. They were Albrecht, the son of Humbert, a knight who served in my father's army, and Dierk, whose father, Johann, was a member of the village guard. Sometimes Hilbert, who was a little younger than us, went too. His father had died fighting against the Slavs and so Hilbert never really knew him.

On the second time visiting our swimming place that summer, I heard splashing not far off to our right. At first I thought it was caused by shore birds or jumping fish, but then I heard voices. Our little cove was bordered by willows that reached their branches out over the water and dangled curtains of leaves that dipped into the lake. I swam over to the barrier and peeked through to the other side. In another, similar cove, three more children were swimming in the cool, clear waters of the lake. One was a boy, a year or two younger than Hilbert, but the other two, I quickly discovered, were girls. One had dark hair and the other the fair tresses and willowy form of the girl herding goats in the meadow. Verena was, even then, beautiful. With long, slender arms and legs, she was as graceful as a young deer come down to drink at the water's edge. Her skin was the color of apple blossoms; especially the parts rarely touched by the sun, and golden hair cascaded down her back.

As it turned out, this other group was as aware of us as we were of them. Occasionally they would swim over to the willow curtain and watch us for a time. Other than that, we never had anything else to do with them despite the fact that their visits to the lake were nearly as frequent as ours. I did find out, however, that the boy was Verena's brother, Niklaus, and that the dark-haired girl was Herta, whose father was a huntsman. I always felt a slight sense of disappointment on the occasions when we would spend an afternoon swimming and Verena wasn't there.

In August I was on my way to visit the horse farm when I came upon Verena at the edge of the woods through which the road passes on its course north of town. She was gathering the late summer berries from bushes on the fringe of the forest and was unaware of my approach until I was nearly past her. I recognized her at a distance for I had become, over the summer, quite familiar with the long blonde hair, the fair skin, and the graceful form that distinguished her appearance. Of course, I had never actually dared to talk to her save for the awkward first encounter with the recalcitrant goat. That time, however, Verena spoke to me first. "*Guten Morgen,*" she said, the inflection in her voice asking the question, 'Were you going to walk by without speaking?'

"*Hallo.*"

"Where are you going?"

Up to that point my excursions to the horse farm had always been solitary and unknown to my friends, so I hesitated before forming my reply. At last I decided that there was no harm in revealing my destination to the girl. After all, I didn't actually think she would be interested in going there. "I'm going up the valley to the place where they keep the horses."

Her face, already illuminated by the morning sun like a rose blossom, brightened with interest. "Oh, can I come with you?"

Taken off-guard by this unexpected response and seeking to deflect it, I stammered, "Well, it's a long walk."

The girl twisted her pretty face into a skeptical look and said, "So long that a *girl* couldn't possibly make it there and back?"

I shrugged and said, "Well, I guess it's not *that* far. If you want, you can come."

Verena looked around for a place to hide her basket, chose a spot under the spreading limbs of a tree and placed it out of sight by the trunk.

We walked for several minutes in anxious silence. The late morning sun bore down on the shadeless road and familiar summer sounds of birds, bees, and wind-rustled leaves were amplified by our lack of conversation. Finally, the girl said, "I'm Verena."

"Max," I replied, without looking up. "How are your goats?" I asked, stupidly.

"They're fine. My brother is watching them in the high pasture right now. He has our dog with him."

"Have you had any problems with wolves?"

"Not lately. We had a kid taken in the spring but in the summer the wolves have plenty of food and don't bother us much. Winter is the bad time."

More silence followed.

"Where do you live?" I ventured.

"If you take this road back, you turn left at the grove of chestnut trees before you get to the edge of the village, go up toward the mill and our house is by the little stream."

After a pause, she said, "I know that you live in *der Ludwigsburg*."

Before I could respond, Verena left the path and knelt down to pick wild berries. In a moment or two she came back with a handful which she held out to me. I took a couple and as we continued down the road we shared the fruit, which was sweet and juicy.

"Do you visit the horses a lot?" She asked as the farm came into view.

I shrugged and nodded yes, beginning to feel a bit more comfortable with my companion.

When we reached the little knoll that allows a view over the whole farm as it stretches up the hillsides from the valley, Verena stopped, as I often did when alone, to survey the scene. Her blue eyes grew wide as she scanned the verdant fields clothed in their mid-summer grasses with small herds of horses in each of them. I was watching her face, fresh and radiant in the warm sunlight as she turned, smiling, back toward me. "Can we go closer?" She asked with excitement.

"Of course," I said, leading the way down the hill.

I picked out a field that had several mares with foals turned out with a few older horses. We climbed up on the fence and watched as the young horses, which were now about four months old, exercised their long legs with bursts of speed. Each would run out from its mother, explore the boundaries of its small sphere and then, as though pulled back by an invisible tether, return to the mare's side. Occasionally one of the lively foals would attempt to play with another member of the herd. The baby would strike or nip or kick, but the older horses would rarely react to this harassment. Sometimes the victim might lower its head in warning or give the offending foal a gentle push with its nose, but even those actions were rare. The most tolerant members of the herd were the mothers themselves. They would suffer countless indignities from their babies that would have brought a swift retaliation from any other herd member.

Verena seemed to enjoy watching the horses as much as I did, especially the antics of the foals. Often, we laughed together at their comical actions. The time went by quickly, and soon the sun had passed its peak. "I'd better get back," said the girl with a sigh. "But you don't have to leave. I can find the way."

"I should get back too; I have some things I need to do," I said.

As we walked back toward the town, Verena said, "I can see why you like to go there. Do you think that I could go with you again?"

"Sure, if you want."

When we got back to the place where Verena had left her basket, she said, "I'd better pick some more before I go home or my mother will wonder what I have been doing."

I helped her fill her basket and then she said, "I'd better go now."

I shrugged as though it didn't matter to me. We walked a short way to the chestnut grove and Verena turned to go up the hill. I felt strangely sad as I watched her leave. About halfway up, she stopped and looked back over her shoulder at me. Embarrassed, I quickly turned and hurried away down the road.

4

Although the rebellion by Eberhard and Thankmar was unsuccessful, their defeat did not bring about an end to the threats to Otto's sole possession of the crown. Thankmar was dead but Eberhard joined with Otto's younger brother Henry to mount a new rebellion. Allied with the conspirators this time was the West Frankish King Louis IV who hoped to gain, from the conflict, dominion over the Duchy of Lorraine. Herman, still loyal to Otto, took his army into Franconia and Lorraine, and my father and his knights were part of that force.

Winter was slow to gain a grip that year, with only light snowfalls at the lower elevations. One day in December, Albrecht and I went out in the early morning to check our snares. It wasn't a particularly cold morning, and there was a light wind coming out of the south-west. The sky was mostly clear but for a few big, billowy clouds that moved overhead. The snow crunched under our feet as we walked into the forested hills that ranged out to the south from the town. We knew we had far to go that day so we had brought with us some bread and meat from the previous night's meal. Setting our snares farther from town seemed to improve our success at catching hares. Thus, we walked for a couple of miles, gradually gaining a higher elevation where the trees were mostly pines and the only footprints in the snow were those of the birds and animals of the forest. Most were small, like hares, foxes, and martens, but then we came upon some chamois tracks and followed them for a time, hoping to get a glimpse of the handsome antelope. We never caught up with him and our tracking took us off course for a while. By the time we got to our first snare (which was empty) we were hungry and sat down on a log to eat.

It was probably while we were eating that the clouds started moving in, but we didn't pay much attention to it. The sunshine of the morning hours was gone, but the air was still fairly warm for the season, and soon after eating all the bread and meat we had brought with us, we engaged in a running snowball fight among the pine trees that left us sweating and out of breath. We finally got back to the task at hand and moved on to the next snare, which had done its job, but the lynx tracks leading to and away from the site (with blood and bits of fur left behind) told the tale.

We were walking along the top of a ravine on our way to the third snare when Albrecht, who was leading the way, stepped in a hole concealed by snow and slid off the edge. Tumbling down the side of the ravine, he tried to gain his feet and got his right leg caught by a tree root. It twisted him awkwardly, and his fall continued down the slope before he came to rest in the small, rocky, stream at the bottom. When I got down to him he was writhing in obvious pain and holding his leg. He said, "I think my leg's broken. I heard it crack."

"Let's get you out of the water and then we'll look at it," I replied.

The water was shallow and I waded in behind Albrecht. I got my hands under his arms, lifted him out of the water and dragged him to the bank. He grimaced when I pulled his boot off but didn't make a sound. Once I had rolled up his pant leg, we were able to confirm what he suspected. The skin was broken on the side of his leg and a white bone bulged through the bloody break. "You're not going to be able to walk on that," I said resignedly.

We were both silent while we thought about the choices. "You could go back and get help," he suggested.

"It gets dark early. By the time I got back into town, organized some help and came back, it would be nighttime. And you would be pretty helpless out here with a broken leg."

Albrecht nodded. The unspoken fear was of wolves. The forest was full of them.

Finally I said, "I can build a litter and drag it out. Most of the way is downhill anyway."

It started to snow as I set to work on the litter. I cut two long poles with my knife and then several shorter ones. I lashed them together with pine boughs and covered the whole bed with more pine branches. It was finished in less than an hour. Once Albrecht was settled onto the litter I lifted one end to test it. It creaked and groaned under his weight but held securely. "The hard part is going to be getting out of this ravine," I said, looking up at the almost sheer sides of the cleft. "I'll follow the creek downstream for a while and see if there is an easier way up."

I started dragging the litter along the edge of the creek, and the going was hard. It was rocky and uneven, and very narrow in most places. The snow was falling heavily by then. We reached a point where the channel was blocked by large boulders, and I knew it was going to be impossible to pass any farther downstream. "I'll have to carry you to the top and then come back down for the litter."

Albrecht got off the litter and stood on one foot. He climbed up on my back, and I began the ascent to the top of the ravine. Finding footholds and moving laboriously across the slope, it took a long time to reach the upper part of the hill. Once we almost lost all of our gains when my foot slipped and I landed flat on my stomach with Albrecht on top of me. Fortunately, I was able to grab on to a couple of saplings with my hands and avoid sliding back down to the bottom. By the time we were able to rest on level ground my energy was completely spent and my legs ached. I lay sprawled out on the ground for a long time with the snow falling on my face. I knew we needed to keep moving if we were to get back to the town before dark, but I just couldn't move until I had recovered from the climb. Finally, I went back down to retrieve the litter. It didn't seem nearly as far going down. I had a length of string in my pocket for repairing snares, and I used it to tie the litter to my waist so that I would have both hands free climbing back up.

Once underway again with Albrecht on the litter, our next problem was finding our way. The snow was falling so heavily that it was impossible to see more than a few feet ahead. The trail had disappeared, and several times I got into heavy brush that was obviously not the way we had come. I had to double back and guess which way to start out again. By then it was late afternoon, and daylight was starting to wane in addition to darkness brought on by the snowstorm.

Suddenly, Albrecht whispered loudly, "Max! I saw eyes!"

I stopped pulling the litter and turned around. "Where?"

"Behind us."

I scanned the trees in the direction from which we came and at first saw nothing. Of course, the snow prevented seeing very far. And then, between the dark trunks of the pine trees, I saw them too. Crouching low was the large grey form of a wolf only twenty paces away. And I knew that there wouldn't be just one. I picked up a rock and threw it at the pair of eyes that gleamed from the growing darkness. They vanished. "They'll only get bolder," I said.

Albrecht drew his knife and fingered it nervously. I drew mine and searched for a long stick. On finding a suitable one, I lashed the blade to the end of the stick with the snare string. "Let's try to get a little farther. Keep watching for them to get closer."

We got about another hundred paces before Albrecht said in an urgent tone, "Max, I can see three of them now."

I set the litter down and turned to see three, then, four dark shapes emerging from out of the trees. I ran at them, shouting and waving my arms, and they stopped and retreated a little. The leader, only about fifteen feet away from me, growled and bared its teeth. I pointed my makeshift spear toward the crouching animal, my heart pounding and hands shaking badly. Snarling and snapping, he charged. I thrust my blade toward him but he was too quick. I missed badly and he was inside my defenses. I wheeled around and caught him on the side of his head with the butt end of my stick and knocked him off his feet. By then I realized that some of the other wolves (and by then there were at least six) had flanked me and were going after Albrecht, immobile on the litter. One of them lunged at him, and he slashed at it furiously with his knife. Another grabbed his leg and shook it, tearing away the cloth of his pants. I swung the spear and made contact with one of the attacking animals and plunged the point of my knife into the other. It made a terrible, piercing cry of pain but then I felt the teeth of another wolf rip into the back of my leg.

Two eleven-year old boys were no match for a pack of wolves. Looking back on it now, we should have died that day. But just when things looked darkest, men on horseback came crashing through the trees into the clearing, scattering the wolves. A search party had come out to look for us when my mother realized that I had been gone too long and night was coming. They had covered the distance from the town to us in less than an hour.

When you are young, the impact of such an incident fades pretty quickly. But later in life, you sometimes wonder if such a close brush with death has a larger significance. In any case, I still carry a couple of scars on the back of my leg from the affair, and Albrecht's leg didn't heal completely straight. He walked with a limp for as long as I knew him.

5

The rebellion of Eberhard and Henry, which was joined by Gilbert, Duke of Lorraine, and aided by Louis of France, was finally crushed by Otto's army. Eberhard and Gilbert were both killed in the fighting, leaving Henry little choice but to submit to his brother. Louis was forced to cede control of Lorraine to Otto.

That summer, Helmut decided that if I was going to hang around the farm all the time, then he would put me to work. I was handed a pitchfork and told to clean stalls and when I had finished with that I hauled water until my shoulders ached. If his aim was to discourage my presence at the farm, it didn't work. It gave me a sense of importance to have a job to do. My mother was dismayed when she saw the blisters on my hands and questioned why a noble's son had to do such work, but when my father returned from France and heard of it he approved. My father always felt that work done with the hands, especially when it came to farming, established a man's worth and earned him the respect of those he was to lead.

The foals that Verena and I had watched the previous year had grown into yearlings, and it was interesting to see the changes that gradually took place in the herd as these new individuals found their positions in it. No longer was their disrespectful behavior tolerated by older members of the herd or even their mothers. They still ran and bucked and kicked and sparred with each other, but when they invaded the space of an older horse with nipping or striking to gain attention, they were quickly put in their place with the threat of a bite or kick. If that proved ineffective, then the physical act soon followed. When this happened, the yearling would usually find its mother's side for security, looking sufficiently contrite until the next time. Through this process the young horse learned to respect individuals higher in importance in the group while still finding accommodation within the herd by its relationship to its mother.

About that time, Verena and Herta stopped coming to the river to swim, at least when we were there. I didn't fully understand it at the time, but I realize now it was because they were becoming young women. We let Nicklaus come with us to swim and soon he was included in most of our adventures.

Verena was still the only one who accompanied me to the horse farm, though, and I came to look forward to our walks together almost as much as visiting the horses. Verena seemed to enjoy going to the farm as much as I did or, at least, she acted like she did. Shortly after the chance encounter when I came upon her picking berries, we began to plan when and where we would meet. Usually it would be in the chestnut grove at the bottom of the hill below her house. That way, whoever got to the rendezvous point first could stay concealed among the trees and not make it so obvious to anyone passing by that it was a meeting place.

One day, when we were returning on the road from visiting the farm, Verena said, "Come, I want to show you something." We were about halfway back to the village, where the river turns gradually to the west. At first, when she left the road and went into the woods, I could see no way through the trees and brush. But soon we came upon a narrow path that was actually just the middle part of a much wider road, paved in stones. The edges of the road had long before been overgrown by grass and trees, leaving only a space wide enough for one person to pass at a time. After about fifteen minutes of winding our way along the mysterious path, we emerged from the tall pines into a large gap in the forest that indicated an area that was once cleared. Within the space were the ruins of a long stone wall. Beyond the low, crumbling rocks of the wall, there were the remains of a number of ancient buildings.

"What is it?" I asked.

"I've heard it called a villa."

"Who lived here?"

"Romans."

"Have you been inside?"

"Yes."

We stepped through a broken place in the wall into a courtyard paved in stones with grass and vines growing up between the cracks. The courtyard was a rectangle and the wrecked buildings comprised the perimeter of the complex. Centuries had passed since people had lived and worked in that place, and the roofs of the houses had long ago fallen away and decomposed. Only rows of weathered stones betrayed the outline of the rooms of what looked to have been a fine dwelling. One of the things that was confusing to me was that some of the floors appeared to have been built on brick pylons that would have created an empty space below them. I wondered what could have been its purpose.

As we moved from the area of the suspended floors we came upon a large basin covered in dirt and mud. Varena's foot slipped while she was stepping down into it and she almost fell. She smiled self-consciously and walked on, but in the mark that her foot left in the mud I noticed a glimmer of color. I scuffed away some more of the mud with my boot and found that the bottom of the basin was paved in small colored tiles. I picked up a sharp-edged piece of debris (which might have been roofing material) and started scraping the layer of mud from the floor. Verena saw what I was doing, and joined in. After a few minutes we could begin to see that the tiles which covered the bottom of the basin made up a pattern, although the space that we had uncovered was too small to reveal whether the pattern was a picture of something or just a design. We resolved to come back and uncover more of the tiles another time.

Another building on the perimeter of the courtyard appeared to have been for storage, having a large open space and a dirt floor, and a fourth structure had the remnants of posts as a part of the construction of stalls to contain animals.

We spent perhaps an hour exploring the ruins of the villa and the sun was descending rapidly toward the horizon. "We'd better go," said Verena, a little wistfulness betrayed in her voice.

As we crossed the low, weed-entangled wall in a different place than we had entered, I stepped on something that made a crunching sound. A quick examination of the spot revealed a large quantity of broken pottery shards. As I carelessly sifted through the pieces, I found that many of them had raised images of plants, animals, and people. The images were only partial, none of them surviving intact, but presently I found one that had a whole image of a female form, with wings but no clothing. It was quite beautiful and I had never seen anything like it. Verena was standing beside me and looked over my shoulder at the remarkable object. "It's lovely," she said, moving closer to get a better look. We gazed at it together for a long moment, whatever thoughts we had in our young minds remaining forever concealed. Finally, I reached out and folded Verena's two soft hands around the piece. Our hands stayed joined for a few seconds, and I thought I could feel her tremble slightly. Unable to look directly into her eyes, I said hurriedly, "We'd better go now."

Verena placed the broken pottery shard in a place of concealment within the folds of her dress. The walk back to the chestnut grove was relatively a silent one. The sun was below the tops of the trees and soft, hazy light filtered through the towering trunks and settled on the woodland plants of the forest floor. Our return through the woods to the road seemed to take much less time than when we first walked the overgrown path to the ruins. Once back on the main road long shadows crossed our path and a few curls of smoke were visible in the distance as evening meals were prepared. When we passed the familiar chestnut trees and were about to go our separate ways, Verena looked around to see if anyone else was in sight, and then quickly kissed me on the cheek. In another second, she was running up the hill, leaving me wonderfully perplexed.

6

During the first summer that I worked on the farm, I constantly pestered Helmut to let me ride. His reply was that if I worked hard and did a good job, 'we would see.' In the meantime, Lanzo, another stable boy, and I took matters into our own hands. When we were done with our work in the afternoons, we would conceal a halter and rope under our shirts when we left the barn and go out to a distant pasture where the horses had been turned out for the night. We would pick out a pair of sleepy wagon horses (neither of us was bold enough to attempt to ride the chargers) and put the halters on them. Then we would lead them to a fence that we could use to gain the height that we needed to mount. Once on, we could experience the exhilaration that only comes from being on the back of a horse. We would have races (very slow races), charge at make-believe enemy lines, and stage mock battles with sticks serving as weapons.

Lanzo was a year older than me but about the same height. He had a wiry build and a mop of curly, dark hair. His blue eyes darted about constantly, apparently looking for trouble to get into. His father was a trader and spent a lot of time away, especially during the summer months. Lanzo was boastful and fearless and liked being a leader. He wasn't, however, very good at catching horses. Once he found that I could catch the horses in less time, he would let me go out into the pasture first, halter his horse and take it back to him.

Unfortunately, our secret riding adventures came to an abrupt end one day when, during one of our more spirited horseback battles, Lanzo fell off and broke his arm. It wasn't the first time one of us fell off; actually, it happened a lot. Usually, we just laughed about it and then led our horse over to the nearest fence and got back on. But that time, Lanzo just happened to come down awkwardly on his elbow, and it was obvious that he was hurt. The injury must have been really painful because Lanzo didn't like to show weakness. His face turned white and beads of sweat broke out on his forehead as he tried to remain stoic. While I took the halters off the horses and returned them to the barn, Lanzo went home, making up a story about how he fell climbing over a fence.

Deprived of the friend from whom I derived much of the courage that I needed to take such risks, I thought about quitting the secretive riding sessions. But the lure of the horses was too great and soon after Lanzo's accident, I was back out in the pastures riding in the faint light of dusk. Our riding methods had not been complicated. We gripped the horse tightly with our legs to stay on, kicked with our heels to go forward, jerked the rope reins right or left to turn, and pulled back to stop. But after the accident, when it was just me alone with the horse, I began to explore different ways in which to communicate with him. I discovered that the horse was much more sensitive to my actions than I had previously assumed and that my movements could communicate my wishes with a lot more efficiency. I gradually scaled down the amount of pressure that I used to get a reaction, and started releasing the pressure as soon as I got the desired response. By timing the release of pressure precisely at the moment the horse tried to do what I wanted, there was a lot less confusion on the part of the animal. I suppose that rather than educating the horse in what I wanted him to do, he was actually educating me on how to respond when he was doing things right.

I started this process with the reins. At first I was giving the horse some unintended signals. I was pulling on one rein but not releasing pressure on the other one. The best responses that I got were when I put pressure on one side of the halter while giving a release on the other side. Using this method, I was able to get the desired response with such a small amount of pressure that it seemed like I was barely doing anything at all. By teaching the horse to move away from pressure, I was eventually able to get him to turn with just the slightest of rein contact with his neck.

I then turned my attention to the way I used my legs. If the horse moved away from the pressure of the reins, then, I reasoned, would the same thing work with leg pressure? I began by pressing in with my leg on the side away from the direction that I wished to turn, and I also tried moving my other leg away from the horse to allow him to move that way. I think the horse could sense my change in body position as I moved my hands and legs to signal the way I wanted to go, because I could gradually get reactions with less and less movement. As my balance improved, I didn't have to grip as tightly with my legs all the time to keep from falling off.

During those times, I always rode the same horse. He was gentle old wagon horse with a cooperative nature. Using the horse behavior that I had learned by observing the herd, I approached respectfully when I caught him in the pasture and kept him at ease by trying to stay calm and self-assured when I was handling him. Over time, I was able to build up a level of trust with him, and communication between us improved with each day.

I grew to love riding. Not content with riding in the pasture with the other horses distracting my mount, I began taking the old horse outside the fence and exploring the countryside. At first the old horse would grow a little agitated when I would take him from the herd and lead him out of the pasture. But once it was just the two of us traversing meadows, crossing small creeks, and padding softly along on layers of pine needles in the forest, the old fellow seemed to trust that I would always lead him safely.

Since I had to ride after activities at the farm had ceased for the day, my rides were always shorter than I would have liked. The long days of summer, however, still provided me with enough waning daylight to spend perhaps an hour on horseback each day. The evenings were cool and still and the changing colors of the sky as the sun moved toward the tops of the hills were different every night.

During that time, Otto continued to consolidate his power through family ties and arranged marriages. He made appointments based on loyalty and faithful service, sometimes passing over nobles who felt their lineage entitled them to advancement. He arranged for his sister Gerberga, widow of Gilbert, to marry Louis IV, thereby solidifying the alliance with France. The King's brother, Henry, however, continued to be a problem, plotting with Archbishop Frederick to have Otto assassinated. Fortunately, the king discovered the plan in time and Henry was arrested.

When I was older, I learned that Otto's reign was quite different than his father's had been. Under King Henry, the dukes were allowed complete internal control of their domains as long as they acknowledged his position as their superior. The kingdom was a confederation of duchies, and Henry was chosen by his peers to lead. Unlike his father, Otto accepted anointment by the Church and felt that he governed by divine right as unquestioned monarch. Also, in a departure from the practices of his predecessors, he did not feel compelled to share the kingdom with his siblings.

The complex workings of politics were, however, beyond my understanding and in my youthful desire for simplicity, things were precisely as they should be: Otto was absolute king of the world as I knew it.

7

About a year after Lanzo and I had started secretly riding the horses in the far meadows after work, Helmut came into the barn where I was cleaning stalls. "Max," he said, "when you are finished here come and see me. I'll be over at the blacksmith shed."

Of course, I thought I might be in trouble. What else does a fourteen year old boy think when an adult wants to talk to him? My mind sought answers to yet unasked questions about acts that I may or not have committed. Finally, I could delay the meeting no longer and walked across the yard to the hot, smoky blacksmith shed. Hammers and anvils clanged rhythmically, and fire belched from the large iron stove. The hissing of hot iron being cooled in troughs of water created clouds of steam which mingled with billows of wood smoke. I found Helmut talking with Jochim, one of the men who trained the young horses. I had watched Jochim breaking the colts ever since I had been coming to the farm and thought I would like to do that when I was older.

I waited at a respectful distance until the men finished their conversation, and then Helmut indicated with a tilt of his head that I was to follow him. We left the shed and walked a short way over to one of the pens where horses were broken to ride. The pens were round and had high wooden fences to discourage the young horses from trying to jump over the sides. We stopped at the third such pen which contained, not a young horse, but a large, old warhorse that I had seen before in the pastures. He was standing serenely at the edge of the pen, eyes looking sleepy, with his head down and one rear leg cocked in a relaxed posture. He was all black except for one white foot. The white extended only an inch or two above his right rear hoof. He had a large, handsome head, a slightly arched neck, and high withers. His back was still fairly straight, his hind quarters powerfully built, and his feet looked enormous. All this I took in at a glance, and then I quickly turned my attention back to Helmut.

"This is Diomedes. He is fourteen years old and has seen many battlefields. But now, when he carries the weight of a fully armored knight, he cannot reach charging speed. We think he has an injury to his left shoulder. The shoulder problem also keeps him from having any usefulness as a work horse. We cannot keep him here at the farm any longer if he has no job. But he can still handle a light load. You can have him to ride and take care of. Your father has agreed to let you keep the horse in his stable."

I looked at Helmut in what must have seemed like a state of disbelief. The old horse master nodded his head slightly in answer to my questioning look. My head swung back toward the horse in the pen. I looked at him more closely now. His black coat glistened as the sun's rays were reflected off of it. His sinewy muscles rippled in spite of his relaxed posture. His huge head had a noble quality. His overall appearance, which was somewhat common before, now seemed extraordinary in its beauty. "Can I…" I started.

Helmut answered, "Go ahead and see how you get along with him."

Resisting the urge to run, I went to the barn and got a halter and rope and returned to the pen to find that Jochim had joined Helmut at the fence. My stomach felt a twinge of nervousness. There was a good chance I would make a fool of myself. I struggled to keep my hands steady as I went through the gate and closed it behind me. 'Breathe' I told myself. Horses can tell when you're holding your breath.

Diomedes' posture changed slightly as I entered the pen. His head came up a bit and his left ear turned toward me. The half-closed eyes opened wider and the weight shifted on his rear legs. I approached to about twenty feet and then stopped. I turned my shoulders at right angles to him and waited. Diomedes' head turned almost unperceptively to examine me. I moved in to about ten feet and stopped again. He turned his head back away from me but watched me closely with his left eye. I moved to five feet but kept my head lowered and my eyes turned away. Diomedes sighed and licked his lips. I closed the remaining distance and put my hand on the powerful shoulder which was nearly at eye level. The huge black horse breathed rhythmically and his muscles were soft in relaxation. When I moved to his massive head he lowered it slightly and brought his nose around toward me. 'This is going pretty well, so far,' I thought. I slipped the halter over his ears and walked him over to the fence.

The great warhorse moved cooperatively along the fence for me and then I climbed up the boards to mount. But before I could get my leg over his broad back, he moved his hips away from me and left me suspended in mid-air. Mildly embarrassed, I got down from the fence, walked around to the horse's left side, and moved his hips back toward the fence. I tried again with the same result. The skin of my neck and face seemed hot as I got down again and moved the horse back toward the fence. I felt that I must be making him fearful by mounting from so high above him, so the next time I started a board lower on the fence and just put my foot on his back and left it there for a moment. When he relaxed, I took my foot back and moved up one board and repeated the process, just resting my foot on his back. Then, when he relaxed again, I slid my leg the rest of the way over. He stiffened a little, took a couple of steps forward, then came to a stop. His ears were turned back toward me, waiting for what I would tell him to do.

Diomedes' back was much wider than the wagon horse I had been riding, and I was definitely higher off the ground. I sat for a few seconds and then gently squeezed his sides with my legs. He responded instantly, and we were soon circling the small pen at a smooth rhythmic walk. I directed him through a few of the maneuvers that I had learned with the wagon horse and Diomedes deftly handled each command precisely. Growing more confident, I urged the black horse into a gallop and the surge from his powerful flanks nearly unseated me. Still, his responses to my cues were executed with a precision that belied his great size. Finally, I brought the horse to a stop at the gate, and he again stood motionless, waiting for my next directive.

I looked at Helmut, whose face seemed to display the faintest of smiles. "I guess all those evenings of riding our wagon horses has provided you with a pretty good education."

My eyes widened in surprise. 'How long has he known?' I wondered. I smiled sheepishly.

Helmut walked over to the gate and swung it open. "Go on home now and get your horse situated in his new home. You can work off the halter tomorrow."

My feeling of elation could not have been any higher on the ride home. I was perched atop a great warhorse looking down upon the world as if all I could see was mine to command. The horse was my own. There is no greater possession for a knight, which it was my destiny to be. I had dreamed of that moment from the first time I saw the wonderful chargers of the heavy cavalry carrying my father's knights as they rode off on campaign. My mind was full with thoughts of places to explore and adventures that lay ahead now that I had been liberated from the realm of ponderous foot-travel. In a burst of exhilaration, I urged Diomedes into a gallop and we flew down the old Roman road toward the town.

I rode through the outskirts of the village like a triumphant general leading his troops through the gates of a city to the cheers of an adoring crowd. Actually, I managed to elicit a few sidelong glances from some of the peasants who were finishing up their work at the end of the day. My greatest moment, however, came when I passed my friend Dierk, who shouted, "Whose horse did you steal, Max?"

"I didn't steal him; he's mine!" I answered proudly.

That night I slept the blissful sleep of one who knows that life can't possibly be any better, and the only dreams that you can possibly have will be pleasant ones.

The next morning I arose early, my excitement from the previous afternoon renewed. After a hurried breakfast, I rushed out to the stables half expecting Diomedes to be gone as though he were part of a fading nocturnal dream. But he was still there, standing in his stall with the patience typical of an older horse. When I opened the stall door, I waited for him to bring his head around to face me. I made a soft kissing sound with my lips and signaled with my hand that I wanted him to come to me. After a moment of thinking about this, he obliged my request and turned so that I could put his halter on.

I brushed the dust from his glossy black coat, and he let me pick up each of his massive feet to check for stones. All the horses in the stables, including Diomedes, had been fed earlier by Claus, the stable boy, so I was quickly on my way. Past the blacksmith shed, the tanners, the candle maker, and all of the other craftsman employed in the compound I rode, proud of my newly elevated status.

Again I elicited a few curious (I thought envious) glances as I passed the palisade fence into the village where the work of the day was just beginning.

Leaving the village, I tried to determine if the injury to my horse's shoulder was causing him any trouble. It certainly wasn't noticeable at a walk, so I urged Diomedes into a trot. His trot was a big, high stepping affair, and we covered ground quite rapidly on the hard packed road. Of course, the trot was difficult for me to ride without a saddle and I soon grew tired of bouncing, so I eased Diomedes back down into a walk. I could feel no inconsistency in his footfalls at the trot, and surely if the shoulder was giving him any pain it would have been apparent at that gait. I moved off on a gallop, as I had done the previous day, and his powerful stride was as smooth as I could imagine it. I felt it must have been as Helmut described, that the injury to Diomedes' shoulder was only a problem when he had to carry the weight of an armored knight or pull a heavy load.

As I galloped my horse into the countryside I saw, ahead of me, the familiar form of Verena with her usual basket in hand, picking berries just past the chestnut grove. Her long blond hair and fair features stood out against the dark forest background, and just her appearance seemed to brighten my day like the morning sun. I slowed to a walk as I approached her, and she looked up in surprise. "Max, where did you get the horse? Is he one of your father's?"

I shook my head. "He's mine. Helmut gave him to me yesterday."

The girl walked out of the brambles to the edge of the road and cautiously approached Diomedes' head. She put her hand out for him to sniff and then stroked him between the eyes. "He's beautiful. What's his name?"

"Diomedes. He was a warhorse."

"Will he go to battle again?"

"No. He has something wrong with his shoulder, but you can't tell it when you're riding him."

"So, I suppose we won't be walking together anymore?" Verena asked, her eyes downcast.

"No, I suppose not," I answered, starting to move the horse down the road and enjoying the moment a little too much. After a few feet, I stopped and looked back at my crestfallen friend. "Why would we walk when we can ride?" I said playfully. Verena's chin came up, and she cast a mildly irritated look in my direction.

"Climb up on this rock and I'll help you up." I said, moving Diomedes close to a large boulder that lay at the edge of the road.

Verena deftly scrambled up to a standing position on the rock, which brought her head about even with my shoulders. I placed my hand under her right arm and grasp it firmly. As she swung her leg over Diomede's back, her left hand went to my left shoulder. Seated firmly and close behind me, she placed her slender arms around my waist, and then playfully jabbed her thumbs into my stomach. "You're bad, Max," she said, "to tease me like that."

As I continued my ride down the old Roman road, with the lovely Verena seated behind me, her body pressed tightly against my back, I thought to myself, 'just when I felt that my life couldn't get any better, it just did.'

8

My walks with Verena became rides most of the time that summer. Often she would prepare food for us to take along on our little journeys, and we would be gone most of the day. Our explorations often included returning to the Roman villa to uncover more of its secrets. By that time we had revealed nearly all of the colorful mosaic on the floor of the bath. The pattern was made up of small colored stones, of which there were thousands. The image that emerged was a sea scene with a man who had, in place of his legs, the tail of a fish. He rode in a cart drawn by creatures that had horses' heads but fish-like bodies.

I wondered if there were other mosaics in the house and, on one visit, I started scraping the thick layer of dirt from the suspended floor of the main room. We discovered that there was, indeed another picture made up of small stones in that place as well. Over time our efforts brought forth a picture of a woman, perhaps a goddess, her torso partially draped, flanked on each side with long-tailed birds with colorful feathers. Farther out were winged creatures that looked like angels, but they were dressed in battle armor. The whole picture was framed in an elaborate multi-colored border.

Riding also opened up new and more distant destinations for our outings. One day late that summer, I started out in the early morning hours and rode to the horse farm so I could clean out the stalls that were my responsibility. On my way there Verena was waiting for me at the chestnut grove as she usually did. Diomedes had gotten quite accustomed to the routine and, with no direction from me, walked up and stood beside the rock that was just the right height for mounting. Verena handed me her basket, which held bread and cheese for later, and then climbed up behind me. As she interlaced her fingers in front of me and pressed her slender form against my back I asked, "When are you expected to come home?"

"I told my mother that I was going to help Herta watch her flock this morning, and then I would pick mushrooms in the afternoon before returning home. We have hours!" She replied in a voice that made her sound absolutely delighted with the little deception.

"Well, we'd better find some mushrooms before I drop you back off."

When we got to the farm, I released Diomedes in one of the grassy fields that ranged out from the central barn area, and Verena climbed up on the fence to pass the time while I was cleaning stalls.

I did my work quickly, deflected a comment from one of the other boys, Erhard, about my waiting companion on the fence, and then headed back to retrieve Diomedes. The great black horse seemed mildly irritated that I was back so soon and interrupting his grazing, but he stood absolutely still, and waited for me to tie the rope back on the halter.

Back astride the great warhorse, we rode on further north and west, following the old Roman road through the valley for several miles. We had been that way before, but that day we turned northeast up into the hills along what was probably a deer path. It climbed gently into the pine forest and then wound its way up and down, traversing the slopes and gradually reaching into higher elevations. We came upon a herd of mountain goats which, startled, ran off in a rumble of hoof beats. They quickly stopped, still within view however, when they realized they had nothing to fear, and resumed their browsing. Diomedes stiffened and raised his head during the incident, but his feet remained firmly planted. Certainly, he had seen much more frightening things in battle and was well-trained to resist the natural urge to run away.

By noon we had travelled many miles but barely realized how far we had come. We came upon a small brook that tumbled down a hillside, gurgling softly as it passed over the rocks in its path. Its course took it into a gently rolling meadow between hills. It was a perfect place to stop and eat our bread and cheese and to rest Diomedes. The horse drank deeply from the stream and then began grazing on the lush grass of the meadow. Verena and I knelt down by the edge of the brook, and cupping our hands in the cold rushing water, quenched our thirst also. We moved up to a fairly level spot on the opposite bank from where Diomedes was grazing.

We sat in the grass, and Verena took out the bread that she had brought. She broke off a piece and handed it to me. It was still soft and fresh, and it had been warmed slightly by the morning sun. She handed me a hunk of cheese, which I cut with the small knife I carried with me. We must have been hungry because we didn't speak at all until the food was gone. Verena sat gazing off in the direction of Diomedes, but her dreamy look didn't seem concentrated on anything at all. I studied the profile of her pretty face. The pale lashes above her blue eyes were long and curved. Her cheeks, slightly flushed by the sun, were round like apples. The downy fine hair over her upper lip was made visible by the gentle glow of the sunlight. I wanted to touch it but I resisted. Below the slightly parted lips was a fine crease that helped form her small, rounded chin.

Verena noticed my scrutiny of her face and, glancing quickly in my direction, she smiled self-consciously and blushed. I looked away. She lay down in the soft grass, and her golden hair surrounded her lovely face like a halo. I picked a tiny purple wildflower and placed it in between the strands of her blonde tresses. The wind blew a wispy strand of hair across her eyes. My hand moved to her face, and I gently laid the errant lock to the side. I touched her cheek with my fingers, and her eyes closed slightly in relaxation. She let out a little sigh. I leaned over and kissed her soft, sweet lips. The kiss lingered longer than I expected, and then Verena pressed her mouth more intensely against mine and I could feel the moist, inner part of her lips moving deeper. That kiss sent a throbbing sensation through my body. I didn't know what to do next so I lifted gently away and lay down beside her and stared at the clear blue sky.

For a while we lay there, each with our own thoughts, not speaking. Then, Verena turned toward me and put her head on my shoulder. I placed my arm around her as she nestled into my side with her hand on my chest. The mid-day sun was warm on our faces as we lay together, contented with the way the day had turned out. I felt drowsy, and Verena's head grew heavier on my shoulder. I thought I should check on Diomedes but I didn't want to disturb the girl.

I awoke to realize that the sun had gone down behind the mountains and the air had gotten much cooler. "Verena," I said, trying not to sound too alarmed. "We fell asleep. It's getting dark. We need to go."

Verena lifted her head, blinked a couple of times, realized how late it had gotten, and then rose quickly.

Fortunately, Diomedes had not strayed very far. He was still on the opposite side of the brook a little ways up the hill from where had left him. But there was no place to mount. I led him up the hill the way we had come with Verena walking along side of me. "I'm sorry," I said. "Your mother is going to be worried."

"It's not your fault. I'll just have to make up a story."

When we reached the forest, we found a rock that we could use to get on Diomedes' back. I wanted to hurry, but the terrain was uneven and the path uncertain so we proceeded at a painfully slow walk. In the meantime, light grew dimmer in among the trees as night approached.

When we were well into the forest, we heard the distant howl of a wolf. Diomedes' head came up, and he turned his ear to the sound. Verena held me tighter. The howl was answered by the voices of other wolves. "How close do you think they are?" Verena ask in a subdued tone.

"Still pretty far away," I answered, trying to offer assurance.

Diomedes' step quickened without any urging from me, and I let him break into a trot. The howls grew closer and shorter, indicating that the pack was on the move. Soon we couldn't hear the sounds at all, which I took to mean that they had picked up our scent and were hunting us. I pointed Diomedes in the direction that I thought we should go to get back to the road, but it was getting so dark and I couldn't be sure. To a large extent, I let him choose the easiest path, but several times Verena and I had to duck low to avoid tree branches. Suddenly, a howl came from just behind us as one member of the pack signaled to the others that we were in sight. Memories of the incident with Albrecht and the wolves were revived in stark detail in my mind. But I didn't have time to dwell on them. We were nearly to the edge of the forest, and I quickly scanned the trees to find the opening that would get us out. There was still some faint light showing between the trees, and when I spotted the path that I thought we should use I kicked Diomedes into a gallop. He didn't require much urging. With his ears back and nostrils flared, his powerful body surged beneath us. Perhaps I imagined it, but I thought I could hear the sounds of the wolves running through the forest behind us just as we burst out of the trees and on to the slope that led down to the Roman road. I didn't look back. Diomedes was in full flight. We hit the dry surface of the hard-packed road, and the sound of his hoof beats changed to a higher pitch. It was marginally lighter once we were out of the trees, making it easier to see the boundaries of the road.

We continued to gallop until Diomedes began to tire. I let him down into a walk and then looked back to be sure that the wolves had given up the chase. It was hard to see anything in the dark, but I was pretty sure that we were no longer being pursued. "Are we safe?" The question came in a whisper.

"Yes. I think we are," I replied.

Verena put her head down on my back and hugged me tightly.

"I'm sorry," I said after a few minutes.

"Why?"

"For putting you in danger."

"I was never in danger. I was with you."

I smiled, but Verena couldn't see me.

"Besides," she continued, "that was so exciting! The feeling...well, riding that fast on Diomedes was like nothing I've ever experienced. It was like being carried along on the wind."

When we reached the chestnut grove, I turned Diomedes up the hill toward Verena's house. She said, "I can walk the rest of the way. You should start home."

"No. I'm not going to let you walk up the hill in the dark. It won't take long for us to ride to your house. Have you thought about what you are going to say?"

"Something will come to me."

When we rode up to Verena's house, candles from within spilled their light out into the night. A woman appeared the doorway. Verena slid down off Diomedes. The woman said, "Thank God you're back. I didn't know what to do. What happened?"

Verena spoke assuredly, "I got lost in the woods looking for mushrooms. I wandered around for hours. Finally, I found my way back to the road but I was far from home. Max came along on his way back from the horse farm and gave me a ride."

Verena's mother came out. She was a tall, slender woman with light hair held back with a scarf. It was hard to make out her features in the darkness. "Thank you Max," she said. "It was fortunate that you came along when you did."

"I'm glad I was able to help. I'd better go home now." I started to turn Diomedes.

"Where do you live?"

"In the village," I said back over my shoulder, hoping to avoid any more questions. I headed back down the hill and wondered how Verena was going to explain why there were no mushrooms in her basket.

9

The first time I noticed the mare was when she was turned out with a large herd of mixed age horses, some yearlings, some two-year olds, and several older mares. She stood out, not just because of her grey color, but also her attitude. Her ears were always laid back tightly to her head, her eyes were narrow and mistrustful, and she stood apart from the rest, showing very little energy or playfulness. Occasionally, one of the other horses would trot over to her and drive her off a short ways. Most of the time, this display of dominance would take the form of just a threatening gesture. But sometimes, if the grey mare didn't move quickly enough, the aggressor horse would bare its teeth and bite her on her neck or side. The victim would then retreat, throwing out a rear leg in a futile attempt at kicking her attacker. As a result, the mare always had a number of crescent shaped marks on her grey coat from the frequent bites.

I decided to watch this mare in various situations around the farm to see if she was always treated this way. It was late winter and because there was no grass to sustain the horses, they had to be fed hay from large stacks which were put into pens. The horses ate from the stack and in behavior normal for them, the dominant individuals would hold off the lower ranking horses for a time before settling into feeding. In these situations, the grey mare was always crowded out and driven away by the group and was the last animal to be let in to eat.

While I was watching this unfold, Helmut walked past the pen and I asked him about the grey mare. "She's an orphan. Her mother died in foaling. We should have let her die too, but the only one who was around at the time was a stable boy who didn't know any better. Orphans never amount to anything, but somebody always wants to try to save them. She's two now, and no one has been able to train her to do anything useful. I don't like to kill sound horses, but we can't go on feeding her forever unless she can be trained. The problem is that the trainers are too busy with the good horses to spend any time with her."

I looked at the mare again as she meekly gathered a few stalks of hay off the ground while keeping a wary eye on the horse next to her. "Can I try to train her?"

"I don't see why not. Just be careful. Don't expect her to act like a normal horse."

Helmut walked away, and I stayed at the pen for a long time thinking about possible reasons why an orphan horse would act differently from a "normal horse." I thought back to my observations of the mares and foals in the pastures. The mare corrects the disrespectful behavior of the foal while it is still young. But at the same time, the mare protects the baby and helps it find its place in the herd. Without a mother, not only does the foal not learn to act respectfully around the older horses, it also becomes something of an outcast, occupying the lowest rung on the herd ladder.

When the feeding was over, I asked that the grey mare be left in the pen while the other horses were let out. I took a halter and a length of rope with me as I entered the pen. The mare eyed me warily through her narrow, mistrustful eyes but stood still. I stood by the gate for a few moments without making any movement toward her. Gradually, I moved a little closer and then stopped again. When I was about twenty feet away, the mare turned and came toward me with her head lowered. As she approached her head started to bob up and down, and when she was nearly upon me she laid her ears back and bared her teeth to bite. I dodged this attempt and moved away from her. As she passed, she kicked out at me threateningly with one rear hoof.

I waited a few minutes before trying to approach the mare a second time. Again, at about twenty feet, she came toward me with her ears back. This time when she got close, she struck out with her front feet. I was slow to move away and one of her hooves struck my leg just above the knee. In pain and anger, I swung the halter at her and caught her on the neck as she raised her head. I drove her away from me, and we stood at an impasse some distance from each other. That didn't last long because soon she came prancing toward me again with her front hooves flying. I quickly pivoted away from the path of her attack and got around to her side where I was, at least, away from her hooves and teeth. She stopped and appeared confused. She tried to turn on me, and I again moved around to the area behind her front legs. Again she stopped. I tried to recall the way horses approach each other. If they approached from the rear, they risked getting kicked. If they approached head-on they faced striking and biting. I decided that the best way to dis-arm a horse is to stand at its side.

I tried to put the halter on her. She tossed her head up and down, and she backed up. When I persisted, she reared up, and when she came down her jawbone hit me on top of the head. My temper again flared, and I swung wildly at her with the halter. She deftly avoided my attempt at hitting her and moved away to the other side of the pen. When the pain in my head started to subside, I tried to think more clearly. I thought perhaps the mare was trying to dominate me like she had been dominated by the other horses in the herd. I felt that I needed to gain her respect. I decided to make her move in the way the other horses made her move. I approached her with the end of my rope twirling and then threw it at her rear end. She took off at a trot around the pen. I didn't chase her because I didn't want her to think of me as a predator so I stayed in the middle of the pen and kept using the rope to urge her on. When she would try to stop, I would take a few steps toward her and toss the rope, and she would take off again. After a while she appeared to get tired, and she dropped her head down close to the ground. I let her stop. I slowly approached and stood at her side as I had done before. I reached out and touched her on the neck. Her muscles quivered a little bit, but she didn't move.

I turned my back to her and started to walk away. She followed me for a few steps and then came up fast and pushed me with her nose. I spun around, throwing up my arm defensively, and she moved out of my space. I decided that I needed some more time to think. I left the pen with the mare standing near the gate watching me go.

I didn't know if the mare's intention was to drive me away or to connect with me. Were her actions based on fear or a desire for companionship? I went out to the pastures to watch a group of horses mingle among each other. I wasn't there long when I noticed two individuals with their heads close together. As they nipped playfully at each other, their heads bobbed up and down in the way that the grey mare had done with me. Suddenly, one of the horses, who perhaps thought she was getting beaten in this little game, reared up slightly on her back legs. The nipping stopped temporarily, and the two horses walked off together to graze. I realized that the mare's behavior toward me was exactly as it would be with another horse. I decided then that horses regard people (and other animals) as either herd members or predators. I resolved to try and see my actions as the mare would see them.

The next day I again separated the mare from her herd-mates into a pen. When I entered the pen I took an armful of hay with me. I knew that the leader of the herd controls the food, water, and space. The leader eats first, drinks first, and decides which horses stand where. I walked up to the mare and stood in the safe zone behind the front shoulder. She shifted her weight slightly in readiness to move, but stayed where she was. After a minute I offered the hay, which she took. While she was eating, I stayed very close to her, stroked her, and even draped my arm across her back.

I placed my rope over her neck and grasped it beneath her chin with my right hand. I then offered the halter in front of her nose. When I started to pull it up over her ears, she tossed her head and backed up a couple of steps. I still had the rope around her neck, and I tried the halter again. She raised her head but didn't back up. Finally, I got the halter tied around her head and switched the rope to the halter. I walked off ahead of her and she followed. I was feeling quite proud of myself when, suddenly, she bit me on the shoulder. As I wheeled around to fend her off, she bolted sideways in quick anticipation of my reaction. I moved closer to her, trying not to act threateningly. She nipped at my arm and again lifted her head sharply before I could react. She was playing the nipping game and probably thought I was going to try to bite her back. I decided that the only way I was going to put a stop to this was to act like a herd leader and move her out of my space whenever she tried to bite me. So the next time she brought her mouth toward me, I pulled the rope toward her hindquarters and swung the end of it at her rump. Her back side moved away from me and we made a tight circle around where I held the rope with my left hand. When we stopped circling, she stood motionless for a moment. As we walked off again she repeated the attempt at biting, and I again reacted by making her back feet move over. We went through this a third time, and the biting stopped. We walked around the pen a few more times and I decided to end the session while I was being successful.

That night at home I asked myself what it was, exactly, that I needed to do to make the orphaned mare accept me as her leader. If the leader controls the space within the herd, then I reasoned that, in order to control her, making her move her feet when she wanted to stand still was the simplest thing I could do that would make sense to her as a horse. Letting her stand still would be the reward for doing the right thing, and making her move would be the punishment for doing the wrong thing. Doing anything more severe, anything that would inflict pain, like when I hit her with the halter, would only make her more afraid of me, as she was of the other horses that were always biting her.

The next morning my thoughts raced ahead to training the grey mare while I got Diomedes ready for our ride out to the farm. There was a heavy fog over the valley as I rode along the old Roman road, foretelling good weather. Thoughts of Verena sprung forth in my mind as I passed the chestnut grove, thoughts that were always pleasantly disturbing. But even these were quickly dispelled as the details of working with the mare came to the forefront of my mind again.

The mare was separated from her herd-mates into the pen as before. As I entered the pen with her, she appeared to ignore my presence, but her left ear betrayed her as it turned toward me. Standing near the center of the area, I squared my shoulders to her rear end and flicked the end of my rope at her. Her head came up, and she made a little jump forward. I took a step toward her and wiggled the rope some more, and the mare took off at a trot around the edge of the pen. Staying in the center of the circle, I turned with her, swinging the rope in a lazy circle and keeping her moving. After three times around the pen, I moved toward her path when she still had about half a circle to go and blocked her progress. She came to a stop. I immediately swung the rope again and she began to circle in the other direction. I moved back to the middle of the pen and kept her going for another three times around. I repeated the change of direction one more time. I felt that it was important for me to control the direction of her movement, otherwise it would seem like she was just running away from me.

I let her come to a stop and approached slowly. I had made a loop on one end of my rope, and I opened it with my right hand. The mare's sides were heaving slightly from the exertion of going around the pen. Her head was down submissively, and she brought her nose around to sniff my hand. I brought my right hand over her back and stroked her on the side of the neck. I then slipped the loop over her head so that it was around her neck. I offered the halter in front of her nose, and she immediately balked and started tossing her head. With my left hand on the rope near her neck and my right waving the end of it I moved her hips away from me as I had done the previous day. We circled a few times, and then I let her come to a stop. I offered the halter again, and she let me put it on.

From that day onward, I didn't have too much difficulty training the orphaned mare. Occasionally, if she started acting irritable because of something that I was doing, I would make her move in a circle and then she would decide that rather than do all that extra moving, it was a lot less work to just cooperate with me. Gradually, over time, her whole attitude changed. Her eyes grew softer, she became less sullen and defensive, she even began to show the playful side of her nature when she was around me. A bond formed between us as her trust grew. I believe now that her aggressiveness stemmed from wanting the attention that her mother was never around to give her. I named her Analie, after a girl that I knew in the village who had lost her mother when she was seven years old. I don't think the girl ever knew that she had a horse named after her, but to me, it seemed appropriate.

10

Analie's training continued on into the following summer, and by then all the talk about how I had taken the un-trainable orphan and turned her into a reliable mount had died down entirely. I did notice, however, a difference in the way the older horsemen regarded me. Actually, the difference was that they regarded me at all. Before, I was just a nameless, faceless, stable hand. The fact that I was the son of a noble was of little significance at the farm, and I'm sure that many of the men who worked there cared little about it. But my success with the mare was something that had earned me some recognition on my own. It wasn't as if the other trainers were coming around and asking my advice, but at least they knew my name and would acknowledge me in passing.

One day, after I returned from riding Analie in a distant field, Helmut approached me as I was brushing the sweat from the mare's grey coat. "I think it's time to transfer that mare into regular battle training and find another horse for you to break."

I realized that I was being paid a compliment, but I really didn't want to part with Analie, to whom I had grown much attached. "She isn't really finished," I replied. "There is a lot more I can teach her."

"Of course there is. It takes years to finish a horse. But what she still needs to learn is her job. Her job is to take a knight into battle, not be your personal mount. You have Diomedes for that."

I realized it was futile to argue. Helmut was right; I couldn't just collect horses for my own amusement. As much as it hurt me to give Analie up, I really had no choice. That was the last day that I worked with her. Over the next few months, I saw her occasionally and she seemed to be doing well in her training. She had spirit; there was no question about that, and she was growing big and powerful, too. At the end of the summer she was sold to a knight named Dietrich, and I don't think I ever saw her again after that.

One day late that fall, while my father was away in Saxony, word spread throughout the village of a missing girl. She had wandered off into the woods in the afternoon, and her parents couldn't find her. A search of the surrounding area was made for the girl, whose name was Liesel, but it failed to discover any sign of her. A larger search was organized the following morning, but by that time hopes of finding the five year old alive were fading. I told my mother that I wanted to help. It was still dark as I fed Diomedes much earlier than usual and headed out to join the other searchers at the edge of the village.

It had snowed a little in the night, which made it even more difficult to find any sign of the girl's trail. It was a cloudy morning, and the new snow covered the branches of the trees as we rode into the pine forest behind Liesel's home. I could see Diomedes' breath in the air coming from his nostrils, and I thought of the child spending the night in the forest in such cold temperatures. I didn't see how she could have survived. I thought of how terrible the waiting and worrying must have been for her parents. There were other men on horseback, and we were spread out over a wide area with men on foot at intervals between us. It was difficult moving through the woods with the dense growth of trees, the underbrush, and many fallen trunks. Occasionally, shouts would ring out in the still morning air when someone would call out the girl's name, and then all would be silent again while we waited and hoped for a reply. It was a grim affair and one that still haunts me today.

Several days later I solemnly described to Verena what happened. "For hours we moved slowly through the woods until we were miles from where she had last been seen. Once we reached the hills we felt there was little chance that she would have continued in that direction even if she had gotten that far. So, half the group turned to the west, while the group that I was in turned east. We again spread out and searched a different section of the forest as we turned back toward the lake.

The cold was numbing and the pace of our search so slow that at times I found myself falling into a sort of drowsy stupor, and several times my head dropped down toward Diomedes' neck as I drifted off. It was during one of those spells that I was brought back to consciousness by the nickering of Diomedes. It was barely discernible at first, but as I shook the fog from my head, I saw that his ears were up and the muscles tight in his neck. He nickered again, a little louder than the first time, and quickened his steps. He sidestepped to the left and his right ear twitched nervously. It was obvious that he sensed something off to our right, and he breathed in and out heavily as if he had caught the scent of something unusual. I gradually moved his head back to the right and his hindquarters moved away to the left. Keeping his feet moving, I continued to turn him back in the direction that his ear pointed, and we made a small arc. I tried to tighten the circle against his resistance until I was certain we were at the spot that was making him fearful. And then I saw it: a patch of color that didn't fit with its surroundings. There was reddish clothing just visible on the other side of a fallen tree trunk. I quickly slid off Diomedes and rushed over to find the girl's snow-covered form lying still on the ground.

I called for help as I lifted the poor girl up and brushed the snow from her head. She was so cold! Her body was stiff and her face was colorless and I thought she must be dead. My arms shook as I put my cloak around her shoulders and held her tightly against my chest. And then I felt her breath on my neck. It was faint and cold, but I knew then that she was still alive. When the nearest man reached me I said, 'She's alive. Help me up on my horse and then lift her up to me.' In a moment I had the little girl up with me on Diomedes and was riding back toward the village. I went as fast as I could through the forest where there was no path, and when I reached the open meadows Diomedes broke into a gallop. It had started to snow again, and the wind made my face feel like it was being struck by needles. But I didn't care. I clutched the girl against my chest with one arm and held the reins with the other as I raced to get her back to her house where she could get warm.

When I reached the house, Liesel's mother came out and ran to me. I handed the girl down to her. I'll never forget that terrible tear-stained face as she hugged the little girl's limp body in her arms. She turned and ran back to the house, and I was left sitting on my horse outside. Soon people started to arrive at the house as word spread that the girl was home. Liesel's father got back from the forest where he was one of the searchers and saw me as he rushed toward the house. 'You're the one who found her?' He asked.

I nodded.

'Come in and get warm.'

I got down off Diomedes and followed the father into the house. There, Liesel was stretched out in front of the fireplace, covered in hides while her mother sobbed softly and stroked her hair. The man knelt down beside them and bowed his head in prayer. I'm not sure how much time went by, but the doctor arrived at the house, and not long after that came the priest. I sat on the floor on the other side of the room while the doctor did something that I couldn't see, and then I heard a few low words of the priest. I felt like an intruder on the family, but I didn't feel like I could get up and leave, so I just sat and stared into the fire. In a little while the mother's sobs grew louder, and she picked the girl up and held her and rocked back and forth. The doctor and the priest stood off to the side. I couldn't help it but I started to cry. Verena, if I had just found her sooner, she might still be alive. She was alive when I found her!"

As I was telling this my throat tightened up and tears came into my eyes and I couldn't speak anymore. Verena took my hand in hers and said, "You did the best you could. They might never have known what happened to their daughter or had the chance to bury her if you hadn't found her and returned her to them."

When I could speak again I said, "I wasn't really the one who found her. It was Diomedes."

11

When spring again arrived in Swabia, Helmut let me train another young horse. It was a bay colt and, unlike Analie, he had been raised by his mother and weaned after spending a year at her side. He had been running with a group of yearlings, and at age two they were assigned to trainers to start them. I used many of the methods that I had found successful with the grey mare, and it wasn't long before I was able to ride him. He was smart, and willing, and had none of the fearful tendencies of the orphaned filly.

At that time I also began my training as a knight. For a large part of each day, I reported to the arms trainer, whose name was Emmerich. Emmerich had fought the Slavs and the Magyars and was one of my father's best friends. He was tall and lean and looked as hard as a tree trunk. His hair was brown and his dark eyes peered out from under dark, bushy brows. He had a strong, square chin and a grim, confident smile.

My father also expected all his knights to be able to read the Bible and write words on parchment. Therefore, along with the other knights-in-training, I had to spend hours in the monastery studying with Father Gabriel, the parish priest. Father Gabriel was a small, thin, middle-aged man, intelligent but somewhat humorless, stern but not mean. He spoke in a soft voice and always looked you in the eye. I wasn't the best student, but not the worst either. But when I was inside the dark, musty monastery, sitting for hours at a time, I longed to be outside and stretching my young and restless legs. The arms training was much more to my liking, especially when we got to ride. Riding was what I did best, which gave me a big advantage over the other young knights when we fought from horseback.

All those things that occupied my day prevented me from spending much time with Verena. In my eyes, she grew more beautiful each time I saw her and indeed, at that time she was reaching the full blossoming of young womanhood. Thoughts of her were so extremely pleasurable that I visited the chamber of my mind in which her essence dwelt often throughout the day. The pull was irresistible, and I found myself being dragged there even when the moment demanded that my thoughts should be on something quite different, like my studies. The satisfaction that I felt from those ephemeral visits to her, however, made up for the rebukes of my teachers and companions for being distracted.

But not all of my thoughts of Verena were serene. Sometimes they were tumultuous and troubling. At times my feelings grew to such intensity that I felt that there was a fire inside me, and the only way to extinguish the flames was to go to her and touch her to make sure she was real and not just a spirit sent to torment me. Other times I would be overwhelmed by feelings of jealousy that she might be with someone else; someone who could steal her affection away from me. Even those feelings that tormented me were intoxicating. I couldn't avoid them any more than I could stop breathing.

One day in mid-summer, when I was able to escape my responsibilities for an afternoon, I arranged to meet Verena at the chestnut grove. Astride Diomedes, we could vanish for a few hours together and not have to worry about the scrutiny of our families and others. It was a warm day, the kind of day that, as children, would induce us to shed our clothes and swim in the cool waters of the lake. It was near noon and Verena's cheeks were infused with a rosy blush and her blonde hair seemed to reflect the sunlight like ripples in the river. The smile which always brightened my soul met me on my approach, and soon, with the lightness of a feather, the slender girl was behind me on the back of Diomedes.

That day we rode up the river valley until we reached a small tributary that flowed down out of the mountains several miles from the village. At that point, the channel was only a few feet wide as the water rushed over and around the smooth rocks in its path and hurried into the main stream of the great river. I pointed Diomedes' nose up the slope and let him pick his way along the bank of the stream where only the animals of the forest had formerly tread. In some stretches, the flow was placid as the ground leveled out, and in others it would grow quite noisy as if fell over steep precipices and crashed onto the waiting rocks below.

After riding a mile or two upstream, a louder a more continuous sound began to drown out the splashing and gurgling of the winding channel. Our course took a turn to the right, and my eyes were arrested by the sight of water spray, illuminated by the sunlight, drifting above the tops of the scrubby trees that clung to the hillside. "It must be a waterfall," I said, as we drew closer to the sound, which resembled the hoof beats of a hundred horses. Finally, we stopped at the edge of a huge clearing where a vast curtain of water cascaded over the side of a sheer, forty-foot drop. The sheets of water crashed into a pile of jagged rocks at the bottom of the cliff, and then tamed, ran timidly out into a placid pool in the middle of the clearing. The whole area was bathed in soft sunlight filtering through the trees that secured the privacy of the spot. For several minutes we sat astride Diomedes, silently taking in the tranquil beauty of the place. The sound of the falls, so angry when unseen at a distance, now took on a soothing natural rhythm, harmonious with the serenity of the scene. On our faces we could feel the fine mist from the falls wafting towards us on the warm summer air.

"What a beautiful place," Verena said softly, her lips close to my ear. "Did you know about it?"

"No. I've never seen it before," I answered.

Verena slipped down off of Diomedes' broad back and ran lightly over to the water's edge. I removed the bridle from the horse and let him graze freely where the grass grew lush along the rim of the clearing. When I caught up with Verena she was stepping from stone to stone in the shallows of the pool. Her ankle-length dress was skimming the surface of the water and she lifted the hem to her knees. I followed her path as she skipped as effortlessly as a dragonfly across the shimmering water. We ended back on the grassy bank where Verena sat, then rolled, then came to rest on her back staring rapturously at the clear blue sky. She was like a kitten whose joyous play could soften even the hardest heart. I knelt beside her and looked at her lovely white face with the pink cheeks and slightly parted rose lips and wanted to cover her with kisses. But before I could put my desires in action she said, "It's hot. Do you remember when we used to go for swims in the lake when we were children?"

"I think I recall that, yes."

"This would be a perfect place to swim."

"It's certainly secluded."

Verena got up and walked to the edge of the pool, leaving her shoes behind. I wasn't sure what she was up to but I had an idea. She stood for a moment looking at the waterfall, glanced over her shoulder at me and then began unfastening her dress. She slipped the heavy material off her shoulders and lowered it to her waist, revealing the graceful contours of her back. She paused for an instance, seemingly to contemplate letting go of the garment entirely. My breathing arrested, I watched as she allowed it to fall to the ground. Of all God's wondrous creations, I am certain there could be nothing more beautiful than what I beheld at that moment. Verena looked over her pale shoulder and with a slight toss of her head beckoned me to join her.

With my heart beating so fast I thought it would leave my chest, I quickly and probably quite awkwardly, undressed and walked to her side. I took her hand in mine and we stood for a moment looking at the glistening water, no longer children, but at the threshold of being grown-up, with all the excitement of expectation and hope that comes with that fleeting moment in time.

We walked together into the pool, feeling the intense sensation of the cold mountain water on our sun-warmed skin. I glanced over at Verena and noticed tiny bumps creeping over the contours of her smooth form. "Come on," I said, letting her hand go and plunging neck-deep into the water. Catching my breath in short gasps, I turned around to see that Verena was still standing in water just above her knees, not yet summoning the courage to go all the way in. I smiled at the sight and felt that seeing her that way, in all the freshness and beauty of an opening water lily, should last in my memory until the end of time. Finally, after taking a couple of breaths, she glided into the water, scarcely causing a ripple in its surface.

Verena came near and embraced me, squeezing out the cold and leaving behind only the warmth of our bodies pressed against each other. She remained there just an all-too-brief moment, and then quickly swam away. We played in the pool beneath the waterfall until we began to shiver and soon we were back on the bank languishing in the warming rays of the afternoon sun.

For a time, I reclined on one elbow admiring the miraculous beauty of Nature's perfect creation. Verena pulled me to her and then the last physical barrier between us fell. There, in that lovely place, our souls became indelibly united as I had always believed they were from our first meeting. Together we rose to such unimaginable heights that the sun and moon and stars could only look up in envy.

12

The following year Otto's wife Eadgyth died. She was only thirty-six. An English Saxon Princess by birth, she married Otto when they were not much older than Verena and I. She was esteemed by the Germans for her good works and often accompanied the king when he travelled. And now, unexpectedly, she was dead. The funeral in Magdeburg was to be attended by many of the Dukes and other important nobles. My father told me it was time I started assuming my proper role in official functions and that the burial of the queen would be a good place to start. Since it took many days for the news to reach us, and a journey of four hundred miles was ahead, we left for Magdeburg the next day. I didn't have time to tell Verena I was leaving.

In the morning we started north toward the Rhein. That was the first time I had been farther than just a few miles from our village. It was an exciting time for me and seeing the mighty river was to be just the first of many new experiences of that trip. We reached its high banks a little past mid-day. There, the water flowing from the wide course of the river falls over a high cliff and through a rocky channel creating a crashing, swirling, white-foaming maelstrom. I had never before, or even since, seen such irresistible power in nature. The spray could be felt hundreds of feet from the falls. We forded the river near the small village of Niuhusen.

Leaving behind the Rhein, it was but a short ride until we reached the Donau which, at that point, borders the Swabian Mountains. For the rest of the day the slopes rose gently on our left, and soon after they fell off in the distance, we stopped for the night. It had been a long day of riding but so exhilarating to me that I lay looking at the stars for a long time before falling asleep, my mind busy with thoughts of the new places I would see.

The next day we turned further north, away from the flow of the Donau and through vast woodlands where we saw few people or settlements for long stretches of riding. In the afternoon we came upon a village which is situated on the Pegnitz and has a large hill fort. We were received by a Bavarian noble named Ingomar who had a daughter, Ermentrud, recently a widow. Ermentrud was several years older than me, but still quite young, and had a son who was about five years old. Later I realized it was no coincidence that I was seated next to her at dinner that night.

Ermentrud had a mostly plain, unremarkable face, but she had beautiful, expressive eyes. In the typically awkward way of two young people who don't know each other, there were many long periods of silence between us at first. "What is your son's name?" I asked.

"Norbert," the girl replied, her lovely eyes joyful at saying the word.

I nodded. "It's a good name." I didn't know what else to say.

After a few more minutes I asked, "Do you have many friends nearby?" I was thinking that the village was small and isolated.

Her look turned a little melancholy. "I have Magda, my attendant, and I have Father."

"Any brothers or sisters?"

"I have a brother. He married last year and lives in Erlangon."

Although she smiled, her voice betrayed a touch of loneliness.

"What about you?" She asked politely. "What is life like in Swabia?"

"It's good. We live on the Limmat near the lake. The soil is good for farming in the valley," I said, sounding like my father.

"Do you like farming?"

"It's all right. But what I really like to do is train horses. Of course, I'm also training to be a knight," I added.

"It sounds like you are very busy."

"Yes, with the arms training and learning to read and write at the monastery, I only have time to train one horse at a time. I'd like to have more horses... Someday, perhaps."

"How do you train a horse? I never really thought about it before."

Ermentrude was probably sorry she asked that question because I spent the rest of dinner explaining in vast detail my methods for training horses. I'm sure it was boring to her, but once I started talking about horses I couldn't stop. The poor girl listened politely, the gaze from her sapphire eyes never leaving my face. Without realizing it I had talked without stopping through nearly the whole evening. When I finally did pause, I was embarrassed. "I'm sorry," I said, looking at Ermentrude's amused smile, "I guess I have been rude to dominate the conversation."

"Not at all; it was fascinating. I will certainly know what to do if I ever train a horse," she said, without a trace of ridicule.

In spite of my humiliation, I felt much closer to Ermentrude by the time we parted that night. She made me feel at ease with her warm and kindly nature. I suppose that was why I talked so freely to her about things that were important to me.

The next morning we left to continue our journey with the intent of reaching Arnstadt by the end of the day. My father brought up the subject of marriage for the first time. "Ingomar suggested Ermentrude as a match for you."

As was his way, he waited patiently for a response from me before speaking again. "I think I am too young to marry," I finally answered.

"It wouldn't have to be right away. It could be a year before a wedding takes place. Think about it. She's healthy and has already shown that she can produce a son."

I'm sure that argument made perfect sense to my father, but marrying and producing heirs couldn't have been farther from my mind at that time in my life. He probably realized that, and the subject wasn't discussed again until weeks later.

Our route took us through the Thuringer Wald which, due to the rugged terrain and dense forest growth was difficult to cross, especially in winter. But my father had travelled its passes many times and knew the best course for us to take. All day we climbed and descended the steep slopes of the mountains where there was still snow on the ground. The layers of snow lay heavy on the branches of the pine trees which grew thick in the vast forest. At one point we stopped to rest at a place called Spitterfall where the stream cascades down rocks that resemble a staircase. The icy cold water that gurgled and frothed and sent spray high into the chilled air paused for a moment at the base of the falls before resuming its course. In the eddy that formed, crystalline lace crept out from the edges near the bank. Despite the cold, my thoughts were called back to the day when Verena and I discovered the falls and pool near home that we had started calling "our falls."

Coming down from the highest elevations on the north side of the mountain range, we arrived at a burg on the edge of Arnstadt late in the day tired and cold and ready for the warmth of a fire and a night to rest. We were in the home of a noble named Raimund, and the rest of his family had retired to their quarters for the night. After being served a hearty meal of game, bread, and beer we slept around the hearth in the center of the great hall along with our host's dogs. The large hounds were actually welcome company to help ward off the cold, and I made an effort to cultivate friendly relations with two of the beasts so that they would sleep in close proximity. One of them, a grey spotted bitch, scratched and bit at her ruffled hair for a time and then circled ceremoniously again and again before settling down with a huge sigh and closing her eyes.

In the morning, Raimund joined us for the rest of the journey. We travelled east for a time until we reached the Saale, then turned north on the trail that follows its banks. Late in the day we came to the place where the Saale flows into the Elbe and my father said that we were nearing Magdeburg. Before long we were in sight of the fortified walls of the city from which Otto ruled all the German lands.

The queen had been dead for several weeks but burial of her coffin had been delayed to allow the nobles to be in attendance. The funeral was held in the Abbey of St. Maurice which is situated at a broad bend of the Elbe. The church itself is not imposing in size, and appeared rather bleak in the midst of winter with the gardens and courtyards covered in white. The austere quarters of the monks, connected to the abbey church by walkways, further contributed to the humble appearance of the holy place that the king and queen had chosen for their patronage. The men in attendance at the funeral, all holding important positions in either the church or in government, filed by the queen's resting place within the chapel in solemn procession. I met many powerful men that day, whose faces and names eluded my young brain almost as soon as they walked away, but one stayed etched in my memory: Otto, the king. His youthful countenance was clouded by grief, but he still looked directly into my eyes when I rose from my knee upon meeting him. He was tall and robust-looking, with a handsome and intelligent face befitting the king of all the Germans. Otto and Eadgyth had ruled side by side for more than a decade and Otto was affected deeply by his queen's death. My father had seen her on several occasions, and said that she was quite a lovely woman, fair-skinned, light-haired, dignified and graceful. The English Saxon princess that had come to Germany to be Otto's wife even before he ascended the throne was now gone and the king was alone. The sorrow that I saw in his eyes that day showed that he had lost more than a trusted advisor. Death had parted him from a person he loved.

The Abbot spoke words of Latin, and I was only able to understand part of his eulogy. My studies of language at the monastery had not occupied a place of importance in my life equal to that of fighting and horses. I wondered if the others comprehended more. When he was finished, the coffin was lowered into the crypt beneath the floor of the church and a stone slab was put in place over it.

A banquet was held that evening for the guests in honor of the queen. It was a solemn affair, absent of the entertainment, boisterous story-telling, and laughter of usual dinner gatherings. I sat at a table with my father and the other members of our party from Swabia and listened to the conversations that swirled around me. Gatherings such as these were rare, and they enabled the nobles to find out what important events had happened in other parts of the kingdom since they had last been together. In West Franconia, the temporary truce between Hugh and Louis had been shattered, and Louis (who was married to Otto's sister Gerberga) was being held prisoner by Hugh (who was married to another of Otto's sisters, Hedwig). Speculation centered on whether or not Otto would intervene in the dispute on behalf of Louis. There was war with the Slavs in northern Saxony, and it was said that the rebellious Slavs had been joined by the Danes. Also, King Henry's pact with the Magyars had long since expired, and raids from the east were a constant threat.

The next day my father was involved in meetings with some of the other lords, so I spent the time walking around Magdeburg. The city showed signs of more planning than our town in Swabia. The streets were laid out in a pattern of parallels and crossings with buildings rising two or three levels along both sides. Since being presented to Eadgyth as a wedding present in 929, the city had been favored by Otto's family and had benefitted from their patronage. It had become a center of political power. Early in my walk I was joined by a thin yellow dog, which sometimes followed at a respectful distance and at others seemed to be leading me along. The streets (or the dog) led me down to the edge of the river, and I walked for a while in the cold winter air. My thoughts were mostly of Verena and the last couple of times I saw her. Our opportunities for meeting were fewer in winter since she didn't have as many excuses to wander away from her house for long periods of time. I knew by then that I loved her and I wanted to be with her forever, but the difficulties of a union between us were great. My father would not approve of my choice of a peasant girl for a wife; that was certain. My mother might better understand my desire to marry someone that I loved, but she wouldn't oppose my father.

I also thought of the horses that were under my care at that time. I had left Diomedes at home. My father didn't think that we should take a chance on the old horse going lame on the long rugged journey. Instead, I rode a well-tested cavalry horse that had seen action in the Slavic wars of 946. When we left, I had been working with a young stallion since late summer that was doing well. I was taking him for rides into the hills and he showed great curiosity concerning new surroundings and also a willingness to trust me when I rode him. His dam was a very smart mare, and the colt seemed to have inherited his mother's good sense.

On the way back up the riverbank, I was approached by an old woman who had evidently seen me pass the first time and had some small items to sell. It was not the time of year for markets, so I didn't think that I would have an opportunity to buy anything for Verena on the trip. The trinkets were all of a religious nature, and I bought a small silver cross with some simple engraving on it. The woman was hunched over and wrinkled and had only a few of her teeth left. She was grateful to make the sale and thanked me repeatedly. Cold to the point of shivering, I headed back to the citadel. The yellow dog stayed with me until I reached the place where he had joined my walk, and the next thing I knew he had disappeared in one of the alleys between buildings.

13

We began the journey back to Swabia the following day. A cold wind stung my face and light snow swirled about us as we again followed the river south. The horses snorted billows of steam and excitedly tossed their heads in response to the cold and snow and wind. By the time we reached the Saale, they had settled into the tasks with which we had entrusted them, carefully picking their footfalls along the trail to ensure their and their riders' safety. Their excitement and anxiety long subsided, head positions were lower, necks were relaxed, and bodies kept in perfect balance regardless of the slope. I was full of wonder at the partnership between horse and rider. There is a mutual trust that flows between the human and the animal. Trust from the horse that the rider won't guide him into a dangerous place where hungry predators lurk, and trust from the rider that a powerful and once wild creature will carry him safely on his back on a rock-strewn hillside.

The snow grew heavier as the day wore on, and the stiff wind portended worse weather to come. By the time we reached Arnstadt it was clear that travelling over the mountains would have to wait until whatever time the storm subsided. Raimund again became our host, and we settled the horses in his stable where there was an abundance of forage and fresh water. It had been dark for several hours when we finally joined Raimund's family in the great hall for dinner.

When we had stayed there on the northward journey to Magdeburg, we ate with only Raimund and a few of his knights that were to accompany us to the funeral. This time, his wife and children as well as several older relatives were also in the hall. Raimund was about forty, with a greying beard and clear blue eyes. His wife was considerably younger and still had pretty features and long curls that gave her a girlish look despite her plump body. Seated next to her was a small boy about eight or nine who, like most boys his age, distained sitting and wanted to leave the gathering as soon as he had hastily devoured his food. For a while, his mother made him stay, but she later looked to Raimund, who silently nodded his ascent for the boy to leave the table, and like a puff of smoke from a fireplace the child was gone.

Further down the table were seated two young girls, one in her early teens and the other about twelve. The older girl had light hair like her mother and the younger dark tresses like her father. They glanced in my direction often and when meeting my gaze, shyly looked away. They talked and giggled and whispered in each other's ear apparently excited to have a new young person in the residence to occupy their attentions. They both possessed the pretty features of their mother, and it was easy to imagine what she looked like at their age. The older girl was slightly more graceful and assured in her movements having reached the threshold of adulthood in which she becomes aware of her allure, while her sister was still suspended in the vaguely awkward, but still beautiful, transition from child to woman.

The next day brought more snow, and by mid-morning the depth had reached halfway up my boots. After checking on the horses, I decided to take a short walk down into the town. The snow had let up, and only a few large flakes floated down from the bright white sky. The wind was much calmer than the previous day, and I enjoyed getting out of the dark, smoky rooms of the burg and into the fresh, cool air. I rounded the east wall and turned down the path to the village below the citadel and saw Raimund's two daughters playing in the snow. The younger girl, on seeing me, raised her hand in greeting. I returned the gesture and continued on down the slope. I had taken only a few steps when I was hit in the back with a snowball. As I turned back in the direction from which it had come, another snowball flew past my cheek. The unprovoked attack brought a swift response. Making loose fluffy snowballs and throwing them as fast as I could, I moved closer and closer to my antagonists. The girls held their ground and kept up their barrage, hitting me several more times. But some of my projectiles found their mark as well, the last exploding upon the face of the dark-haired girl. I immediately regretted the act, and rushed over to the small figure which had turned away with her hands covering her face. "I'm sorry, I'm sorry," I sputtered, placing my hand on her back and feeling like the worst villain in the world. Her sister rushed over and comforted her as girls do, without looking up at me. A terrible minute passed as my victim kept her face buried in her hands. Suddenly, her narrow shoulders shuddered and then began to shake convulsively. At first I thought she was crying and that thought filled me with further remorse. And then I realized instead that she was laughing. Guilt lifted from my shoulders, I laughed with her, and we were soon joined by her sister who first looked at us as though we were mad.

The dark-haired one looked up at me with large, moist eyes, fresh cherry-red cheeks streaming with a mixture of tears and melted snow. Wet, dark curls framed her tiny face. How lovely she was! Arrested for a moment by her beautiful dark eyes, I had no words. Finally, I blurted out, "I'm Max. And you are a most worthy opponent."

Her wide smile held me captive for another awkward moment before I said, "Reveal your name, mysterious warrior!"

"Nadja," she finally answered in a musical, child-like voice. A silence ensued that quickly became awkward, and then the sound of throat-clearing broke in. "Oh," Nadja said, breaking off eye contact with me, this is my sister Svenja."

I looked at the older sister for the first time. Svenja's pretty face was rounder than her sister's and was framed in waves of thick blond hair that cascaded far down her back. Her fair skin, unmarked by a single blemish, had a bright pink patch on each cheek. The blue eyes that looked out at me from beneath long pale lashes caused my breath to catch in my throat, and I would have been unable to speak had I thought of anything to say at that moment. The girl was probably accustomed to the enchantment that she held over men, and the corners of her lovey mouth turned upward in a sly smile. I made a slight bow.

"Would you help us build a snowman?" Interrupted Nadja.

Putting aside the dignity that I had assumed as part of my father's envoy to the queen's funeral, I agreed to help the girls build a snowman. Working shoulder to shoulder with the sisters, talking, joking, and laughing, I again became a child along with them. The snowman toppled before we could get the head attached, but that only became another cause for laughter. Nadja was the first to drop on her back in the snow to make the outline of an angel, and was quickly joined by her sister, making two angels holding hands (or wings). They convinced me to do it as well, and the three of us lay happily in the snow together catching, on our tongues, snowflakes falling from the bright sky.

The morning playing in the snow with Nadja and Svenja, is still a fond memory. It was light-hearted and completely frivolous, and when it was over I was left with a vague feeling of wistful happiness. I suppose there was a small element of romance in the episode. Although my companions were quite young, their beauty was undeniable. They exuded a freshness and unaffected charm that was irresistible. But for the most part, our morning romp in that fairyland of new-fallen snow was just childish fun. I was, after all, still a young boy at that time, unencumbered with the grim responsibilities of manhood.

That afternoon, the two girls and I found further entertainments. The household dogs, perhaps sensing our youthful exuberance, joined us. We played games of dice. We played knucklebones. We baited each other in a game of hoodman's blind. Each episode was filled with teasing and laughter. Nadja was clever, whimsical, and completely uninhibited. Her wonderfully musical laugh was always just below the surface ready to burst forth even in moments of feigned seriousness.

Svenja was more reserved. She good-naturedly let her sister's bubbling personality dominate the games. But her smile was always there; sometimes bemused, other times breaking widely and illuminating her beautiful face. When the focus of the game centered on her, she blushed self-consciously, and tried, with uneven success, to remain dignified. In the end, the child which remained in her could not be restrained, and what was revealed was something sweet and vulnerable.

Each of the two girls, still charmingly unaware of their just-awakening feminine allure, would have produced a pleasing effect. However, their combined power was absolutely intoxicating. By evening I was completely under their spell.

Nadja and Svenja ate hurriedly that night, I thought, and were excused from the table. As they were leaving, Nadja caught my eye and with a gesture of her head indicated that I was to join them as soon as I could get away. After a discreet amount of time had elapsed, I too excused myself and left the great hall. The excited girls, like two conspirators, led me to a part of the burg I hadn't been to yet, and proposed that we play hide and seek. Nadja decided that she and I would find hiding places and that Svenja would search for us.

Unfamiliar with our location, which was away from the primary residence area of the home, I found a place to conceal myself among some stores from the kitchen. After some time had elapsed, I don't know how long, I heard the approach of footsteps. I was crouched down close to the floor and trying to be very still when I felt something run across my hand. I involuntarily recoiled in surprise. I turned to see a large rat disappearing between the sacks. Svenja, standing nearby, immediately discovered my hiding place. "Betrayed by a rat!" I exclaimed in mock anger, actually glad to be off the floor and back in the company of such a lovely companion. We went in search of Nadja, who was much better at the game than I was. Fortunately, Svenja knew most of her sister's favorite hiding places, and it wasn't long before we were all together again.

It was Nadja's turn to search, and Svenja and I headed off in roughly the same direction. I scoured the corridors looking for a place that would not be too obvious. I turned into a store room that didn't have food in it and thought, 'At least there shouldn't be rats in here.' I was contemplating climbing into the window ledge to get above eye-level when I heard, "Max!" in a whispered voice. I turned to see Svenja's face peeking out of a closet on the other side of the small room. "Come in here," she said. Knowing that Nadja was in close pursuit, I quickly slipped into the closet as Svenja backed up and made a space for me. When I closed the door, all light was extinguished, but I soon realized that it was very close quarters. The girl's small body was pressed against me and she couldn't, or wouldn't, move farther away. The cold air in the far reaches of the burg that had seemed so inescapable only minutes before was replaced by an all-enveloping warmth. We stood motionless for a time, and it was so quiet that the sounds of our breathing seemed to merge in rhythmic unison. Slowly, the girl put her hands around my waist and laid her head on my chest. I could feel her breath on my neck and smell the sweetness of her hair. I placed my hands on her small back, and she nestled closer.

Some minutes later we heard Nadja's approaching footsteps. We made no sounds or efforts to move, but when the younger sister threw open the closet door, our arms dropped to our sides, and we stood stiffly as though we had been caught stealing cookies. "Well! How cozy!" Said Nadja tersely. She spun quickly around and rushed out of the room.

"I think the game is over," said Svenja demurely. "I'd better follow her."

I walked back to the great hall with my head spinning in happy confusion. What a day it had been. Those girls had burst upon my consciousness like two beautiful yearlings racing each other across a meadow in spring. When I returned to the great hall, I sat before a warm fire in the hearth and stared into the orange flames. The members of the household had retired for the night and only my father's party remained there with the ever-present dogs. The events of the day rushed in and out of my mind pushing and jostling for space. The strongest of all of these was Svenja. Her essence remained embedded in my soul for many weeks to follow.

My thoughts were interrupted by my father's words: "The weather has cleared. We leave tomorrow." At first the thought of leaving Arnstadt made me feel a bit sad. And then I thought of what might happen if I stayed longer and said quietly to myself, "It's just as well."

Early the next morning I was standing in the great hall, dressed to ride, petting one of the great hounds that had become a friend over the past two nights. My father said the horses were being brought out of the stable, and I was about to walk outside when I heard my name in a loud whisper. I turned toward the sound, and in a doorway off the main hall was the slim figure of Nadja, beckoning me to come to her. I walked over as the girl retreated back into the corridor and both girls were there. Nadja showed none of the anger that I had seen in her the previous day when she discovered her sister in the closet with me. Instead she was bright and vivacious as before. Svenja stood behind her quietly in the usual unassuming demeanor that she adopted when in the presence of her more outgoing sister.

"Were you going to leave without saying goodbye?" Asked Nadja, in a stern voice that made me smile.

"I didn't know if you would be up yet," I said seriously. I glanced in Svenja's direction and her eyes were turned downward.

"Well," Nadja continued, "I hope you will come back to see us soon." With that she stepped forward, and raising herself on tip-toe, turned the side of her face to me. I reached down and gave her a quick brotherly kiss on the cheek. She smiled and suppressed a giggle, then stepped aside for her sister. Svenja came forward, still with eyes lowered under long lashes. When she finally looked up, her blue eyes were moist with tears. Looking into that angelic face, I felt the blood rushing up my neck and into the back of my head. I hesitated a moment, then bent down to kiss her left cheek as I had with Nadja. But Svenja had other ideas. She quickly tilted her head to the side and pressed her lips against mine. As surprised as I was, I couldn't bring myself to draw back. Her lips were soft and caressing. A tear rolled down her cheek and trickled between my mouth and hers.

"Svenja! Ooh! You promised!" Wailed Nadja. She stomped her foot.

I held Svenja at arm's length. Her beautiful melancholy face tore at my heart. "I have to go." I turned and rushed back into the great hall where my father was calling me. "Where were you?" He said, "We need to leave."

"Just saying goodbye," I said as we walked out into the cold winter air. The taste of Svenja's tear was still in my mouth as we rode away.

14

It was a clear morning, and the sun threw long shadows across the white landscape. The air was still and cold and billows of steam rose above the horse's heads. Their steps were higher than usual as they lifted their feet out of the deep snow and plunged back into it with each step. Hours in the saddle rolled by almost unnoticed as my thoughts returned again and again to the events of the last two days in Arnstadt. The memories, fresh as a new wound and undulled by healing time were both sweet and troubling. As much as I tried to push them out of my mind, they continued to flash back into my thoughts, like a fire impossible to extinguish.

When we were near the village of Saalfeld we came upon a contingent of knights riding towards us on the trail. They were led by a severe-looking knight on a black horse who brought his troops to a halt upon seeing us approach. "Ludwig!" He hailed as we grew near. "What are you doing so far north?"

"We are returning from the queen's funeral, Carsten." Replied my father. "Where are you going?"

"There is a band of raiders nearby. Slavs we think. They have staged several raids to the east and are moving this way."

"Strange that they would be raiding in the middle of winter."

"It's been a mild year. They might be renegades, just hitting villages when they wouldn't be expecting it."

"How far away do you think they are?"

"We sent out a rider yesterday. He just returned this morning and said that he saw them on this side of the river about twenty miles from here."

"How many of them are there?"

"He said about sixty. We're going to be outnumbered. It's hard to gather many knights this time of year. We could use your help."

My father looked at Parsifal, his first knight. Parsifal nodded. Then my father glanced over his shoulder at me. He pondered his decision for a moment. Then he said, "All right, they won't stand against us. We'll help you drive them back across the river. That should give you enough time to raise a bigger army to disperse them."

Carsten had about forty well-armed knights, and we added our party of nine. We weren't in full armor, but we all carried swords. I also had a small battle ax lashed to my saddle. What had occurred in Arnstadt was quickly submerged in a flood of thoughts much more urgent. Perhaps it would be just a brief skirmish, I thought, and our foes would retreat beyond the river as my father had predicted. I felt fear rising in me like I had when Albrecht and I were trapped by the wolves. My weapons training had been no more than a game. I didn't have to kill anyone, and I never had a fear of dying. But it all became real to me that day.

We rode south at a gallop over an old road that provided us with firm footing beneath the new snow, but after a couple of miles we turned east and slowed our mounts to a walk when we encountered a dense stand of pines. Emerging from the woods, we came to a small village that overlooked the river valley. It was not much more than a few huts scattered on the hillside with a tidy stone chapel perched above it like a watching bird of prey. Not a soul was to be seen. Finally, a man in a priest's robe came out of the church. He was of medium height, thin, and had thick black eye brows and a receding chin. He approached

Lord Carsten timidly and said, "We heard that there was a raiding party nearby. When we heard your horses we thought it was them. Our women and children have fled into the hills nearby with a few of the younger men. We are defenseless."

Carsten replied that the raiders were, indeed, nearby and that we were riding to intercept them. He asked the priest if we could rest our horses in the village and have a meal. It was well past noon, and we had been riding for hours. The priest seemed relieved that we were in pursuit of the raiders. He asked us to wait at the church while he gathered food from the remaining villagers to bring to us. Soon, the priest returned with about fifteen villagers, mostly old men, and they were all loaded down with bread, smoked meats, cheese, and some pots of rye porridge. There was a meager amount of hay in the village, but the men willingly shared what they had with our hungry horses. I felt bad about leaving the village with a depleted supply of hay for the remainder of the winter, but if we drove off the raiders we would prevent them from losing a lot more.

Once on our way again, we moved rapidly with the horses refreshed. We wound our way down the snowy hillside into the valley where Carsten's scout had located the Slav camp. The dense pine forest helped conceal our presence coming down from the higher elevation. It wasn't long before we could see wisps of smoke curling skyward from the enemy campfires. We stopped on a relatively level plain about half a mile distant from the edge of the camp. "They may already know that we're here," said Carsten, "so we need to close quickly from this point on. Once we reach the camp, let any surrender that wish to, but kill any that resist. Stay in close formation so you can protect each other's flanks. Ludwig, keep your men to the rear during the initial charge, since you don't have lances. Defend our backs."

With that, Carsten drew his sword, put spurs to his black stallion, and started galloping straight toward the campfires. His courage and leadership helped a little to dispel my fears. His men lowered the tips of their lances and, throwing up snow in their wake, bolted after their leader. My father, letting Carsten's knights move ahead of us, looked sternly at me and said, "Stay right behind me. I don't want you separated from us when we get down there."

I nodded, and like the others drew my sword. My horse, wanting to move with the rest, tensed his muscles and leaned into the bit. Holding him back, I fell in behind my father's horse and eased into a slow gallop. Lord Carsten's men gained speed, and we urged our horses on to close the gap that developed between us. Snow flew back past me from the horses in front, and the cold air stung my cheeks and made tears form in my eyes. Soon my powerful charger was in full stride as my left hand moved in rhythm with each huge forward surge. The sword I held in my right hand felt heavy as I struggled to keep its point straight ahead despite the resistance of the wind. An image flashed before my mind of plunging that deadly point into the body of a man, and a shudder ran through me. Swept along on that torrent of destruction, I felt that I no longer moved of my own will. I was part of a roiling, cascading mass, the parts of which had no identity but instead were merged into pure, un-haltable momentum.

I could hear voices shouting in a language I did not understand as we closed on the perimeter of the Slav encampment. Just seconds later some of the shouts turned to screams, and I heard the crash of weapon on weapon. Carsten's men carved a wedge into a crowd of men, campfires, and equipment. Once inside the camp but still in the wake formed by the leading knights I found no one to fight. My horse tried to veer to avoid a man on the ground, but the lifeless form was crushed beneath pounding hooves. As we advanced deeper into the camp, the Slavs started to regroup at the far end of the clearing. Some of them reached their horses and fled toward a copse of pines east of the river. Moving together in close formation we were able to prevent the remaining Slavs from gaining their mounts. They scattered on foot, making it difficult to concentrate our force on them. In the meantime, a number of fighters that had survived the initial attack formed behind us. I was turning my mount to pursue one of the running men when something hit my right leg with so much force that I thought I heard the bone shatter. The searing pain flashed up into my hip and down to my knee. I looked quickly and saw that an arrow had pierced my thigh. I reached down to pull it out but the shaft was buried so deep in the muscle that I couldn't move it. Trying to budge the arrow caused so much pain that I nearly slipped out of consciousness and swayed to one side of my saddle. I regained my balance, shook free of the dark shadows that formed behind my eyes, and tried to get my bearings. Other knights were moving in the direction that the arrow had come from, so I turned my horse to follow them. It was then that I realized I had dropped my sword. I quickly grabbed the ax from behind my saddle. The archers began to scatter when they could no longer bring their bows to bear on us as we closed in rapidly. My horse ran up the back of one man and trampled him as he fell. In a nearly blind fury, I overtook another man and, swinging wildly with the ax, I hit only air.

Suddenly, the fight was over. Their numbers decimated, the Slavs that were unable to get to their mounts surrendered. The ones that gained their horses and escaped into the copse were later seen crossing the river downstream. We didn't have enough men to pursue them and still be able to contain the prisoners that we had taken. As the captives were gathered up, the wounded, both ours and theirs, were tended to in an area by the river. I rode over to it and, with great difficulty, dismounted. Every movement sent excruciating pain through my leg. I sat down on the cold ground and waited. Battlefield treatment is mostly about trying to stop bleeding and then applying bandages. One man who was trying to help, saw the arrow sticking out of my leg and just shook his head. He said, "It will do more damage to remove the arrow than to leave it in. We need to get you somewhere for better care."

I tried to lie still with my back propped up against a log, since every movement caused throbbing pain in my leg. My father came over to me and knelt by my side. "I just heard that you were wounded. I'm sorry, I didn't know or I would have come sooner."

"It's all right. There wasn't anything that you could have done anyway," I answered.

"We need to get you to a place where that arrow can be safely removed. And it can't wait until tomorrow. We'll get the wounded together and leave immediately. Fortunately, we have no dead to bury on our side. It will just be a short time now."

Then I asked, "What will happen to the prisoners?"

"The leaders have been executed. The rest will be taken across the river at the shallows and turned loose without weapons or horses. They will take their wounded with them. God will decide their fate."

My father got up and started to walk away and then turned back toward me. "The Slavs had taken a number of prisoners from two nearby villages. We found them bound together at the back of the camp. There were both men and women. They would have been sold as slaves. Because of us, they are free again."

I nodded. He smiled at me and started to say something else, but changed his mind and continued on.

A short time later Walther, one of my father's best knights, brought my horse to me and helped me get mounted. My leg had stiffened up quite a bit while I was sitting, and once on my horse I just let my right leg hang down beside the horse without putting my foot in the stirrup. I know there were others that had been wounded and were riding their horses, but I was in so much pain at the time I couldn't tell you how many there were or what their condition was.

There was a brilliant red-orange glow on the rim of the clouds to the west when we left the camp, and it was rapidly getting colder. I asked Walther where we were going, and he said we were going back to the village where we had stopped earlier in the day.

Before the last light faded from the western sky, a nearly full moon rose in the east. It illuminated the valley and surrounding mountainsides and cast long shadows across the ground. The glistening crystals of the snow spread out before us like thousands of tiny white jewels. For a while I was able to keep my mind off of my injury, but when we started the climb into the hills, the rocking motion of my horse sent lightning bolts of pain up my leg and into my hip. Several times I was unable to suppress my groans, and I know that Walther, riding nearby, heard them. I hated my weakness and clenched my teeth to prevent any more sounds from escaping my mouth.

With darkness, the cold grew menacing. Wind swept through the valley and cut into us as surely as a knife. My fingers and toes, first feeling pain, began to feel nothing at all. I recalled stories of men losing parts of their feet and hands to the cold, and I wondered how long it would take before that would happen. When I finally saw lights from the village, faint and distant, I wanted to shout and urge my horse on, but I couldn't move my jaw to utter a word and any movement of my right leg brought renewed pain. So I sat in my saddle like the others, painstakingly making my way up the mountainside to the fires that awaited.

We stopped upon reaching the church and the priest came out as before. Sir Carsten said to him, "We have wounded that need care. Do you have someone in the village skilled in the healing arts?"

"I will send for Tiedemann. He will know what to do. Bring the wounded men into the church," replied the priest.

On hearing these words I began to dismount. I knew that the act would cause me great pain, but I also knew I would have to endure it sometime. I swung the injured leg over the back of my horse and lowered myself to the ground. My left foot had no feeling and my right leg was stiff as a plank. Only holding tight to my saddle allowed me to stay standing. Walther saw my plight and supported me as we moved with the others into the church.

It was a little warmer inside the church and blankets were brought and gradually the feeling began to return to my hands and feet. The throbbing pain in my leg intensified however, and I had difficulty lying still. I looked around at the other men whose wounds appeared to be worse than mine. One man had an arrow in his torso and was unconscious. Several others had bandages that glistened red with fresh blood. When the man named Tiedemann arrived at the church, he went first to the unconscious man. He shook his head sadly and moved on to another man. When he finally came to me he looked at the arrow protruding from my leg and said, "I can remove it, and you will bleed a great deal. But that will be a good thing, for much of the swelling and pain will be relieved."

I nodded and replied, "I'm ready."

Tiedemann was old and grey with a pock-marked face and several missing teeth. His blue-green eyes showed warmth and intelligence, though, and I was reassured by them. He unfolded a cloth that contained several steel implements and selected a long slender knife from among the array. The old man's eyes shifted momentarily to Walther who was sitting nearby, and the knight moved closer and put his hands on my shoulders. My gaze caught a glimpse of my father's concerned face just before the blade was pressed into my flesh. I involuntarily stiffened and felt the pressure of Walther's hands holding me down. I suppose that only a few minutes went by but I thought the pain would never subside. I was aware of the shaft being pulled out, but that only made my agony worse for a time. Finally, the pain started to release me from its grip. The sweat that soaked my clothes turned cold, and I started shivering. I heard old Tiedemann say, "The point came out cleanly. That's good." In contrast to the cold that I felt in the rest of my body, there was something warm under my leg. I then realized that it was the pool of blood coming from the wound. Tiedemann let the blood pulse out of the cut for a few minutes and then gently pressed a cloth against it to stem the flow.

The wound was bound, the pain dulled slightly, and my chills subsided. I was more comfortable and gradually lapsed into sleep. I awakened once and was confused about where I was. It was quiet and dark, and I strained to see some recognizable features of the room. Finally, I realized that I was still in the sanctuary of the church. I tried to recall where things were before and noticed that the man with the arrow in his side was gone. A chill ran through me, and I pulled the blanket up around me. Any movement of my leg caused me pain. I fell asleep again.

The next time I woke, I was vaguely aware that I was being moved out of the church. It was daylight and snow was falling. I was taken to a hut a short distance away and placed by a fire. The room was small with the only furnishings being a rough-hewn table and a couple of chairs. A woman in ragged clothes fed me some rye porridge. The aroma of the porridge mingled with the smells of wood smoke, onions, animals, and sweat. The warmth inside the small room made me drowsy, and I again drifted off into sleep.

During my waking moments, I was aware that the pain in my leg was growing worse. Also, my entire body ached and I couldn't get comfortable. One time that I was awake I heard Tiedemann talking to my father. "He is feverish. Arrow wounds are dirty and deep. He may lose the leg."

"No!" I protested. "Father! Don't let them cut off my leg!" My father's eyes showed distress, and his mouth was set in a grim line. "Isn't there something else that can be done?" He asked.

"I can try to drain the wound again. And try a poultice of herbs that might draw out the poison." He sent the woman out with some instructions that I couldn't hear and took out his tools again. As he cut into my leg I couldn't feel it as much as the first time, and it scared me. 'Was my leg already dying?' I thought.

After a while, some of the pain in my leg subsided. The woman returned and Tiedemann, mixed the herbs that she brought into a wet mass and packed it into the wound. The old man left, and my father started out too. "Don't let him cut off my leg while I am asleep!" I implored.

"I won't." He replied.

Terrible visions sprung up in my imagination. I had only one leg. I couldn't ride anymore. Verena could only look at me with pity. My friends came to see me but couldn't hide their revulsion and left with heads bowed.

My fever grew worse. I thrashed uncomfortably under the coarse blankets. The woman went out for a moment and brought back a bucket full of snow. She took a handful and rubbed it on my forehead. Her touch was gentle, and the cold felt good. She continued applying the snow to my face and neck and then uncovered me and took off my shirt. My skin hurt terribly, but the ice didn't make it any worse so I submitted peacefully. Once she had applied the snow to my whole body and covered me back up, I felt more relaxed and fell asleep again.

I dreamed. At first the dreams were pleasant. I was home again. It was summer, and the fields were green and full of life. There were herds of young horses running in them. Then the mood grew dark and confusing. Diomedes was there, but he was in his stall and no one was caring for him. I grew alarmed, and then he was gone. Verena was at my bedside, but she seemed to be with someone else. Then she disappeared. Tiedemann was suddenly beside me and started cutting into my leg. I felt the blade sink deep into my flesh and I screamed. The scream sounded terrible to me and not like my own voice at all. I woke in a sweat. I was shaking. The woman, who was sitting beside me, said some calming words and stroked my forehead.

Once my fear from the dream faded, I realized that I felt a little better. Instead of shivering under the blankets, I was warm. The aching was gone from my body. I reached down and put my hands on my leg. It was still there, and I could move it. It hurt, but I was happy to feel the pain. At least I had a leg in which to have pain.

I looked at the woman for the first time. Her face showed the lines of age but she wasn't old. Her blue eyes shone from out of creases in her weather-worn skin, and a few wisps of silver mingled with the fair strands of hair that escaped her scarf. The corners of her wrinkled mouth turned slightly upward when she detected that I was feeling better. She had probably been pretty once, but time and a harsh life on the mountainside had stolen the freshness from her face and what was left was plain. I said, "I am grateful for your kindness. Am I in your house?"

"Yes," she replied. "I live here with my son. He is staying with my sister. You are not much older than he."

I started to ask about the boy's father but decided that it was a question that might have a painful answer.

"What is your name?" I asked instead.

"Gerlinde," she replied. "What is yours?"

"Max," I answered.

"You seem so young to be a knight," she started again.

"I'm not really a knight yet," I replied. "I'm just in training. We were returning from the queen's funeral when Carsten asked for our help."

"You attended the queen's funeral? In Magdeberg?" Her eyes widened.

"Yes," I answered, finally realizing the great significance of being included in such an important event.

"I've never been off this mountain," the woman said wistfully. "What was it like in Magdeberg?"

"It is a fine city, with many stone buildings." I tried to describe it to her, realizing that she would never see the home of the king or anything else beyond a few miles from that village. I began at that moment to understand my position.

94

The nobles were privileged to travel to far-away places and make decisions that affected the peasants, like that woman. As nobles, it was our responsibility to protect the peasants, like we did against the Slavs. In return they work our fields, make our boots, shoe our horses, tan our leather, forge our weapons, and do hundreds of other necessary tasks—tasks that I seldom thought about.

In the ensuing days I was able to get up and walk around with the aid of a crutch. Carsten's men left with their wounded, having buried the man who died. I felt like I was delaying my father's return to our village, so after three days I told him that I thought I could ride a horse and that we should resume our journey home.

Once I was strong enough to stand, I left the woman's house and moved to another where Walther was staying with an old man of the village. On the day of our departure, I went to say goodbye to the woman who had cared for me. When she opened the door of the hut and the morning sunlight shone on her face, just for a moment, I could see the beauty that lay beneath that tired and aging exterior. When she smiled at me, I felt that she was the embodiment of kindness and mercy and that perhaps instead of looking skyward for angels we might find them among us on earth. "I came to say goodbye and to thank you for caring for me and sharing your house," I said, looking into her eyes which held the depth of a mountain lake.

"I wish you good fortune always, Max."

I reached into my pocket and withdrew the small cross that I had bought for Verena. "I want you to have this," I said. "I bought it in Magdeberg."

Her eyes grew wide as she beheld the simple item. "I couldn't accept something so fine," she protested.

"Please, take it. I will always remember your kindness. I want to show my appreciation."

Her eyes grew moist as she took the cross and pressed it to her breast. "Thank you," she said, her voice filled with emotion. "Have a safe journey."

Mounting my horse was difficult since I had to spring up on my right leg. But with the assistance of Walther I was soon in the saddle, and riding was not particularly painful to my leg. As we rode away from the village on that sunny morning, I looked back and saw Gerlinde standing in the doorway of her hut. I lifted my hand, and she returned my gesture of goodbye.

15

For two days we had favorable weather on our journey. Skies were clear, breezes gentle, and there was no deep snow to contend with. On what should have been the last day, however, just after we crossed the Donau, heavy, dark clouds gathered on the horizon. It began to snow, and the wind came up, but for a few hours we were still able to make some progress traveling along the river trail. Eventually, though, the snow became so heavy that we were unable to see where we were going, and we were forced to seek shelter. We came to a small village built around a mountaintop fortress that overlooked the Donau and sought refuge within the walls of the burg. It was only because my father knew of the burg's location that we were able to find it at all. It was well past sunset when we arrived at the village, and the low clouds and heavy snowfall completely obscured our view to the top. Reaching the summit of the mountain was treacherous due to the fresh snow on the trail. Disaster nearly struck as Walther's horse lost its footing and slid backwards into mine. His horse's hind feet went off the edge of the narrow pathway and dislodged a number of stones. Just when it appeared that both horse and rider would fall off the side of the mountain to certain death, the agile animal scrambled back up and regained its footing.

Finally inside the citadel, we were admitted into the knights' quarters along the outer wall, where we ended up staying for the next three days, so severe was the storm. The long, low building had adequate space for us, there being only four other knights in residence at the time. We took our turns at tending the fire and carrying water from the well, in addition to trading stories with the men there to help pass the time.

One of the knights, Rainer, was big and loud and brash. He was the son of a Saxon noble but apparently not a legitimate heir. His father had two daughters with his first wife and then Rainer by a peasant woman. His father then had another son with his second wife, and Rainer was passed over for the title. He fought in the war with France and was wounded in the Battle of Andernach.

Another of the knights, Petrus, was only a few years older than me. He was tall, slender, and blonde-haired and was the son of a local lord. Being the youngest, he was quiet and hung on every word from the boisterous Rainer.

The third knight, Meino, was a bit older than the other two and grew up in Muhldorf am Inn, a village in Bavaria. He was a short, thick-built man that had fought in campaigns against the Magyars and the Eastern Slavs.

The oldest of the four, I think, was Quirin. White-haired and with deep creases in his weathered face, Quirin was from Lorraine. His mood was always serene; one of confidence and moral strength. He spoke sparingly and softly, as if to imply that what he had to say was worth saying, that his listeners could themselves, choose to listen or not, and he was unconcerned about their choice.

These four (or at least three, for Petrus rarely spoke), confined in the knight's quarters for the winter months, had obviously had many discussions on various matters and were well aware of each other's views. They seemed happy to have new ears in which to present their positions, and the arguments went on nearly non-stop.

One particular discussion concerned the presence of evil in the world. Rainer took the position that a perfect God could only create an ideal world and instill in humans His values of truth, beauty, and virtue. But that evil is necessary and inevitable, he said, because without the contrast in values, people wouldn't know the perfection of God.

Meino felt that if there was a God, He was weaker than Satan and that the world was inherently evil. He said we could fight for the values instilled in (some of) us but that we were destined to lose in the end.

To this, Quirin said, "The world is imperfect, but it is not evil. It is improving, for good will always be dominant over evil. We are instruments of God, and through us the world will progress toward perfection. *That* is what is inevitable."

The storm abated after a few days, and we resumed our journey homeward. The break in the weather was a short one, however, and another snowstorm hit shortly before we arrived at the lake. The rest of the month that year consisted of one storm after another. The snow increased to nearly waist depth, and it made even the shortest of journeys nearly impossible, so I was unable to see

Verena. Even though from *der Ludwigsburg*, I was only minutes away from her house, in those conditions there was no pretense that would allow a visit.

The long weeks of confinement did allow my leg to heal a bit more, and in March, when the snow melted, I was finally able to venture out on Diomedes. The great black charger had been turned out daily in snow-covered pastures to romp and play with other horses during my inactivity, so he was in in fine condition when we first ventured out together, even though I wasn't. His walk was brisk as we started out along the road, and when I let him have his head he pranced enthusiastically, splashing through the many puddles left by the melted snow.

It was good to be out riding again; to breathe the fresh, spring air and feel the warm sunlight on my face. The swelling green leaf buds covered the trees and likewise, bright green grass shoots poked their heads from beneath the dead brown vegetation of the previous year.

In spite of the great pleasure that I gained from that early spring ride, I eventually returned home feeling frustrated. I had gone searching for Verena, and had failed to find her. I rode to all the places that I had seen her before: the oak tree at the bottom of the hill, the berry patch along the road (of course, there were no berries at that time of year), the meadow where she grazed her goats, and the creek where she washed clothes. I even rode to the crest of a hill that overlooked the house in hopes of getting a glimpse of her.

The evident coming of spring turned out to be premature. Rain started the next day, the temperature dropped, and by nightfall it was snowing again. For the next two weeks, the weather alternated between rain and snow. The mud and the ruts in the road became so bad that it was nearly impossible to travel. The time passed slowly as I contemplated my next meeting with Verena. I tried to picture myself going to her house, but I knew that would never happen. In the first place, it would have been exceedingly awkward in that one-room house with her parents there. And it would reveal our relationship at a time that would cause family problems for both of us. Of course, I didn't know when we would be able to come forward about it. Marriage to a peasant girl was never going to be acceptable to my parents.

Finally in April of that year, warmer weather moved in, and I was again able to take rides that brought me in the proximity of Verena's house. The countryside was cloaked in signs of spring. Leaves burst from their tightly furled buds, meadows were lush in grass cover, and wildflowers sprinkled a profusion of colors along the roadside and in the woods and fields. At last, I found her in the meadow above the millpond with her new kids, much as I had the first time I saw her.

Our meeting was restrained, as it had to be where we were in open view, but I saw on her face the joy that it brought her. I smiled, as I always did, upon finally seeing her again. It seemed impossible, but she was more beautiful than ever, the pale of her complexion caused by the long winter only seeming to emphasize the blue of her eyes and the red of her lips. I got down off Diomedes and joined her as she strolled slowly around the herd of goats. "I looked for you weeks ago when there was a pause in the snow storms."

Verena thought for a moment. "About three weeks ago? Mother was very ill, and I couldn't leave her to go out. How long have you been back?"

"Almost two months. How is your mother now?"

"She's better, but awfully weak. She seems much older. You've been back for two months?"

"We got back during a snowstorm, and until that one break, there was no way to find you outside. And I was wounded."

"You were wounded?" She turned and looked up into my face with concern in her eyes. "How? All I was able to find out was that you went to the queen's funeral."

"On the way back from Magdeberg, we were asked to defend some villages that were being attacked by Slav raiders. I was hit in the leg with an arrow."

"Oh dear. Is it all right now?"

"Yes, it's fine.

"Are you sure?" she said, looking at my legs. "Which one?"

"The right. I got a fever and was sick for a few days," I said, secretly relishing Verena's sympathy.

"Well," she said, looking up into my eyes slyly, "I'll have to see the scar to be sure that you're not just making this all up." Then she blushed and looked embarrassed about what she had said.

"Maybe when we go swimming again," I said.

She smiled and more color rushed to her cheeks.

After a few quiet minutes, she said, "Will things ever be different for us?"

"Different?"

"Will we ever be able to see each other without depending on these chance meetings?"

"These meetings are anything but chance. I come looking for you."

She smiled. "You know what I mean. It scared me when you left, and I didn't know where you had gone or when you were coming back."

"I wanted to tell you but there wasn't any time."

Verena shook her head and the wind caught her long blonde curls and wrapped them across her face. She brushed them back and said, "There's really no hope for us is there?"

"All I know is that I love you, Verena," I said. "And I will find a way for us to be together always."

She looked at me in wide-eyed surprise and tears came into those lovely eyes. She took a step toward me, then looked around to see if we were being observed. Apparently satisfied as to our momentary privacy, she put her arms around my neck and kissed me. Like a wave that had crashed upon the shore and receded back into the ocean, she quickly retreated and stood apart from me again. She started walking again and put her hand out behind her. I reached out and lightly grasp the tips of those delicate fingers as I followed her. By that tiny bond we were linked together, as we would be forever.

16

In 947, Duke Hermann's daughter, Ida, married Otto's son, Liudolf. That year also saw the marriage of Otto's daughter Liutgarde, to Conrad the Red, Duke of Lorraine. Otto arranged for his brother Henry to marry Judith of Bavaria, the daughter of Duke Arnulf, thereby putting Henry in line to become Duke. Through these marriages of close family members, the king continued his quest to unify the German duchies into an empire completely under his control.

I finished my knight's training but still spent most days working with horses at the farm. I rose eagerly each day to ride to the farm where my time among the horses sped by all too quickly. Helmut assigned four young horses to me that summer, and I continued to develop the training methods that I learned while working with the mare, Analie. In the mornings, I would feed them, and while they were eating, I would stand close and pet them all over, getting them used to my touch. After that I groomed each one, picked up their feet and had them move forward, backward, and both right and left and in circles. By my using the lightest touch possible to ask for these movements, the young animals became supple and responsive. In the afternoons, I would begin again with each one in the fenced enclosure, having them move away from me and then return. They watched for the most subtle of cues from me as I became the leader that they needed now that they were separated from their mothers. When they returned to my side at the time they were supposed to, I allowed them to stand and relax and rubbed them on the head, neck, and shoulders. I returned home each day tired but satisfied and tranquil, as if the horses in my charge had somehow transferred their simple serenity to me.

In August, my father was ordered to travel to the Arab Kingdom in southern Iberia to begin establishing trade relations with the Umayyad Caliph. He told me that I was to accompany him on the journey. I was excited by the prospect of seeing a strange, far-away land, but I also had some misgivings about leaving Verena again so soon and about leaving the horses that were under my charge. But I knew I really had no choice and resolved to tell Verena the next day.

We met at the usual place along the road where the berry thicket was producing copious amounts of its summer harvest. Verena climbed onto the back of Diomedes, and we started off in a different direction than was custom. "Where are we going?" She asked.

"That will have to remain a secret for a while." I answered.

We were heading back toward the village where we never went together but soon veered off on a secluded path that I had used alone many times in the past. It skirted several farm fields and looped back toward the base of the mountain. Diomedes climbed a long, grassy slope and, near the top, I guided him into a grove of oaks. On the far boundary of the grove was a small clearing, around which I had built a rail fence. The grass within the enclosure was lush and green, and Diomedes pricked his ears and nickered a little bit upon seeing it. It was a familiar place to him and one with associated good memories.

We slid down off Diomedes, and I removed two rails from the fence. I took off his bridle and turned him loose within the little pasture and replaced the rails. He eagerly began grazing. I turned and looked at Verena, and her eyes were wide with wonder and curiosity. "How many other girls have you brought here?" She asked.

"Oh, hundreds. I've lost count," I answered with mock seriousness. I reached out my hand to her.

Verena frowned. "Am I the first?"

"The first and the only."

She smiled and took my hand. We circled the fenced enclosure, and I led the way to the entrance of a wooded trail that started up the mountain. It was narrow, not quite wide enough to allow us to walk side by side, but after a time it merged with the wider main trail, the one that my father and I had used the first time he took me to the mountain. "Have you ever been to the top?" I asked.

"No. I didn't know there was a path."

"My father showed it to me when I was a little boy."

We didn't say much as we walked steadily upward along the winding trail. It was a fine day, and the birds that flew from tree to tree in advance of our steps announced our coming with their songs. The warm sunlight filtering through the leaves above our heads cast intricate patterns of shadow on the ground beneath our feet.

I asked Verena if she needed to rest. "How much farther to the top?" She asked.

"We're about half-way."

"I'm used to walking. I don't have a fine horse to take me everywhere." She replied with a sly smile. "Let's keep going."

At last we reached the section of the path that leads to the promontory, and I asked Verena to close her eyes. "Did you bring me here to play a game of hoodman's blind?" She asked.

"I told you it was a surprise. I want you to get the full effect."

"The full effect of falling to my death?"

"I won't let you fall. Give me your hands and close your eyes."

105

Verena put out her soft, small hands, and I took them in mine. She closed her eyes and set her mouth grimly. I slowly guided her out on to the rock. "All right, you may look."

The view unfolded before her eyes: the shimmering blue lake, the white peaks reaching for the cloud-flecked sky, the green fields and forests stretching out in the distance. But I saw none of it directly. I saw it reflected in Verena's wide-eyed expression. Her great beauty was never more vivid than at that moment: her fair skin faintly colored by the sun, her blond curls ruffled by the breeze, the sweet smile of pleasure on her lips, and the wonder in her eyes at seeing the valley in which she lived as if viewed from heaven. For a long time we didn't speak. Eventually, she found the location of her house not far from the village and pointed to it. Then she pointed to the near shore of the lake and said, "That's where we used to go swimming." On and on we located familiar places viewed from an unfamiliar perspective. Finally her gaze lingered on the distant white-capped mountains. "I would like to go there," she said wistfully. "Italy is on the other side, is it not?"

"Yes, that's right." I didn't want to spoil the moment by telling her I was leaving. We continued to enjoy our eagle's perch there on the mountain until Verena decided that she needed to get back home before her mother started to worry. But before we started back down the mountain she hugged me tightly and said, "Thank you for bringing me here, Max. It's beautiful."

As we walked hand in hand down the path I said, "I have to leave for a short time, Verena."

She looked at me briefly and then back down at the path. She was silent for a while and then she asked, "Where are you going?"

"I'm going with my father to Iberia on a trade mission."

"Won't it take a long time to get there?"

"Yes, I suppose so."

"Then you aren't leaving for a 'short time.' You're actually leaving for a long time."

"Yes, it will be a long journey. And I don't want to leave you. But the important thing is that I will be back. And when I return we will talk to our parents of our intention to marry."

Verena stopped and looked at me with questioning eyes. "Do you really think that is possible?"

"I will do whatever is necessary to make it happen."

She shook her head resignedly. "I really don't see how."

"It will happen because we are meant to be together. Nothing can change that."

Verena smiled. "I don't want anything to change. This day, this place, being with you, why does it ever have to be different?"

"Only the times and places will change. Being together will always bring us happiness."

We walked on for a while. "How will you get to Iberia?" She asked.

"We'll cross the mountains into Italy to get to the coast and then travel by sea."

"I wish I could go with you."

"I wish you could too."

"Will it be dangerous?"

"It shouldn't be. We won't cross any hostile territory. And we're going to trade, not fight."

When we got back to the fenced enclosure Diomedes was laying on his side in the thick grass with his neck stretched out along the ground. When he assumed that position, it was impossible to tell whether he was sleeping or dead. I called out, "Dio!"

There was no sign of movement in the large body. My stomach lurched a bit. "Dio!" I called louder.

The ear of the great black horse twitched. I exhaled after realizing that I had been holding my breath. His head came up momentarily while he looked sleepily around, and then settled back into the grass. I walked into the enclosure, and Diomedes finally raised his huge form up to standing and shook himself vigorously. "I guess you feel pretty safe here to sleep so soundly," I said softly to him as I put his bridle on.

Verena and I spoke little on the way back to the berry thicket, but she held me a little tighter than usual and laid her head on my back. When we arrived I said, "I'll walk with you."

We slid down off Diomedes and started walking back along the road towards the Chestnut grove. When we reached it, Verena led me into its cool, shady depths so that we were hidden from the rest of the world. She drew me near, her eyes lowered. I lifted her chin with my fingers, and there were tears in her eyes. We kissed long and tenderly, and in our embrace, every contour of her young body found a place to nestle within mine. "Return to me safely, my love," she whispered softly in my ear.

As I watched Verena walk up the hill toward her home, my soul ached as I contemplated being away from her for even a day, let alone the undetermined number of months my journey would take.

Our journey took us south, and for the first two days we were able to travel easily along well-trodden trails that crossed gentle terrain. Our route took us past the lakeshore village of Zug and by several more inter-connected lakes. The summer sun was bright, and the blue surfaces shimmered with the light of a hundred thousand lanterns. The lakes were surrounded by green-clad mountains, and deep inside I had to admit that their beauty rivaled even that of the lake at home and the majesty of "our mountain." On the third day, however, the terrain began to change hourly, becoming much more steep and rocky. Our progress was much slower as we had to wind through narrow passages and negotiate difficult changes in grade. Waterfalls cascaded straight down the vertical sides of the black rocks that towered menacingly above us. Many of the higher passes were still impassable, but in the ones at our elevation, the snow came only to our horses' knees. I asked my father if we were following the same route that Hannibal used when he crossed the mountains with his army to attack the Romans. "There is no one alive to tell us what exact route Hannibal used," he answered, "but if this isn't it, I wouldn't think it would be much different."

In the high meadows there was abundant grazing for the horses, and tiny streams of snow melt wound their way through narrow rocky channels. On the hillsides and in the crevices of the rocks a profusion of red and blue and yellow wildflowers basked in the warm sunlight of late summer. Although it took many days to travel across the slopes and valleys of the mountains known as the Alps, such was their beauty that I was almost sorry to leave them behind as we began a gradual descent into the lush, fertile plateau below. The breezes were much warmer there, and the vegetation was unfamiliar to me. We arrived at a lakeside trading village called Lugano. It was late in the afternoon, and it had been a long and tiring day when we first spied the placid basin nestled in the mountains. There was a small but well-defended fortress on a hill overlooking the lake, and it was there that we spent the night. The fortress commanded an expansive view of the surrounding countryside, and I stood for a long time at sundown gazing across the lake. Dark green hills rose straight up from the deep blue waters, and the course of the lake wandered off between the walls of rock and into the distance. Behind me the sky was streaked with rose-colored clouds as the sinking sun threw up its last rays. Verena would have loved that view, I thought.

The next day we continued our journey south into the broad, flat Po River Valley and its vast grain fields. The snow-capped mountains were to our backs, and the rich, fertile farmland stretched out endlessly before us. There were eleven of us in all: my father and I, Walther and Parsifal, plus a third knight, Berthold, and four attendants who were armed and could fight if we were attacked. Also travelling with us was a man named Friedemann, sent from Magdeberg to negotiate on Otto's behalf, and his attendant.

It wasn't long before a large settlement came within our view well before we reached it. It was Milan, the Italian city that controlled not only the east-west trade routes but also all goods coming across the Alps. That it was once a Roman city was obvious by the street patterns and the presence of so many old stone buildings still in use. The marketplace was huge and crowded with merchants, farmers, and travelers from distant lands. There was a colorful profusion of fruits and vegetables of types I had never seen before as well as many strange forms of bread. Smoke from cooking fires clouded the air. The smells of food, oils, leather, and bodies mingled confusingly. There were fine fabrics in brilliant colors on display and gleaming weapons with finely tempered blades. Conversations and bargaining hummed on in many languages. The scene as a whole assailed my senses as nothing had done previously.

We met a trader named Agostino, and Friedemann talked to him about serving as agent to make purchases and arrange for goods to be shipped across the mountains. Agostino was a short, stout man who wore fine clothes and had large gold rings with jeweled settings on nearly every finger. He was deferential in the extreme and obviously pleased to obtain such a lucrative opportunity. I sensed, however, that his avarice knew no boundaries and that if having our throats slit could bring an even larger treasure, then he would have no hesitation in carrying it out. But I suppose that such men are a necessary element of commerce and that they remain useful as long as they are well paid for their services. Agostino introduced us to a man named Cecilio who would be the one to assure that the goods purchased would be safely transported through the mountains. Cecilio was, in sharp contrast to Agostino, a large and powerful man, dressed plainly, with a square jaw and dark, penetrating eyes. There were no rings on the fingers of his rugged hands. In fact, he was missing the last two fingers of his left. Moving trade goods in the frontiers and across the lawless mountains was a dangerous business.

While we were in Milan we were warned more than once that bands of thieves were operating in the countryside. Most were small and elusive, managing to evade the large, well-equipped armies that maintained order near the towns and villages. We weren't sure how far south Milan's control extended, so it was with a watchful eye that we headed out of the city and toward the Po.

We reached the river without perceiving any threat and crossed at Valenza. Since it was late in summer, the water level was relatively low, although signs of flooding earlier in the year was evident. Valenza was much smaller than Milan but showed some of the same characteristics, such as the street grids and mix of old Roman buildings and more recent buildings in the style of the Lombards and the Franks. Friedemann knew a man there named Ferruccio who dealt in fine cloth from Iberia and the Far East. He had an opulent villa that was situated in the midst of olive groves. He invited us to stay there for the night, an invitation that was gratefully accepted. Our generous host was a tall, thin man with dark wavy hair streaked with grey. His quiet and gracious manner caused me to reconsider my opinion of merchants. We dined sumptuously on lamb and pork and exotic fruits and nuts the like I had never seen before. Red wine flowed freely, and that night we slept between sheets of silk. We were well rested when we continued our journey the next morning, but a bit too much indulgence in the wine left me with a head that throbbed with every hoof fall.

It wasn't long before the mountains called the Apennines came clearly into view and our elevation increased as we moved out of the Po valley. The foothills gradually rose around us, and the far-ranging view of our surroundings that we enjoyed in the valley diminished. A group of riders approached from ahead. My father, riding in the lead, turned and cautioned "Everyone be on guard." It was an unnecessary warning. We had all heard the stories. I counted eighteen men, variously armed with swords, axes, and maces. Their equipage and armor did not indicate that they were part of a regular army. The man at the head of their procession nodded and smiled as we passed them on the narrow trail.

When they had passed, Sir Walther said, in a voice just loud enough for all of us to hear, "They are checking our strength and trying to decide whether to attack us."

Evidently deciding that their numbers were sufficient to defeat us, the group of bandits circled and formed two columns. When they did this, we quickly turned our horses so that they all faced in the direction of the attack. We formed a wedge, with the five knights, including myself, across the front. As they charged, the two columns of our attackers split and clashed with us on both sides of our formation. I was on the right, behind Walther. Fear rose in me once again, as it had against the Slav raiders, but I controlled it more easily. The mountain thieves were savage killers, but they lacked skill and discipline. They were no match for our superior armor and training. One by one they fell to our blades as we fought tightly quartered, flank to flank. Realizing the futility of engaging our front, several of the horsemen swung wide, coming around to our rear.

Our armed servants came under attack. As I swung my horse around to meet the second charge, I saw one of our men suffer a mortal blow. I rushed forward to engage his killer. The bandit was a formidable fighter, and I was immediately locked in combat with him. I blocked several furious blows, but one of them slid off my blade and hit my mount's head. The brave animal remained steadfast in the fight despite the injury. Indeed, it was his agility that eventually allowed me to prevail, for I was able to out- maneuver the other man and bring my sword crashing down on his neck. He slumped forward in the saddle, wavered for a moment, and then fell heavily to the ground. By that time, the skirmish was over. The bandits, their number reduced by half, retreated into the nearby hills. We had suffered only one casualty, the rest sustaining only minor wounds.

I jumped down off my horse and examined his head. The flesh between his eyes was laid open and a stream of blood ran down his face. A sliver of white bone was visible under the flap of skin. Walther came up to me and said, "Detlef is dead," referring to the servant who had been killed in the fighting, "but his horse is uninjured if you need another mount."

"I can sew up this gash if someone will hold his head for me," I replied.

"I will do it."

I got a needle and string from our supplies as Walther wrapped his arm securely around the horse's nose. Walther was a large man and very strong, but hugging the horse could not have stopped him from pulling away if he really wanted to. However, the horse was trained well to yield to pressure and gently lowered its head. "Have you ever sewn up a horse before?" My companion asked.

"Once. One of the horses at the farm cut its leg, and Helmut had me close the wound."

I carefully inserted the needle next to the wound and then waited to see if the animal was going to tolerate what I was doing. A barely perceivable flinch was the only reaction I got. With each stitch the horse grew less apprehensive of the needle pricks, which were probably not much more painful than a fly bite. They were most certainly less significant than the pain of the sword wound. I was able to close the cut and stop the bleeding. I washed away the dried blood. "Well, he isn't so handsome as he was before, but I think he will still be useful," I said.

The servant Detlef was buried as we apprehensively surveyed the surrounding mountain passes for another attack. No further incidents ensued, and we were again on our way. I rode Detlef's horse and led mine. Late in the afternoon we reached the southern slope of the Apennines and arrived at the termination of the overland portion of our journey, the seaport of Genoa.

17

How does one adequately describe his feelings upon viewing the sea for the first time? It is similar to the awe with which one regards the night sky, with its seemingly limitless boundaries and mysterious depths. The sky is unattainable, surely, but the sea has just enough accessibility to cause men to risk their lives upon it. The sea also has a smell and a feel that is missing from the sky. Even when we were still far from the rocky shores of the great sea, the wind carried upon it a distinctively salty smell and a heavy moist feeling that contrasted greatly from the dry air of the high mountains.

Beyond these tangible elements, there is a strong feeling that emanates from deep within me now whenever I am near the sea. Certainly part of it is the disquietude that comes of realizing how insignificant we are in comparison to such might. Yet, we still dare to risk total ruin by challenging such infinite power by riding its surface on feeble man-made conveyances. But the sea also has a strangely calming effect on me as well, as if its great power could also be benevolent and hold me in a reassuring embrace.

The city of Genoa had been sacked and burned by the Fatimids a few years earlier, but signs of rebuilding were apparent. Walls and buildings were under construction amidst the ruins of the old Roman structures. On the approach to the city our trail, which had been no more than packed earth in the north, merged with the remains of a road paved with square-cut stones. Over-grown with weeds, with broken and dislodged stones, the road led us through the gates to the city and gradually improved in condition within the remnants of the wall. It branched off into narrow streets where it became slippery with odious wastes, both human and animal. As we got closer to the busy waterfront, the stench of the foul street air mingled with the smell of fish and salt water. Hundreds of noisy gulls soared and dove to snatch bloody fish heads and entrails left on the docks or thrown into the water by men processing their catch.

We arranged for passage on a galley with double rows of oarsmen and a large square sail. We could not bring our horses so we left them in the care of a man named Leandro who took them to a farm outside the city. We gave him a purse of gold with the promise of another on our return if the horses were in good shape.

We set sail aboard the long, graceful craft on a calm morning with the sun ascending the sky behind us. With each powerful thrust of the oars we gained speed until it seemed as though we merely skimmed over the surface of the waves with the water providing little impediment to our progress. The rocky coastline off our right side rose and fell in elevation and small villages seemed to cling precariously to the vertical faces of the cliffs. I stood in the bow of the vessel looking out over the broad expanse of the sea with the wind and the saltwater spray caressing my face and wondered if there would ever be again in my life such a grand adventure.

The days went by at a languorous pace as we glided along the rocky coast, making our way southwest. On the fourth day out, there was a flurry of excitement as a ship was spotted on our left rapidly approaching on a course that appeared to be in a direct line with ours. The captain gave an order that had, as a result, the effect of a much quicker cadence of the oarsmen. Our faster pace allowed us to avoid the path of the other vessel, but it swerved to pursue. The glimpse that I got of the men in the other craft as our paths nearly intersected was fleeting, but I clearly saw individuals with dark skin and black robes. Their heads were covered.

Walther came up by my side, and I gave him an inquiring glance. "They are pirates from the north shore of Africa," he said. "They prey on merchant ships that travel these coasts—ruthless killers that don't leave survivors."

"Pirates," I repeated the word, which was new to me. Thieves that plied the seas for their victims. "Well," I said, "they could die at the end of a sword just like a bandit on land."

Walther smiled. "True enough. But this is their battlefield," he said with a wave of his arm, "and it's not the fight I would pick if I had a choice."

The chase wore on for an hour, the pirates hoping to gain on us as our rowers grew tired, but the pursuing boat gradually fell further behind and eventually curled off and left us to go on our way. The captain slowed the stroke cadence with a command and, after a time, the rowers resumed the normal system of rotation that took a number of oarsmen out of service periodically in order to rest.

Our voyage stretched on for a week. We kept the shore in sight off the starboard side during the day and navigated by the stars at night. One night a beacon emerged from the blackness of the sea, first as a pinpoint of light like a star resting on the horizon, and then growing larger as we drew nearer. Its flare danced capriciously against the dark sky, and soon we realized it was a large fireball that held our gaze. As we cautiously drifted closer, the flames revealed the outline of a large galley that was being consumed by an inferno. No one spoke as we picked up speed and glided by the dying ship. I wondered to myself how many of the occupants died in the struggle and how many were sold into slavery. I felt my anger rising that such vermin should thrive making their livelihood preying on innocent seagoing traders and travelers.

We reached Malaga on the southern coast of Iberia, the region called by the Arabs, 'al-Andalus'. As we sailed into view of the old city, my attention was arrested by an ancient fortress perched on a hill above the harbor. At the bottom of a steep descent from the walls of the fort was the old town that had changed rulers many times over the centuries. Under the Umayyad, the city was expanding across the waterfront, becoming the most important trading center of the Iberian Peninsula.

Malaga is an interesting mix of sights to catch the eye. Sort of like wildflowers on a hillside in spring. The Phoenicians and the Carthaginians, the Romans, the Byzantines, and the Goths all seem to have left their identity in the mixture. And now the Arabs with their grand mosque and graceful towers have cultivated flowers that dominate all the others.

Friedemann purchased horses for our overland passage to the caliphate in Cordoba. Before our departure from the city we procured a quantity of figs, pomegranates, and almonds, all of which were abundant in the central market.

We were barely outside of the busy heart of town when a profusion of grapevines began to spread across the green slopes. These vast vineyards were soon joined by neatly laid-out groves of olive trees. In every direction on the road between Malaga and Cordoba we saw the agricultural methods of the Arabs thriving. After the long days spent at sea, it was good to be travelling on land again. Having a horse beneath me was reassuring in a way that a ship's deck could never be. The Spanish horses were, for the most part, smaller than the animals I was used to. But they were sure-footed and nimble and well-suited to their job of carrying riders. It appeared that much of the farm work that we use large horses for is done by donkeys in Spain.

In two days we reached the enormous city of Cordoba. Long before we reached the seven gates of its old town, however, we could observe proof of a society of great wealth and innovation. Ingenious irrigation systems brought water from the mountains, beautiful ornamental gardens flourished within the city, and magnificent buildings seemed endless in number as the city spread to the east and west. The grandest of all was the mosque, which surely must be the most elegant structure ever built by men. I marveled at its hundreds of columns and intricate mosaics, thinking of not only the thousands of skilled hands that it took to build it, but also the genius of the architects who could conceive of such an edifice.

Near the great mosque stood the Emir's palace, splendid in its own right. But when we sought to gain entry we were told that the Caliph had moved his residence to the new city of Medinat al Zahra. We were directed toward a road paved with perfectly fitted stones which surpassed the finest Roman road that I had ever seen. The three mile route between the two cities was lined with date palms and lemon trees. A distant sea of sugarcane gently swayed in the wind.

Almost immediately the city where the Caliph resided came into view. Medinat al Zahra is constructed on three terraces, each surround by a wall. The lower level, although heavily populated, is spacious and efficiently organized. A fine mosque is located there, as well as markets, gardens, and public baths. We were told by a soldier there that court officials were on the next level up. We left our horses and made our way up the steps to the second terrace. By then it was quite late in the day. We were told that the Caliph would be informed of our visit, and we would be notified when we could have an audience. In the meantime, we would be shown to quarters. A lower ranking officer led us back down to the first level and to a row of white-washed structures that housed soldiers. Our quarters were simple but adequate. The most surprising feature was a compartment located within the building that took away our wastes on a flow of water.

The Caliph did not see us the following day, and I occupied myself with exploring the wonders of the city. Expecting to see only Muslims, I was surprised by the large numbers of Christians and Jews in Medinat al Zahra living and working and even worshiping there. The markets displayed an enormous agricultural bounty, with olives, rice, almonds, lemons, pomegranates, dates, and sugar in abundance. Also growing within the city were small trees that bore a sweet fruit the Arabs called 'naranj.' Fish swam in large man-made pools throughout the city. Water was carried by aqueducts from the mountains and filled gigantic cisterns and then ran through pipes to wherever it was needed. Thousands of workers labored on new construction. Surely, I thought, the prosperity I saw there must rival that which existed in ancient Rome.

On the third day we were granted an audience with the Caliph. His palace sat atop the uppermost terrace. Ranks of soldiers held aloft their swords on both sides of the path where we made our entrance. Richly embroidered fabrics adorned the chamber inside. We were led into a room with gilded designs on the ceiling and walls and colorful floor mosaics. We were greeted by a distinguished looking man in a turban and fine robes. We were a bit confused by this personage and were starting to bow when we were told by our escort that the man was merely one of the Caliph's slaves. We crossed a great hall with pillars and statues and marble floors and finally reached an inner courtyard with a large tree in the center that spread its limbs like a canopy. A man in a white robe knelt in prayer beside it. We waited silently until he rose to his feet and turned toward us. We were then allowed to approach the Caliph of al-Andalus.

Abd Ar Rahman III was soft-spoken and courteous, and his manner quickly put us at ease. He talked of his eagerness to establish safe trade routes with the Frankish realms and expressed his opinion that a peaceful Italy would benefit both the German lands and al-Andalus. Indeed, the man himself embodied a merging of east and west. Unlike other Arabs, his eyes were blue and his hair was reddish in color, a result of his mother's heritage. When my father introduced me to him, he asked if I would like to be shown around Medinat al Zahra by his son, who was the city's architect. I replied, "I don't wish to interfere with your son's work, but I would be very interested in learning all I can about the city and life here."

The Caliph sent for his son, who arrived at the palace a short time later. Al Hakam ll was a few years older than me, taller than average, with dark hair and eyes. He wore a serious expression on his face at all times and although he was methodically polite, there seemed to be a slight undercurrent of displeasure at being burdened by my presence. His ability to speak our language was better than his father's, and it rapidly became apparent that he had an excellent mind and could converse intelligently on a broad array of topics. As we walked around Medinat al Zahra he pointed out, with obvious pride, elements of planning and construction that might not be readily visible to a casual observer. With thoughtfully conceived questions, I drew out more and more detailed answers from my guide and gradually his shell of formality began to melt away.

Some of my questions hinted at the great cost of building a new city completely from nothing, for many of the materials, such as marble, had to be imported. Hakam explained that the great wealth of al- Andalus comes from its agriculture. Olive oil, wine, dates, lemons, rice, sugar, saffron, and cotton were exported to distant places such as Alexandria, Bagdad, and Byzantium. Other industries such as leather goods and metalware also provide income. We came upon a grove of trees that I didn't recognize, and I inquired about it. He said that they were mulberry trees and that the leaves provided food for the silkworm caterpillars used in the production of silk fabric, which is also a valuable export.

We reached the northern edge of the city where, from the first terrace, we could look out over the surrounding countryside. Not far from the city I could see a herd of horses and a large camp filled with tents. "What is that over there?" I asked.

"That is where our horses are trained in the traditional way."

"I am very interested in seeing that. Would it be possible for me to go there?"

"I could take you there tomorrow. Bring your horse to this place an hour after sunrise and I will meet you here."

"That would be extremely gracious of you. I hope I am not being too much trouble."

"It is no trouble."

I awoke at dawn the next day full of excitement. I hastily ate a few bites of bread and a naranj and got my horse from the stables. I arrived at the arranged location early and looked with anticipation at the horse camp in the distance, anxious to learn something of the Arab methods that might help with my own training.

Not much later, Al Hakam, alone, rode up on a beautiful grey Arabian horse with a long flowing mane and a tail that swept the ground. Dressed in white robes that fell upon his steed's back Al Hakam bowed quickly and touch his forehead in the gesture of greeting that I had seen numerous times since coming to al Andalus. I returned his greeting and he seemed pleased. We rode down a winding path that led away from the city, and when we reached level ground Al Hakam urged his horse into a gallop. Faster and faster the grey horse went, and I spurred my mount on in an effort to keep up. The easy stride of the grey devoured ground, and my horse fell further and further behind. I felt I was being tested. The tail of Hakam's horse was raised like an ensign flying in the wind. I took aim at it and tried to get as much speed out of my animal as I could. Striding effortlessly, the grey was not expending maximum effort, and I reached its flank just as we got to the outskirts of the Arab camp.

What I saw was a fully contained tent camp which seemed devoted to raising horses. Hakam explained: "Although in al Andalus we have fine cities, we are descended from desert tribes in which our relationship with our horse means either life or death. Our horses go everywhere with us, and sleep in our tents. Our children play around the mares and lie on top of them in repose. One day their lives may depend upon the loyalty of the mare that was raised in their tent. Our horses must be able to cross wide expanses of desert in extreme heat with very little food or water. If we fall from a horse it must stand perfectly still until we get back on or help arrives. If we need to rest upon the ground at night the horse will stand guard over us and warn us if danger approaches. The young horses are handled almost from the moment of their birth, and their education begins then. Once the horse reaches the age of two, it is ridden hard on a journey of many miles as a test of its courage and stamina. Would you like to try it?"

Again feeling like I was being tested, I hesitated a moment, and then answered yes.

We walked to where a small herd of young horses was browsing among the sparse forage. Along the way I observed men handling and riding horses of varying ages. Their methods were gentle and quiet, and the horses were very relaxed and calm. I never witnessed any harsh treatment of the animals—no striking, no loud voice commands, and no restraints were used. The horses were responsive to the most subtle cues of their riders and handlers.

Two horses were selected from the group, one black and the other grey. They were small, but well filled-out, the muscles of their hips and shoulders rippling beneath glossy coats. "Neither of these has been strenuously ridden. It is time for them to show us their worth. Which one would you like to ride?"

Except for the difference in color, the two horses were nearly identical. The black had a slightly softer, more trusting eye so I walked over and took his reins from his handler. "With your permission, Prince."

Hakam nodded, then quickly jumped up on the grey. Neither horse had a saddle, but since they were small, mounting was not difficult. I thought to myself, 'getting on was the easy part. Staying on might be a lot harder.'

I had barely gained my seat when Hakam and the grey took off across the plain at a gallop. It took little urging for the black to follow his companion. His initial jump was so rapid he almost left me suspended in mid-air. I regained my balance and started my pursuit. At first I didn't think I would be able to close the gap, which had grown wide while my horse and I were working more against each other than together. Soon, however, I started to trust him and let my hands move in rhythm with his huge stride, and the ground raced by us like the flight of an arrow. Foot by foot the distance to the grey narrowed as I bent low over my horses' neck, his long black mane swept back into my face. I had never felt such speed under me. It was almost as though his hooves flew over the ground without coming back to earth.

Miles of mostly empty terrain sped by, and I finally reached the grey's flank. The prince and I were not riding the horses hard. We were giving their heads almost complete freedom, but the two young horses were competing with each other. I drew alongside and the grey let me pass, but only briefly. He surged forward again, seizing the lead.

I could see ahead of us a broken line of trees and wondered if Hakam would draw his horse up. He didn't. Closer and closer we came to the trees, which I could see bordered a river. Surely, I thought, the prince would stop before reaching its banks. We veered down into a dry creek bed which led into the larger stream and galloped over the smooth channel toward the shallow water at its mouth. Without slowing, the prince drove his horse on, sending up a spray as he entered the water. Farther and farther they splashed until the grey plunged into the deeper pool of the river. My horse showed no hesitation on approaching the water and followed his companion into the river channel. Soon both horses were swimming and I clung to my mount's neck to keep from floating off his back. When we finally reached the other side of the river, the horses clamored up onto the bank, their sides heaving in exhaustion. Only then did Hakam let the animals rest. He slid down off the dripping wet horse which shook itself vigorously, and then dropped its head to nibble some grass.

"We will ride them back in the same manner, and if they eat heartily we will know that they will be great horses."

"Did you know that they would enter the river without hesitation?" I asked, also getting down off my mount.

"An Arab's horse must go wherever it is directed, even if it risks death."

Once the horses had returned to normal breathing, we re-mounted. Hakam rode his horse in a wide loop, first away from the river, then back toward it. The bank on that side was several feet above the surface of the water and the prince gained speed as he approached it. 'This could end badly,' I thought to myself, but urged my horse to follow. The grey collected his steps, but did not hesitate. I watched as they took off from the bank and stretched out through the air toward the water. I thought the black would duplicate what his companion had done, but just as we got to the edge, his back legs came under him and we stopped. I didn't know whether to make him go forward or turn him around for another try. He made my decision for me. Gathering himself, he jumped awkwardly off the bank and landed with a huge splash in the water. I lost my seat but managed to hold on to the reins. For an embarrassing moment, I swam alongside my horse before I could grab a handful of mane and regain my position as rider.

After swimming the river in reverse, we emerged in the sandy creek bed and continued on at a gallop until we could climb the bank to level ground. The rest of the ride back to the tent camp was done at a slightly slower pace than the outward journey, and we rode mostly with the horses side by side.

On dismounting at the camp, we gave the horses back to their handlers. "They will be given water, some hay, and then barley," Hakam told me. "They will be given a day off, watched carefully for any soreness, and if they are sound, we can ride them again in two days."

'Was this an invitation?' I asked myself.

As we rode back to the city, we talked about horses and training. "The methods that you employ are not greatly different than what we use," I ventured. "By the time you take the horse on its first journey, it has learned not to fear people and accepts you as its leader."

"Yes, the horse must obey without questioning."

"But a horse will not naturally place itself in danger. What we call courage in a horse is actually trust. It believes that as its leader we will keep it safe."

Hakam thought about this for a moment, then nodded. "It is unfortunate that we must sometimes put them in dangerous situations."

When we arrived back at Medinat al Zahra the prince said, "Shall we meet here day after tomorrow and go riding again?"

"I will look forward to it," I replied.

The next day passed slowly for me as I passed the time waiting for the day on which I would again ride with the Prince.

The morning of our second ride was hot and hazy. Hakam had the same two horses outfitted with saddles. They needed to get used to a saddle's weight and stirrups as well as various equipment flapping against their sides. We started out along the same route as before, but at a slightly slower pace, and after a while we turned off north and travelled toward a line of hills. "The change of terrain will strengthen their legs and teach them how to carry a rider up and down slopes," the prince explained.

The first incline was a gentle rise that leveled off at the top for a time before it descended into a grassy valley on the other side. The far side of the narrow valley was a bit steeper and the young horses labored to climb to the second ridge. We reached the top with Hakam slightly in front, and the grey started the downslope a few yards ahead of us.

The ambush was well-planned. Shielded by the rise, the black-robed riders converged upon us swiftly, with no chance for us to flee. I saw three men close in on the prince, and one of them threw a rope around him, trapping his arms. That was the last thing I saw before something slammed into the right side of my head and the ground spun around me. I landed hard on my side and my left arm jammed violently into my ribs. As I lay writhing in the sand, gasping for breath, I was barely conscious of four riders speeding away with Hakam under their control.

The earth became solid beneath me again, but the pain in my side remained. My head throbbed as I slowly got to my feet. The black stood motionless about fifty feet away, his head held high, ears pricked, and eyes intent on the receding image of his companion in the distant dust cloud. As I walked over to him, he gave me a quick glance and then returned his gaze to the fleeing horses. I climbed into the saddle and said to him, "Let's go get our friends."

I didn't have to ask twice. The black leaped forward and was in a full gallop in two strides. I didn't really have a plan, but my other option, going back to the camp and admitting that the prince was abducted while in my company, wounded my pride.

My foes weren't escaping quickly. They probably didn't expect to be pursued, and Hakam was doing his best to slow them down. With each stride the black gained ground, and it wasn't long before my pursuit was detected. One of the riders peeled off from the others and circled back toward me. I drew my sword. My attacker's curved blade reflected the sunlight. He was on me in an instant. The blade was in his right hand, so I veered right to pass on his left side.

I blocked his blow with my sword and swung the agile black around behind him. Before he could turn in his saddle, I slashed his right arm and his sword fell to the ground. I hit him again across the back of his neck, and he slumped forward in his saddle.

My chances were improving. A second warrior came back to meet me. I hugged the neck of my horse with my head on the left side, my sword held low on the right. My enemy's sword was raised, exposing his right side. I extended my right arm as far as I could reach, and an instant before his blade fell I thrust the point of my sword into his rib cage. The impact wrenched my weapon from my hand and unseated the other rider. I circled back and found him lying on the ground with his horse standing over him. He was still alive, but impaled on my steel blade. I withdrew my sword and dispatched him quickly by plunging it into his throat. The coldness with which I performed the act chills me now to think of it, but at that point I felt only rage.

The two remaining riders flanked Hakam's mount, with the one on the left side holding his horse's reins. The one on the right showed no inclination to leave his position beside the prince and held fast. I stayed close behind waiting for my chance. The man on the left seemed most vulnerable since one hand was occupied holding the grey's reins so, urging my tiring horse on, I took a quick run at him. It almost worked. But at the last second, the other rider dropped in behind his comrade and fended me off. I had anticipated his maneuver, however, and dropped back slightly. I waited until the second rider was abreast of the one holding the reins, then darted in on the undefended right side with my dagger drawn. I cut the rope that held Hakam's arms, then handed him the knife. In an instant, he had dispatched his captor. The last of the abductors, now facing two foes, veered off from us and fled. "Should I pursue him?" I asked.

"No," answered the prince. "We should save our horses for the long journey back."

"Who were they?"

"Radical Muslims. Not everyone approves of my father's policies of tolerance."

We rode at a walk back in the direction from which we came. We passed the bodies of the two men I had slain and collected their horses to take back with us. Hakam shook his head. "If all of Otto's knights fight like you, I hope the German King never invades al-Andalus."

When we went our separate ways back at Medinat al Zahra, the prince grasped my hand warmly and said "Shukran Jazilan."

My ribs ached for several days after that, especially when I took a deep breath. The caliph's physicians bound my torso in linen bandages, which helped some. Our visit was nearly at an end and seemed successful. The caliph was grateful for the assistance that I had given his son, and assured my father and Friedemann of favorable trade status for Otto's merchants.

On the day that we left Medinat al Zahra to begin our journey home, Hakam came to say goodbye. We were loading our horses with the last of the products of al Andalus that we were taking with us as trading samples and gifts. The prince rode up on his fine grey and dismounted in a flourish of white robes. He respectfully greeted my father and then turned to me. "You must someday return to al Andalus and help train more young horses, my brother. Please accept this gift as a token of my gratitude." From a folded piece of linen he produced a fine dagger with a gleaming blade. The pommel was gold inlaid with large precious stones. "This dagger was made in Toledo. The steel from Toledo is the finest in the world," he said.

I took the wonderful gift from him and bowed in thanks. He bowed in return and then started back toward his horse. After a few steps he turned his earnest eyes back to me and said with a slight smile, "May you have a long life. I predict your enemies will quake with fear at the coming of the great cavalier of Swabia."

18

Two days out from the port of Malaga, we were experiencing calm seas and steady winds on our return to Genoa. Around mid-day, we sighted a skiff off the port bow that appeared to be drifting aimlessly. As we got closer, it was apparent that the small boat had a broken mast and the two occupants were hailing us. Our captain slowed and steered our galley closer to the disabled craft and tried to speak to the two men, who appeared to be fishermen, in Italian. He received no response from them, and so tried Spanish and then Portuguese. Still the men were silent.

Suddenly, a large, sleek galley appeared in the near distance behind the skiff, under full sail and with its rows of oars cutting the water. It had emerged into the open sea from a well-concealed cove and was heading for our bow. Our captain, turned his sail to catch the wind and ordered our oarsmen into action. But it was quickly apparent that he was too late. The skiff had served its purpose by slowing us down enough for the corsair to intercept us. "Ramming speed!" Came the order.

The cadence of our oars rose faster and faster as the other craft grew larger in our view. The wind and spray stung my face as I tried to calculate where we would strike the pirate vessel. I was vaguely aware of Walther nearby. He tied a rope to an iron ring at the base of the mast behind me, then shouted, "Sit down!"

I looked at him questioningly. "Sit!" He yelled, and pushed me to the deck. He brought the rope across my waist and looped the end through another ring. With just seconds before the imminent collision, he sat beside me, bringing the rope across his body and securing in on the other side. I realized then what he was doing. The impact of the two ships would make it impossible to remain upright, and being thrown forward could result in injury. I braced myself against the rope. However, just before we rammed into the pirate vessel, it veered off to port, causing us to slide by on its starboard side. The ships groaned and screeched like two huge quarreling sea creatures. Immediately, boarding hooks began clanging over our bulwarks. Despite the captain's efforts to cut the lines and pull away, the two ships were drawn together.

Walther and I, and all the members of our party, rushed to ward off the attackers that were swarming over the entire length of the port side. Like denizens from hell, the black robed devils fought their way onto our ship, and the deck soon ran red with blood and seawater. Many paid with their lives, but the ruthless onslaught continued until we were pushed back to the other rail by overwhelming numbers. It was clear that our deaths were not what the pirates wanted, for once they had established their superiority they merely held us at bay. I felt trapped like a deer must when surrounded by wolves.

Walther was on my left and Father was on my right. How many others were still alive I couldn't tell. A large man, with a greying beard and narrow slits for eyes, emerged from the line of black robes and bloody blades. A voice came from behind us on the right. I recognized it as the captain's. The voice spoke in Arabic, and the leader of the pirates listened but kept his baleful gaze straight ahead on us. After a moment, the pirate spoke a few guttural sounds in reply. The captain then spoke to us in Italian: "We will not be harmed if we surrender now."

My father asked, "What does he intend to do with us?"

"You will be held for ransom."

"You know this from what he said?"

"This is not the first time I have been taken by pirates. Those that can pay are ransomed."

"What about those who can't pay?"

"They are sold as slaves."

"What choice do we have?"

"Give up or keep fighting and die."

A man's instinct for survival is strong. No one willingly throws away his life. Starting with my father, we all put down our swords. I seethed inside as the black-robed assassins roughly searched me for weapons. They found the dagger Hakam had given me and presented it to their tall, silent leader. 'I will kill him and take it back,' I thought to myself.

We sat at the rail while the dead were lined up on the deck. Berthold was dead, and so were three of the four attendants. It sickened me to see their lifeless bodies lying there in the squalor of blood and slime and seawater. They were friends, who just an hour before had been talking and joking and taking in the sunlight and air of life. Their lives had been senselessly ended. And for what? A small share of whatever ransom money that could be exchanged for the ship and a few prisoners. Surely a life is worth more than that. And yet, at that moment, I would have taken all of the lives of our captors in revenge.

Our ship was guided toward the cove from which the pirates staged their raids. I could see the masts of three other ships that lay at anchor in silent testimony to the raiders' treachery. As we reached the mouth of the inlet, a large swell surged against the side of the vessel, causing the deck to list abruptly to port. Our two guards, who were standing, lost their balance and lurched clumsily in the direction of the shift. One, slightly forward of us, caught himself against the rail, while the other one, more aft, slipped on the blood stained deck and fell sprawling headlong on the deck.

What I did next could not have been considered for even an instant, for if I had thought about it I certainly wouldn't have purposely ended up lying face down amidst the corpses on the center deck. But in the moment that the two guards were regaining their footing I lunged forward and assumed a place among the dead. I lay motionless, restraining even the slightest exhalation, waiting for a shout, or a blow, something that would indicate that my deception had been discovered. But nothing of the kind occurred. I was left to lie between two lifeless bodies, my still warm flesh touching the cold dead skin of the man next to me. My cheek was flush against the hard planks of the deck and each time the ship rolled with the waves the putrid slime in which I lay sloshed over my lips. But still I remained inanimate, waiting for whatever fate the pirates had in store for the departed. I was soon to find out. One by one, the bodies of the slain were roughly picked up and thrown over the side. When my turn came, I resisted a sudden urge to cry out that I wasn't really dead. My captors showed little respect for my deceased state, however, with one man grasping my ankles and the other my wrists. I was swung toward the rail and released, my knee and my arm striking the bulwark as I tumbled into the dark, cold waters of the sea.

I kept up my imitation of a corpse, in case anyone still observed me, letting my body remain limp and sinking beneath the roiling waves. I stayed down as long as my inflated lungs would allow, then slowly bobbed to the surface. The boat was gliding away toward the rocks in the distance. I watched as two more bodies were hurled over the side, to spend eternity at the bottom of the sea.

My knee throbbed in pain, but I gradually began to regain the usefulness of my arm which had gone numb from striking the bulwark. Once the boat was at a safe distance from me, I began the long swim toward land. The tide was favorable, and even during my frequent rests, I still drifted toward the gaping mouth of the inlet that seemed to gulp huge draughts of seawater with a rhythmic cadence. It was with great effort that I avoided being sucked into the breach where the rushing tempest calmed and became a refuge for the ships. With all my strength I swam toward the rocks to the right of the opening. Tossed by the surf, I was nearly dashed upon the rocks that lurked in the dark water. Like a child's toy I was plunged under the waves and nearly drowned only to be returned to the surface by the capricious sea. By chance I was able to catch hold of a jagged stone and prevent having my head bashed against the final bastion of rocks that protected the shore. There I pulled myself up into a crevice, shielded from the sight of the pirate lair. The sea water washed over bleeding wounds rent in my flesh by the jagged rocks. I rested, waiting for total darkness to come so that I might seize the opportunity to free my imprisoned comrades.

Throughout the afternoon I waited among the rocks. No other boats entered the harbor. Storm clouds gathered on the western horizon, eventually blotting out the setting sun. The winds picked up and the air grew colder. I could see a curtain of rain slowly moving across the water toward me and streaks of lightning illuminating the low, black sky. The angry storm swept over me like an attacking army. The cold, wind-driven rain stung every inch of my body. I could barely take a breath, so intense was the onslaught. Thunder crashed again and again as the storm hurled itself upon the land. I clung to my rock, defenseless against the beating, which seemed to go on without end. Finally, as suddenly as it begun, the rain subsided. The clouds parted slightly, and a glimmer of light emerged shyly from beyond the horizon. No warmth was to be gleaned from the sun which had set. I shivered, wet and cold, against the rock but was grateful to have survived the wrath of nature.

Eventually, complete darkness swallowed the cove. Only the flickering light from a few lanterns pierced the utter blackness. Beyond the ghostly silhouettes of the boats, more lights were concentrated on the slope that led upward from the harbor. Perhaps, I reasoned, the majority of the pirates spent their nights on land, leaving only a few guards aboard the vessels. Gradually, as the hours wore on, many of the lights were extinguished leaving only a few, and none of them on the boats. Still I waited. The later into the night I made my move, I thought, the better the chances were that the guards would be asleep, or at least, drowsy.

Finally, I slid down into the water and swam to the silent form of our captured ship. Carefully, I pulled myself up over the side and peered onto the deck. My eyes had gradually become accustomed to the dark. In the flinty greys of night, I could see no prisoners on deck. A single guard dozed by the rail on my side. I knew I would only have one chance. Noise would bring more guards and all would be lost. I surveyed the area around me. A line dangled over the side of the boat and was secured tightly at the other end. I made a loop in the loose end and tied a knot. With the rope between my teeth I inched my way, hand over hand, down the bulwark toward the sleeping guard. When I reached him, I threw the loop around his neck and immediately dropped over the side, grasping the rope in both hands. The line snapped taut, and I was left dangling in the darkness. I hung for a minute, waiting for a struggle at the other end. It never came. I pulled myself up unto the deck and found the guard dead, his neck broken.

I quickly took the man's weapons, which consisted of a long, curved sword and a short dagger. I had not aroused any attention yet, so, sword in hand, I crept down the steps to the galley. The steps creaked loudly and alerted a guard at the bottom, who turned just in time to have my sword plunged into his chest. I quickly surveyed the dark galley which was illuminated only by a candle. The oarsmen were seated in their positions with their hands tied. A rapid glance around the low, dark chamber revealed my father, Walther, and the other members of my party who were placed at intervals on the benches beside the rowers, also with bound hands. I met my father's gaze, and his eyes grew large and alert at seeing me. He was about to speak when my gesture silenced him. Sound would travel far across the water into the quiet night. Seizing the second guard's dagger and handing it to Walther, I went to work cutting the ropes that bound the captives. "Where is the captain?" I asked my father in a low voice.

"He isn't here."

I looked at him questioningly.

"He's with the pirates."

I sighed and shook my head. "Well, let's deprived him of his ship."

Once all the men had their hands freed, I crept quietly back up on deck and found where the anchor had been dropped over the side. I tried to lift it out of the water, but my greatest exertions were to no avail. I signaled to Walther, who had followed me to the top of the galley steps. Together we were able to budge the heavy anchor from the bottom of the bay and gradually draw the rope deckward. Finally, we had the iron anchor in hand and placed it as quietly as we could on the wooden deck. I made my way to the stern and un-lashed the rudder. Walther returned to his position at the top of the steps. On my signal, he quietly gave the order for the oarsmen to heave into their tasks with all their strength. I swung the rudder hard to the left, and the boat surged forward. Slowly at first, then gradually it gained speed toward the opening in the rocks that would lead us to the open sea. I thought if we could make it beyond the mouth of the bay without our movement being detected, our escape would be assured.

Unfortunately, a guard on one of the other boats saw us and raised the alarm. By the time we reached the cataract, the whole pirate's lair had been aroused and a ship was being readied for pursuit. With quiet no longer necessary, I shouted to Walther to move to the bow and help guide us through the rocks. The going was treacherous in the pitch black of night, especially since I was unfamiliar with the narrow passage. Maneuvering the large vessel in such a tight space was awkward, and I struggled with the balky rudder. The current threatened to sweep us into the rocks as it surged through the opening. Walther shouted and gestured desperately that I was too close on the port side, but I was straining with all my strength against the rushing tide. Father had taken Walther's place at the top of the galley steps and helped me to communicate with the oarsmen below. I yelled to him that I needed the men on the starboard side to stop rowing and the ones on the port side to pull as hard as they could. The maneuver worked. We barely slid by the rocks on the left and cleared the opening of the cove.

Once out in the open sea with all the oarsmen pulling together, we rapidly gained speed, cleaving the black of night as we rose and fell on the waves. We sensed that at least one of the swift pirate vessels was in pursuit, but it was impossible to see that far back in the dark. Throughout rest of the night we followed the coast to the east, resting half the rowers at intervals so that we might have all of them at full strength should the need arise.

Gradually, almost imperceptively, the sky lightened. At first it seemed no more than my eyes grown accustomed to the dark, but then the dark silhouettes around me took on tones of grey, then began to take on form. A streak of silver light was visible on the horizon and grew wider by the minute. The new light revealed what we had feared: a pirate vessel had come even with our stern and was preparing to board us. We had no weapons except what we had taken from the two guards, so we had no way to ward off a boarding party. I ordered everything that was not nailed down to be brought to the stern. Boxes, barrels, tools, and hardware from the ship's rigging became projectiles that we rained down on our attackers. Some simply caused a delay; others found their marks and caused injury. The pirates succeeded in throwing a hook over our side, but I was able to cut the line which fell harmlessly into the water. With that, the threat from the pirates subsided. Gradually, the gap between our vessels widened, and eventually the raiders gave up the chase.

There was a great sense of relief at having escaped from the pirates, but we had lost all of our possessions: our trade goods, our weapons, our gold, and for me, the jeweled dagger given to me by the Prince of al-Andalus. It would take us a week to make it back to Genoa. We were still easy prey for pirates, and we had no food. Our fresh water supply was low. We had to make a stop somewhere along the way to take on provisions. If we chose our port badly, we could fall back into the hands of raiders who controlled much of the coast. We sailed on through the second night, our water nearly gone and our stomachs burning with hunger. On the third day, desperate to find a safe port, I spotted a tower in the distance. As we got closer, we could see that it was part of a fortification built on top of a rock that overlooked a small town. The town had a protected position at the back of a natural harbor. I decided that the town looked defensible enough to be able to hold off pirate raids, so I took a chance and guided our ship through the narrow passage between the rocks and into the harbor. We were met by armed men on the wharf who had obviously seen our approach long before we even made the decision to put in. We were not allowed to tie up until I had assured their leader of our peaceful intentions and that we lacked the means to attack them in any case. A few of our men were allow to disembark and bring fresh water and foodstuffs on board. We had to rely on the charity of the townspeople since we had no money with which to pay. The next morning we thanked the villagers and pledged to send payment back with an agent on the next trade voyage to Iberia. Back on our way, we followed the coast east and faced no more serious difficulties in reaching Genoa. There, we were able to find a buyer for the ship, and Friedemann borrowed some additional money from a wealthy Jew of his acquaintance. Thus, we were able to retrieve our horses and the necessary weapons and supplies for our trip back across Italy.

19

Our numbers were greatly reduced for the journey back across the lawless plains of the Italian peninsula, making us vulnerable to attack by bandits. Outside Genoa we stopped at a hill fortress governed by a minor noble named Alphonso. He was able to spare four knights to accompany us until we crossed the Alps back into Swabia. The men were probably pleased to relieve some of the boredom of burg life, and Alphonso was probably glad to have someone else pay them for several weeks. This brought our number to ten, all able-bodied fighters except for Friedemann, the trade envoy.

Many long, dull days of travel brought us back to Milan where we were able to take on supplies and replace one of our horses, which had come up lame. It was late October and nearing the season for early storms in the mountains, which would make our crossing much more dangerous. When we reached the foothills, our fears were realized when we could see that it was already snowing in the higher elevations.

One night in camp, we were alerted by the sounds of our horses signaling the approach of intruders. It barely gave us time to seize our weapons before the assault came. Arrows whistled through the chilled night air striking trees and rending flesh. Riders thundered into camp, and we met them on foot. Fighting from horseback in a dense forest is difficult however. Maneuvering from the ground between the trees, I brought two men down with my sword and killed them where they landed. The sounds that came out of the darkness gave little indication of our success or failure in fending off the enemy. Hoof beats, the clanging of metal, the cries of wounded men, all mingled in the confusion of battle. The Italian knights acquitted themselves well and, almost as quickly as it started, the skirmish ended. The raiders fled into the night, leaving behind eight dead and several wounded who met their fate at the end of a sword. Silence returned to the forest, and upon the scene of so much bloodshed, a light snow began to fall. On our side, one of the Italian knights was badly wounded and died within a few hours. Parsifal had an arrow in his shoulder, and several others had minor injuries. We decided that, rather than wait for another attack, we should pack up our camp and continue into the higher mountains, taking our chances with the snow. We briefly considered returning to Milan but decided that we would be more vulnerable at the lower elevations. We hoped that the bandits might be more reluctant to pursue us into the snowstorm where they might get trapped.

After burying the Italian as best we could, and leaving the bodies of the bandits on the hillside for their companions to claim, we started off in the dark. It was difficult following the trail at night, but we stayed on course and by morning we had gained a couple of miles. The snow grew heavier, and the cold wind stung our faces as it blew through the mountain passes. For two days we trudged on through the storm before it subsided. Fortunately, the Alpine winter wasn't ready to set in for good, and the cloud cover broke up just as we reached the highest point of our crossing. The meager warmth of the November sun was welcome on our faces, and we no longer had to negotiate snowy trails.

Parsifal still carried an arrow in his shoulder, but we found no villages in the higher mountains to get attention for it. He bore up well and didn't utter a complaint, but it was obvious that the wound was making him weaker by the day. Finally, in coming down the northern side of the mountains we were able to find a village with physician tools and a man skilled in using them. The arrow was removed, but fever had set in, and it was nearly a week before Parsifal was strong enough to travel. During the time we were in the village, we ate well and had warm homes in which to sleep. We repaid the villagers' kindness by helping with the work that went on daily to prepare for winter. Firewood needed to be put in, roofs needed repair, hay and grain needed to be brought in and stored in barns, and game could still be hunted in the forests before the snowstorms made it scarce.

Although life in the village was pleasant, especially after coming through the mountains, I was restless to continue on our way and get back home. It had been nearly four months since I had seen Verena, and the ache inside me that had been there through the journey had grown stronger as we appeared to be reaching its end. Of course, no one knew about us, so I had to keep my feelings concealed until the proper time. The thought of speaking to my parents about our intentions filled me with dread. At last Parsifal was able to sit upon his horse, and we left the village behind us. The late autumn weather was mild, and on well-rested horses we made good progress moving from town to town through the familiar countryside.

The time finally came when we could overlook the shimmering lake and the town that sat beside it. The cool wind foretold the coming winter, but the sky was bright and the few clouds that moved across it cast patchy shadows on the still-green hills. My eyes impulsively searched for the small house where Verena lived, even though I knew I couldn't see it from where we were. In spite of my weariness from the long journey, I felt an exhilaration inside at the prospect of seeing her beautiful face and holding her in my arms again. But first we had to return home, and by the time we got to the burg it was nearly dark. My mother was excited to see us return safely and wanted to hear every detail of the trip. We had a hearty and very welcome meal and told of our adventures long into the night. The stories of al-Andalus seemed, even to us in the telling, almost beyond belief. The reality of the place pushed past the boundaries of imagination. The dangers of our journey, however, were all too real, but these were downplayed when we related our encounters with bandits and pirates. I think my mother knew, the way mothers do, that we weren't being completely truthful about them, and the men that didn't return provided hard evidence. But Frankish women are strong, and she didn't betray her worry on the outside, only the joy of having her husband and son back safely, this time.

Fatigue completely overtook me that evening, and despite my anxiousness at the possibility of seeing Verena, I was asleep in my bed almost before my feet left the floor. By the time I woke up, it was nearly noon the following day. I was pleased to see Diomedes after all those months, and he had grown fat and lazy in my absence. We rode out along the road on a bright, brisk, sunny afternoon. The trees still held on to some of their colorful leaves, but the ones that had already fallen swirled in the wind ahead of us and crunched beneath Diomedes' hooves.

Shortly I was at the bottom of the hill that led up to Verena's house. I rode up and down the path a number of times trying to decide whether or not to ride up to the house and ask to see her. After perhaps a half-hour of this, I saw someone walking up the road toward the chestnut grove. Spirits rose when I thought it was Verena but then sunk again when I saw that it was not. I did, however, recognize the figure in the distance about the time she looked up and saw me. It was Herta, the huntsman's daughter and Verena's best friend. I rode up to her and said, *"Guten Tag, Herta."*

"Guten Tag, Max."

I thought there was a slight look of apprehension on her face. "Have you seen Verena today?"

She shook her head, and her look grew worried.

"Has something happened, Herta?" A feeling of dread welled up in me.

"She's gone, Max," the girl blurted out.

"What do you mean, gone?"

"They wanted her to marry Wolfram."

"The old man?"

"Yes. His wife died last year and he was ready to marry again. He had his eye on Verena, and asked her parents to consider it. He's very wealthy. Verena avoided him as long as she could, but finally her parents told her the decision was made. In her desperation to avoid the marriage, she told them that she had been with another man."

"What?"

"She wouldn't tell them who it was, but I knew it was you. She had sworn me to secrecy, and I haven't told anyone. But of course the wedding was called off and Verena was sent to a convent."

"Which convent?"

"The one to the north. Outside Winterthur."

Without another word, I turned Diomedes and left Herta standing in the road. I started riding north in the direction of the convent. It lay in the hills just south of Winterthur, about eighteen miles away. I thought I could reach it before dark if I rode hard. After galloping for a few miles, I realized that Diomedes could not keep up that pace and dropped down to a walk. After being idle for the long months that I was away, his condition was poor. He quickly broke into a sweat and blew loudly through wide nostrils. I had to make frequent stops to allow him to recover every couple of miles. The sun dropped low on the horizon, and the air grew colder. The end of the short November day closed in on us. Soon it was dark on the road, and we were still a couple of miles from the convent. I began to think that it would have been better for me to have departed from home the next morning and on a different horse. But it was too late for that. The road to the convent wound up and down through the hills. The remaining light that trailed the sun in the western sky faded, and we were left in total darkness. At times I feared for our safety.

Finally I saw, in the distance, a pinpoint of light. As we got closer, the walls of the convent loomed dark and shadowy on a hill ahead of us. A lantern flame barely illuminated the entrance, which was closed for the night. I got down off Diomedes and pounded on the heavy wooden door. After a lengthy wait one of the sisters opened a panel in the door. "What is it that you want?" She asked.

"You have a girl here. Her name is Verena. She is my betrothed. She was sent her by mistake while I was away. I wish to see her."

"It is late. All the young women have gone to bed. Come back tomorrow."

"There is no place for me to go at this late hour. Can't I stay here until morning?"

"No men are allowed in the convent at night. You can use the stable if you insist on staying."

I started to get angry. I was cold, hungry, and anxious to see Verena. But I was relieved to know that she was there. I held back my anger. "Thank you for the use of your stable," I said as politely as I could. It would do me no good to make an enemy there.

I walked Diomedes to the stable, which lay about fifty yards down the hill. An old man with a lantern came out to meet me. "I'd like to put my horse in your stable for the night," I said. "I need to stay here too," I admitted.

Without speaking (perhaps he was mute), he led the way into the stable which was adequate for a night's stay. I unsaddled Diomedes, rubbed him down and then gave him some hay and water. There were a couple of wagon horses in the stable, and a few chickens roamed the area, pecking at the floor. The old mute pointed to a corner where there was clean straw, evidently where I was to sleep. My return to my bed at home had lasted one night. Hunger gnawed at my belly. I was, however, close to Verena, and I felt certain I would see her the following morning.

The next day dawned grey and damp, and the cold penetrated my bones. I splashed some water on my face, straightened my clothes, and strode up to the walls of the convent. I was admitted through the door this time and led to a small, drab room that contained a couple of chairs, one small window, and a crucifix on the wall. The sister who led me there stayed standing by the door as if she expected me to attempt an escape. Soon the Mother Superior came in the room and beckoned me to sit down. I complied, and she sat down across from me. She appeared old, deep lines marking her face like ripples in a stream. Her thin lips were set in a firm line, but behind her blue eyes there seemed to be a glimmer of kindness. "You are here to see Verena?" She inquired.

"Yes. I wish to take her away from here."

"By what right have you to do this?"

"We are betrothed."

"Verena's parents have no knowledge of this."

147

"It was a secret."

"Why?"

"I wasn't sure my parents would approve of the marriage. They wanted me to choose a wife from another noble family."

"What makes you think that they would accept Verena now?"

"I will have to convince them. But I won't be deterred. I will marry Verena even if it means leaving home and making my way on my own."

"Are you sure that Verena feels the same way?"

"Have you asked her?"

"She did seem sure that you would come for her."

I felt a sense of elation at that statement, but I waited for the sister to continue.

"Her parents sent her here because of the shame that she brought on them. A girl who has been cast out by her parents and has no husband has few choices. Verena is not a prisoner here. She is old enough to make a decision about who she is to marry. If this is what she wishes, then we will not stand in her way."

"Does she know that I'm here?" I asked anxiously.

"Not yet. I wanted to meet you first." She nodded to the other nun, who left the room. "Will you try to reconcile with your parents?"

"Yes. They don't even know where I am right now. I intend to return home immediately with Verena."

"I will pray for your safe return and their acceptance."

"Thank you."

We sat for a few minutes without speaking. After what seemed like an interminable wait, the old nun looked up at the doorway behind me. I rose from my chair and turned around to see Verena standing there, dressed in the drab grey habit of the nunnery. The coarse fabric of her long robes completely hid her slight form and seemed to stand by itself, unsupported by a body underneath. In contrast, the white skin of her tiny face was radiant as the sparse light from the window fell upon it. Wisps of golden hair escaped the confines of the dark scarf upon her head. Her eyes shone brilliantly as they found mine. Her pale lips quivered slightly as they evinced a relieved smile. I walked over to her and held out my hands. She looked toward the Mother Superior, who nodded her assent. Verena placed her small, delicate hands in mine. Tears began to glisten in her blue eyes. I bent down and kissed her gently on her cheek.

The Mother Superior asked, "Do you wish to leave here under the protection of this man and to become his wife?"

Verena answered "yes" in a voice distorted by emotion. She repeated her answer stronger and more clearly.

"So be it. Go with Sister Magdalene and change your clothes. You have my blessing."

"Have you had anything to eat?" Asked the nun after Verena had left.

"Not since yesterday morning," I answered.

"Wait here," She said and left for a short while.

149

While I waited for the nun to return, I felt a great relief and happiness that Verena was safe and that we were together again. I even began to plan what I would say to my parents to break down their objection to our marriage, but my thoughts became fragmented and drifted away before they were complete. We still had to make the journey back home and, riding double on Diomedes, we would have to make a lot of stops.

Finally, the Mother Superior returned, and she brought a loaf of bread. "Eat some now, and take the rest with you to share on your journey."

I thanked her, and ate a few mouthfuls of the hard bread. Feeling a bit awkward, I excused myself and went outside to get Diomedes from the stable. The morning chill numbed my face and hands, and thick fog blanketed the hills. Diomedes tossed his head and blew billows of steam from his nostrils. He was rested, and the cold air excited him. Soon Verena emerged from the convent, attired once more in simple peasant dress and wrapped in a long cloak with a hood that framed her lovely face. She embraced Sister Magdalene, and then I helped her climb up behind me on Diomedes. As we rode away from the walls of the convent and down the mountain, she squeezed my body tightly into hers and lay her head on my shoulder. "Who told you where I was?" She eventually asked.

"Herta."

"Did she tell you that they wanted me to marry Wolfram?"

"Yes. You were very brave to refuse."

"I knew you would return someday."

"You were sure?"

"I trusted you."

"But what if I had died?"

"Then I would have spent my life in that convent, living with the memories of you."

"You aren't a very practical girl, are you?"

The road from Winterthur to Zurich is a good one and the weather, although cold, did not impede our short journey. We did, however, have to take many breaks along the way to rest Diomedes, and darkness closed in on us before we reached our destination. Since I had not returned home the previous night, I thought we should continue travelling until we got to my home to assure my parents that I was all right even though it would be late. By the time we reached the gates of my father's great fortress in town, all the light had gone from the sky and it was very cold. Verena was shivering and exhausted as we dismounted and walked into the great hall. There was a good fire in the hearth, and Verena and I stood in front of it warming ourselves and staring into the flames. The blood was just beginning to return to our faces and hands when Mother and Father came into the hall. "Max! Where did you go?" My father's deep voice sounded calm but serious in the large, empty hall.

"Winterthur," I answered.

"For what reason?"

Verena was still facing the fire. I put my arm around her shoulders and timidly, she turned around. She still wore the long cloak, and the hood obscured her downcast eyes. I gently lifted the hood away to reveal her face, and she raised her gaze to meet the scrutiny of my parents. Although she trembled slightly, her uncontrolled shivering had ceased, and the fire had returned the color to her cheeks. "Mother, Father, this is Verena. She is the reason I had to go to Winterthur. Because of me, she was in the convent there."

Verena bowed and there was a long awkward silence while I let this last statement sink in. Then I said, "We're going to be married."

Finally, my father said "Nonsense. We can discuss this later. Right now the young woman needs to go home."

"She can't go home. At least not now. Her parents are the ones that sent her to the convent. She needs to stay here."

"Stay here? No."

"If she doesn't stay, I don't stay."

My father started to protest, but my mother put her hand on his shoulder. "It is late," she said. "The girl is exhausted. She can stay."

Mother put her arm around Verena and led her out of the room. Verena looked back over her shoulder and gave a slight, fearful smile. I tried to nod reassuringly.

When they had gone, Father asked, "Where does this girl come from?"

"She lives just outside of town near the mill."

My father sighed deeply. "This is foolish Max. I'm sure you like her; she's a pretty girl. But...well, in your position you can't just marry someone because you like them."

"I can, and I will."

"That's very selfish of you."

"I'm sorry, father. We can go away. Verena and I *will* be together."

"I hope you reconsider. Let's talk about it again tomorrow."

"Nothing is going to change tomorrow. You just have to decide whether I stay or go."

"Damn it Max! You're as stubborn as your mother. Don't put this on me."

"But it is on you. I've already made my decision. It was made years ago. Verena is the most important thing in the world to me."

"You would give up your inheritance, your family, your horses, everything for this girl?"

He knew that, if he had any chance of changing my mind, bringing up the horses would carry the most weight. "She *is* everything." I answered without hesitation.

He was furious. I thought he was about to launch a new attack, but instead, he turned and strode out of the room, leaving me there alone. I felt remorse. I hated going against my father. We had never really argued before. I had never taken a stand and held it. Part of me still felt like a boy who should never defy his father, but the other part felt like a man who needed to determine his own destiny. I had been taught to pick my fights carefully. I had thought about this one for a long time and decided, unquestionably, that this one was worth fighting.

20

Verena and I were married in the spring, and we took up residence in *der Ludwigsburg*. Verena's parents reconciled with her and came to the wedding. Of course, her marriage into a higher station greatly improved their situation as well. My mother's affection for Verena grew quickly, her sweet and gentle nature nearly matching that of my wife's. My father took a little longer to accept the marriage, but eventually Verena was able to soften the edges of his opposition, and finally the barrier between them fell completely.

I returned to working with the horses at the farm, and one day I saw Dietrich, the knight who had bought the grey, orphaned mare Anelie. He didn't know me, so I went up to him and said, "I'm Max. I trained a grey mare that you bought. I was wondering how she was?"

For a moment he studied my face as if to see if it brought forth any recollections. Apparently it didn't because his thoughts seemed to move on to memories past. Finally his perplexed expression changed and he said, "Yes, the grey mare. Bravest horse I ever took into battle. In the north, against the Slavs, she took an arrow in the chest."

His words punched me in the gut. He continued: "In spite of her wound, and several others, she carried me until the victory was won. She even waited until I dismounted before she fell. She died on the battlefield. An exceptional horse."

A huge weight crushed my chest. I couldn't speak. As I turned away from Dietrich, I vaguely remember him asking if I was all right. I walked off without answering. I headed toward the woods behind the row of barns, barely aware of my surroundings. I didn't want to talk to anyone. In my mind I could picture Anelie the way I last saw her, trotting around her pen, tail held up like a flag. I remembered her coming up to me, smacking her lips, waiting for me to pet the top of her head. I had her trust. I felt like I had betrayed her.

Away from everyone, I sat on a log, alone with my thoughts. A cool breeze rustled through the treetops, swaying the branches with their cloak of new, pale green leaves of spring. In the distance. I could hear frogs chirping, their voices mingling with the territorial calls of birds. At my feet were tiny wild flower blossoms interspersed with fresh young grass. How the horses love this time of year! I thought. Horses are the gentlest of creatures, only wishing to be allowed to graze in peace. But we take advantage of their willingness to trust us, to follow us, and we turn them into instruments of war. We take them into situations that normally would cause them to flee to safety, but because we teach them to trust our leadership, they get hurt and often killed. I understood as well as anyone the usefulness of a horse, but the way we take advantage of them seemed cruel to me then, as it still does now. I never stopped loving horses, but from that moment on, I lost my enthusiasm for training them for warfare.

Anelie taught me more than any other horse I ever had. From her I learned patience. She taught me how to communicate with my actions instead of my words. I learned to use the lightest possible pressure to get a response before using more pressure. I learned to wait for my request to be processed before expecting a response. I learned to reward effort instead of always expecting perfection. I learned that I had to earn respect before it was granted to me. I found that all these lessons were also useful in dealing with people.

Although Anelie's life was short, in it she made me a better horse trainer; a better man. And perhaps she also saved the life of Dietrich, who put his trust in her. Not bad for an orphan that no one thought would ever amount to anything.

In the fall of 949, I accompanied my father to Constantinople. Otto's efforts to arrange a marriage to link his family with the Eastern Empire had failed thus far, but he still had good relations with Constantine VII Porphyrogennetos, the Byzantine emperor. The Eastern Empire was in a constant state of war with the Arabs and maintained an uneasy truce with Bulgaria, so having good relations with the Germans was of great importance to the emperor.

As in our mission to Al Andalus, we set out across the Alps to the south. However, once into Italy, we turned east toward the Adriatic and headed for the Venetian coast. We followed the broad flat valley formed by the Po, and after many long days of travel, we reached the great marsh that leads to the city of Venice. We had all heard stories of the city built upon a hundred islands, but it sounded like a myth until we saw it with our own eyes. There, spread out over the wide expanse of the lagoon, was the largest city that I had ever seen. Protected for a hundred and fifty years by the Byzantines, and favored by its position on the Adriatic, Venice had become a naval power and a huge center of commerce. We hired a boat to take us to the island of Rialto where we were to be guests of the Doge. Construction seemed to be going on all around the lagoon. Bridges were being built to connect islands, and there was dredging of soil to raise the land areas above the tides. New buildings were being constructed atop wooden piles driven into the sea floor. As always, I wished that Verena could have been there to see that wondrous ocean city with me. But even my stay was short. We boarded a Venetian galley the next day to continue our journey to Constantinople.

We sailed south along the Italian coast for many days, eventually turning east across the Strait of Otranto. From there we followed the Greek coast, stopping several times at islands to re-stock our supplies of food and fresh water. The people we encountered there were mostly fishermen, friendly toward us, with dark hair, dark eyes, and skin tanned by the intense sun of that southern region. There was little worry about pirates to that point in the journey, the Adriatic being controlled by the Venetians and the Byzantines. We were cautioned, however, that once we rounded the tip of Morea that the seas would grow more dangerous, since the island of Crete was in the hands of Andalusian Muladis, fierce raiders that had been able to resist the efforts of the Byzantines to oust them.

I recalled the treachery of our captain on the voyage back from Al Andalus and wondered aloud to Walther if we should have similar concerns about the one that we presently employed. He replied that he had personally talked with the mariner and assured him that if we suspected in the least that his best efforts to avoid capture were not being made that he would be the first to die. The passage between Morea and Crete was made without incident. There were, however, ships in the distance that might well have been corsairs, but they were kept at such a distance that there was no chance of their making a successful pursuit.

We entered a long stretch of the voyage in which, in addition to hugging the Greek coast, we were nearly always within sight of one or more islands. Our heading was north into the Aegean and to the island of Lesbos, which was a Byzantine stronghold. We spent a couple of days there while the ship took on supplies. It was a welcome respite from being aboard the cramped galley, and I took advantage of the time to walk among the ancient Greek ruins and re-acquaint my legs with solid land.

On leaving Lesbos, we continued north to the narrow strait called the Dardanelles. The currents in the strait are treacherous and caused us two day's delay before the captain felt it was safe to continue our passage on its dark and churning water. Our boat carried a cargo of Italian wine, and two casks of it plus six silver coins were forfeited at the customs house to allow passage. The strait has a narrow and winding course, at times resembling a river. Slipping through it undetected would be extremely difficult.

We emerged from the Dardanelles into the Sea of Marmara and sailed toward the other narrow passage between the Aegean and the Black Sea, called the Bosporus. On its banks lay the seat of the Eastern Empire, Constantinople. The main part of the city to the south of the Golden Horn is constructed on a succession of seven hills beginning at the strait and continuing to the west. The whole city is protected on both land and sea sides by a line of walls, the outermost making a line that encompasses the sixth and seventh hills. When, at last, the city came into view, I fairly gasp in wonder. I never saw the Rome of Italy, but the "New Rome" of Byzantium had a size and grandeur unlike anything I had seen in my life or ever saw again.

We sailed into the Golden Horn, a river that borders the old city of Byzantium on the north and forms a large harbor as it spills into the sea. There were a vast number of ships in the harbor, and the various sails created a patchwork of hues much like the leaves of autumn. I wondered at the number of vessels, for it seemed too many for ordinary merchant trade. The sun was shining brightly, and it reflected off the golden crosses that topped the many churches located on the hills of the city. Most prominent of the structures that were visible was the enormous cathedral, Hagia Sophia. The central dome of that church seemed to reach into heaven itself, guarded by four graceful towers on its ascension.

We were met by a representative of the Emperor when we got off the boat. His name was Evangelos, and a more agreeable representative you could not hope to find. He had a relaxed, friendly nature, spoke German very well, and immediately put to rest any anxieties that we might have had about our visit to this far-off place. As we walked into the city, our eyes fixed on the magnificent Hagia Sophia, my attention was diverted to a palace of immense size and an adjacent racing track. We were told that we would meet Emperor Constantine at the Great Palace. I ask about the track, and Evangelos said that it was called the Hippodrome, the name itself coming from the Greek words for "horse" and "path". He went on to explain that it had been used for centuries for chariot racing and that some racing was still done there. I replied that I would be very interested in finding out more about chariot racing, and he said that he would introduce me to one of the horsemen, who could answer all of my questions.

The next day, we met with Emperor Constantine VII Porphyrogennetos and his son and co-emperor Romanos II. We went to the palace and entered by a great bronze gate on the north side, the Hagia Sophia to our left. The palace was a series of pavilions built on a hillside that sloped toward the shore. For this purpose, the hill was terraced, and columns of different lengths supported each section of the building. Through the gate were many statues and religious icons. The floor beneath our feet was a colorful mosaic, which brought to my mind the intricate designs that Verena and I had seen during our exploration of the Roman villa ruins.

We had heard that the emperor was more a scholar than a politician and that we would find his son and wife, Helena, to be more active in diplomacy. This proved to be true when we met him, for when Romanos was present, the emperor grew more taciturn and let his son discuss foreign relations. However, when the subjects of the arts, history and his library came up, he had much to say. He seemed passionate about improving the condition of the peasantry. He felt that a prosperous landed peasant class was necessary for the strength of the empire.

I asked about the number of ships in the harbor. Constantine replied that he was gathering a fleet to attempt to regain control over the island of Crete and that it was nearly ready to launch.

I went away from our audience with the emperor impressed with the man. Although unpleasant to look upon, Constantine seemed a capable ruler, willing to delegate responsibility as needed. As we were leaving the palace, Evangelos said that he had arranged for me to meet one of the chariot drivers in the afternoon. He called on me after mid-day, and we went to the Hippodrome where there were several drivers exercising their horses. Each two-wheeled chariot was pulled by a team of four horses harnessed side by side. We went to the northwest side of the track where there was a pavilion with stables and a hitching area busy with horses, caretakers, and trainers. There Evangelos introduced me to a horseman named Stylianos. Stylianos was not a noble, nor was he a slave. He was of the peasant class and, as I was to discover, a skilled handler of horses. He appeared to be a few years older than me, short and thickly built, with dark hair and eyes. He didn't seem to mind when Evangelos told him that I would spend the afternoon with him learning about chariot racing. Instead, he seemed glad to display the vast knowledge that he had accumulated. Evangelos stayed to help us communicate with each other. Stylianos said, "So you have no chariot racing where you come from?"

"No," I replied, "I have never seen it before."

"Have you been around horses much?"

"Yes. I train the horses that carry knights into battle."

His look showed a little surprise as well as curiosity. I wondered if he thought that training horses was a job for peasants and slaves.

The horses were brought out one at a time and harnessed. All were black, three with a few white markings. The slowest of the four, Lefteris, was hitched first. "Lefteris travels the shortest distance around the turns," said Stylianos.

The next one to be hitched was Ionannes, the youngest. "Ionannes needs to be placed between the two steadiest horses," I was told. The third horse, Vangelis, was the strongest, to exert the most pull on the shafts.

The last horse, Spiridon, was placed on the right side because he was the fastest, and his speed would allow him to make up the extra ground around the turns. Once the horses were all hitched to the chariot, it was led out onto the track inside the massive Hippodrome. Stylianos told me to climb in behind him, and I held on as we surged forward along the upper part of the course.

We started slowly with the short, choppy strides of the horses causing a rocking movement of the chariot. The harness jingled and squeaked and groaned with each lurch forward. We kept up that pace along the long first side of the track. We rounded the end of the spina (the low wall that ran up the center of the oval) with Stylianos holding the horses in check, but coming out of that turn, he allowed them to lengthen their strides. Our speed increased, and the wheels sped over the dirt more smoothly. Going down the other side of the track, the horses seemed to reach full gallop, urged forward by the energy that they sensed from each other. Their necks were stretched forward as they leaned into their bits, and their black manes flew behind them like four battle flags. I thought we could go no faster, but I was certainly proved wrong. We approached the other end of the spina at a dangerous speed, and I didn't see how we could possibly make the turn. But with skillful hands, Stylianos guided the team around the end of the spina, Spiridon eagerly churning up the extra distance that his outside position made necessary.

Stylianos had put me on the left side of the chariot, and I quickly found out why. The tight turns caused the rigid axle to tip to the outside, and it was necessary for the driver to lean hard to the inside to keep the chariot from turning over. Faster and faster the horses galloped, with no apparent urging from Stylianos. They were trained to run the course as fast as they could, and it was as though they were racing each other. Around the track we flew at an exhilarating speed, and I steadied myself by holding on to the chariot rail in spite of my pride. Seven times we were to round the course, and as if the horses could count, they slowed their speed as soon as we completed exactly that number. Stylianos easily brought the team to a stop, and the horses were unhitched and led away one at a time.

Another team was readied. In this one the horses were bay, their red-brown coats shining glossy in the sun. Their long manes and tails were black as raven feathers. Again they were hitched according to their strengths. From the left there was Akakios, then Neofytos. The next two were brothers, Photios and Sotirios. Stylianos placed me in the front of the chariot and showed me how to hold the four sets of reins. He asked, "Are you ready?"

I replied that I was, although my answer might not have been convincing.

"Don't try to hold them back," he instructed. "It only makes them pull harder against the bit. Just keep a slight pressure on the reins. And stay away from the spina. You don't want to come too close going around the end or you'll run the inside horse into it."

We began with a lurch and a jerk as the horses started forward unevenly, but they soon moved in unison up the track. Four horses pulling at once gave me an immense sensation of power in my hands. As we gained speed going toward the far end of the spina I steered the outside horses, Photios and Sotirios, slightly to the right and found that the direction of the team did not change immediately. I pulled harder, and we gradually began to drift away from the spina. Stylianos said, "Give yourself a little more time to change your path since you are giving cues to four horses, not one."

As we approached the turn Stylianos said, "Be sure to give the outside horses their heads so they can swing out farther going around." I did as instructed, and the cadence of the hoof beats of the outside horses quickened and they thrust their heads forward to keep up as we rounded the end of the spina with plenty of room to spare.

I felt a little relief that I had successfully executed my first turn, but my satisfaction was brief. The horses picked up speed going up the other side of the track, and I was soon faced with making a much more difficult turn at the other end. "Wider!" Stylianos shouted as we approached the end of the spina. I pulled hard on the right reins and, as before, nothing happened. The horses were headed straight for the barrier. My heart seemed to rise in my throat and every muscle in my body tensed. I continued to pull and finally, just before we got to the end, the team drifted slightly to the right. Akakios missed hitting the barrier by the thinnest of margins.

For the rest of the seven laps I stayed in the middle of the track, not chancing another close call. I let the horses dictate their own speed, neither urging them on nor holding them back. I relished holding such power in my hands and watched with great interest the way in which each member of the team did his job. I wondered how difficult it was to start with a new team, one in

163

which the horses had never worked together. The one I drove had had many hours of practice and meshed like a flock of birds in flight. I had spent countless hours observing the movement of horses in the fields at home. Each horse is extremely sensitive to the movements of other individuals in the herd. Every posture, gesture, and action has a meaning and response. That sensitivity not only enables the individual to adapt to life in the herd, but also allows the herd to function as a unit in times of danger, such as when there is a predator. Harnessing horses together to pull a chariot challenges each horse's nature as an individual within the group, but once they have spent enough time together, their ability to sense each other's cues allows them to function as a cohesive whole.

When we were finished for the day I thanked Stylianos for taking the time to teach me about chariot racing. He said that the horses would have the next day off, but that if I wanted to come back the following day we could take the teams out together. I assured him that I would be there.

The day after my experience at the Hippodrome, the fleet assembled by the Emperor sailed for Crete. Walther and I went down to the harbor to watch the spectacle. One hundred ships comprised the fleet, led by twenty huge Dromons that had rowers above and below deck. I estimated that there were one hundred and twenty rowers for each ship, but there may have been two men at each oar on deck, which would have brought the total closer to one hundred and ninety. Shields lining the sides of the vessels glimmered in the morning sun, and the triangular sails filled with wind as each glided out of the Golden Horn. The procession of warships continued on throughout the morning until finally the last galley sailed out into the Sea of Marmara.

The same day that we watched the Byzantine fleet sail, Walther and I procured two fine Arab horses from the Emperor's stable and rode around the perimeter of the city to study its defenses. We passed out through a gate that stands between the second and third hills on the side of the city that faces the Golden Horn. Once outside the walls, we turned north and rode along the narrow strip of land between the harbor and the defenses. Upon reaching the northernmost extent of that boundary, we turned inland and followed the Blachernae wall which connects the Golden Horn defenses to the land side Theodosian walls.

I looked out over the distant hills dotted with various hues of green and said to Walther, "It would be a shame to take these spirited horses back to the stables without giving them a proper degree of exercise."

He looked at me with a slight smile, and before he could answer, I pressed the sides of my mount and raced off. The finely built grey took the bit and with very little urging from me settled into a smooth gallop across the dry hills. I could hear Walther's horse, racing to catch up to me, the cadence of his hoof beats more rapid than mine. I looked back and saw his horse, a black, driving against the bit, and Walther leaning forward over the horse's neck. Down a slope we raced, then up a bald hill. At the top, Walther and his mount overtook us, and we raced side by side with them past a small village where the chickens and the people hurried out of our way. On we ran, the scrubby bushes flying past on both sides as we created a cloud of dust in our wake. Our horses began to tire, and our pace slowed slightly. We reached the edge of a dark green forest and came to a stop. My horse's neck and shoulders were dark with sweat. The trees, while not tall compared with those of Swabia, offered a cool respite from the warm afternoon sun.

We got down off our mounts and walked them along a narrow goat path through the woods and eventually found a small, nearly round lake, set down between the tree-studded hills. The still water reflected the cloudless blue sky, and birds soared above its surface. We let the horses sip at intervals until their thirst was satisfied and then we, too, drank from the cool, clear lake. My horse began to browse in the vegetation on the banks so I sat down on a sun-bleached log. Walther, ever vigilant, stood looking around at the surrounding hills. "Walther," I said, "relax. Enjoy the day."

Walther gave me a severe glance and then continued to survey the approaches to the lake. "You worry too much. You are giving yourself grey hair," I said. It was true. My friend's black hair was beginning to be streaked with grey, especially in his beard and moustache. "You see bandits behind every rock and tree."

"*Every* rock and tree may not conceal bandits, but it will be me who discovers the ones that do," he answered.

The warm afternoon sun, which bore down upon us, began to bring on a sort of drowsy stupor, and my head dropped to my chest as I succumbed to sleep. When I awoke sometime later, Walther was sitting on a nearby rock scrawling pictures in the wet soil of the bank with a stick. Seeing me awake he said, "We should head back before the sun goes down."

I yawned and stretched and reluctantly retrieved my horse. Our return trip was leisurely as we meandered up and down the hills with the sun at our backs. We came up over the crest of a hill, and the great city rose before us in the distance. That was the first time we had seen Constantinople from the landward side as an invader might see it. Its great size alone made it intimidating. As we drew closer, the westward boundary stretched for miles before us. The high inner wall shone like gold in the low afternoon sun. It seemed unassailable, especially since an attacker would first have to find a way to breech the outer wall and all the defenses that could be assembled on its top. The outer wall looked down over a wide moat which could only be crossed at great peril. It was easy to see why the city had never been conquered, and it seemed inconceivable that it ever would.

As we rode south, following the walls which loomed massive and intimidating like a man-made mountain ridge, we passed a succession of huge towers at regular intervals. When we finally reached the Sea of Marmara, the double Theodosian walls met the sea wall, which seemed to rise straight from the water. We re-entered the city at the Golden Gate and continued to follow the perimeter from inside the walls. By the time we returned our tired horses to the stable, the sun had dropped below the distant hills, and the western wall began to spread a lengthening shadow over much of the city.

The next day I arrived at the Hippodrome early, but the place was already alive with preparations for training. Stylianos was there and was checking each of the horses personally. He brushed them, picked up their feet, and ran his hands over every part of their bodies. Finally, when he was satisfied with them, both sets of horses were brought out to be hitched. I watched as each strap and buckle was secured and tightened and then checked by Stylianos himself. "Follow me out," he said. "And then stay close behind for the first six times around. Then, move to the outside for the last two turns and try to draw even with me by the end of the seventh. Stay wide on the turns and…good luck."

Both teams were led out, and Stylianos had the blacks. I climbed aboard the chariot with the bays. Excitement filled every inch of my body as we started forward on the floor of the massive Hippodrome. At first all I could concentrate on was the back of the other chariot. My horses wanted to move much closer than I did. I wasn't comfortable running right up the back of Stylianos, so I held them back. We settled into an even pace, and I glanced around the Hippodrome, taking it all in. Graceful statues marched by in silent succession, having seen races there for five hundred years. I imagined what the crowds must have been like on race days, cheering for their favorites.

We took the first turn slowly, and I kept Akakios, my inside horse, in line with the inside horse of Stylianos. Going down the other side of the track, Stylianos let his horses speed up, and the gap between us widened. I didn't want to fall too far behind and look ridiculous, so I let the horses have their heads, and they surged forward with great enthusiasm. Still, the black team stayed well out in front and reached the next turn with a sizable lead. I was careful to stay out from the spina on my approach, fighting the tendency of the team to bear in. I was still far behind going up the other side, and Stylianos' chariot appeared to be getting smaller. The dust that he stirred up from the floor of the track flew in our faces. It choked me and stung my eyes and obscured my vision ahead. I was embarrassed to be so far behind and was aware of a crowd of stable workers watching from the pavilion. I lashed the flanks of my horses with the reins and got a response. Our speed increased well beyond that which I achieved in my first practice two days previous. We took the next turn so fast that the inside wheel left the ground momentarily, and I shifted my position in the chariot far to the left to bring it back down. The next few laps were a blur to me as I try to recollect them now. I remember having the sensation of almost flying above the surface of the track, so perfectly my team was pulling in unison.

I began to gain ground on the black team, and soon the dust cloud raised by them was behind us. I lost count of our laps, but I thought we had reached the sixth. My horses were eager in pursuit, straining at their bits. I decided to let them go and moved them to the outside. They responded with a tremendous burst of new speed and would have drawn abreast of the black team had not the new turn caused us to lose ground. Up the straight we again moved beside the other chariot, and Stylianos looked back at me. His face was calm, and he looked like he was doing no work at all. Again we fell back slightly on the turn, but not as much that time.

On the last straight my horses, with the greatest of effort, pulled nearly head to head with the blacks. It was like being in the midst of a storm. Thirty-two hooves beating the track sounded like thunder. Nostrils flared and blew almost in perfect rhythm with each gigantic stride. Saliva and dirt flew back and hit me in the face. It was one of the most exciting things I have ever experienced.

Once past the finish line, the storm began to subside. The horses' heads came up a little, and gradually we slowed down. Their powerful flanks, dark and wet with sweat, bulged under their taut skin. My hands and arms and back and shoulders ached with fatigue. My legs felt as weak as willow saplings. Despite my weariness, I was supremely happy. As we brought the teams back to the pavilion, I expected some words of praise from Stylianos for my performance. None were forthcoming. He went about his work, supervising the cooling out of the horses and checking them for injuries. All came through in good shape.

With work at the stables drawing to a close, I found that I didn't want to leave. I never felt as at home anywhere as I did around horses. But finally it was time to leave. I shook Stylianos' hand and thanked him for letting me drive the team. His grasp was firm and friendly. As I turned to leave, he said to me, "I think you would have made a good charioteer."

21

We departed from Constantinople in October. It was our intention to be home before storms impeded our journey. Both the sea and the mountains were dangerous foes during the winter months. It was a bright, calm morning as we sailed out of the Golden Horn and into the Sea of Marmara. I looked back at the immense sun-washed city of the seven hills with a little melancholy. I was anxious to get home, but the sights and sounds and smells of Constantinople had infused me with a feeling of excitement. It was exotic and seductive, and I felt that its impression on me would last a long time.

We reached the Dardanelles and negotiated its passage without difficulty. The sparkling Aegean beckoned us into its vast, island-studded expanse. On the third day out, we started watching for pirate vessels as we widened our distance from the areas tightly controlled by the Byzantine navy. What we should have been watching more closely was the weather. Dark clouds gathered on the western horizon, and the winds calmed ominously around us. We were not close to the mainland or any islands at the time, but the captain knew where we might find landfall. The oarsmen pulled hard as we steered eastward away from the oncoming storm. Eventually land came within sight, but the rapidly moving wall of clouds was nearly upon us. The wind came up in advance of the storm, and our sails filled as we fled. With the rocky coastline clearly visible, it appeared that we might make it to safety, but the raging tempest hit us with its full fury. Wind-driven raindrops stung our skin like thousands of bees, and the ship was as a leaf being tossed about on the turbulent ocean. Waves washed over our decks and knocked men down like toddling children. We fell into a deep trough, and I heard a loud crack. As we rose again the mast, splintered as though it was no more than a stick of kindling, came crashing down, the sail flapping on deck like a dying fish.

We were being driven before the storm toward the land that was to have been our sanctuary. But by then the rocks that rose out of the crashing waves looked to be our executioner. The captain bravely tried to steer our hapless ship through the gauntlet of jagged rocks, but then the rudder shaft splintered into pieces. We were spun sideways, and our stern ran up on a partially submerged boulder. For a moment we came to a stop, the wooden hull creaking and groaning as it attempted to free itself. Helpless, we were hit by a huge wave and spun around the other way. The next rock that we hit signaled the end of the ship. It began to break in half, and dozens of men were immediately thrown into the water. Walther and I, in the half of the ship that was teetering precariously on the rocks decided to enter the water on our own terms with Father so that we might stay together. I went first, sliding down the broken deck, which was sloping downward into the dark water, and easing myself over the side. Father followed, and then Walther made his way into the torrent. Once past the barrier of rocks, the sea calmed slightly, making it possible for us to swim, and we made it to the rocky beach upon which we were thrown roughly by the surging breakers.

Exhausted, we dragged ourselves out of the surf and got to our feet. More men were being washed ashore, some able to walk out of the water, others limp and lifeless. Many had serious injuries caused by the jagged rocks. For the next couple of hours, we walked up and down the shore, collecting the dead in one area and helping the injured as best we could, although we had no supplies. The storm gradually abated as darkness closed in around us. We tried to sleep, but the rocky beach afforded little comfort and our clothes were soaked. The moans of the injured and dying mingled with the sounds of the breakers to disturb the otherwise lonely solitude of the place where we had been stranded.

The next day broke grey and chilly. Those of us who were able met to determine a plan. We had decided to explore further inland to find people to help us when those very people arrived on the beach. One of the inhabitants of the island (as it turned out) had seen us and summoned help from the nearby village. Nikodemos, the interpreter traveling with us on the journey to Constantinople, was able to communicate with the people there, who spoke Greek. The village leader, an old man named Pavlos, said that ships came infrequently to the island, especially in winter, and that it might be months before we saw another vessel. It was decided that each of us would stay with a family, so as not to burden any one household with more than one additional mouth to feed. When, at last, a ship did come that could take us off the island, word would travel fast in the small community and we could all, hopefully, depart together.

I went with a man named Fillipos, who was probably about thirty years old. He had deeply tanned arms and face, black hair that was beginning to grey, and weary brown eyes. He walked rapidly, without speaking, swinging his muscular arms by his sides. We walked for perhaps half an hour, skirting fields that had mostly been harvested. We crossed grassy meadows where occasionally we saw herds of goats being watched over by old men, and we waded small, shallow streams. In the distance I saw, on the hillsides, rows of grapevines and orchards of olive trees. Fillipos had a farm situated among the hills on the south side of the island. He lived with his family in a small stone house with a mud, straw, and wood roof. As we approached the dwelling, there was a young girl, about eight, feeding chickens in the yard. She looked at me with curious eyes but no discernable change of expression as I passed. I nodded and smiled at her.

Inside the dwelling Fillipos' wife, whose name was Despoina, was busy spinning thread at a wheel. She stopped when I came in and looked a little apprehensive at the stranger in her house. She was a short, plump woman with a round, pleasant face and dark hair covered partially covered by a red scarf. Fillipos introduced us and after a brief conversation amongst themselves, Despoina cut a large chunk of bread for me and poured a cup of water from a clay pitcher. I was extremely hungry and thirsty, having had nothing to eat or drink since the previous day, so I was grateful for the humble repast.

Not long after that, a young man came in carrying an armful of firewood. He looked at me suspiciously as he passed but apparently had been forewarned of my presence. He stacked the firewood by the hearth and quickly went back out.

I met the last member of the household when Fillipos' father, came in for supper. His name was Georgios, and he looked very much like an older Fillipos. He was slightly smaller than his son (perhaps because of his stooped posture) and leaner, with narrower shoulders and thin, sinewy arms. His hair was completely white and thin, with the darkly tanned skin of his scalp showing through. When he smiled, he showed the gaps of several missing teeth.

It was awkward for the family having a stranger living in their house. It wasn't bad when everyone was involved in their work, but when they came in for meals, it was obvious that no one was acting naturally. The silence at the table was particularly uncomfortable, but eventually, Despoina began to speak to the other members of the family in order to get them to talk. Once conversations began, they seemed to forget that I was there, which was fine with me. After a couple of days of this, Natasa, the little girl, took pity on me and started teaching me words at the table. At first the others smiled and laughed at my attempts to repeat the Greek words for objects on the table, but after a while they all started to join in. Soon, it became a family project to teach me the language, and the lessons spilled over into situations beyond the supper table.

Natasa took me under her little wing and welcomed me into her daily activities. We fed the chickens together, tossing grain to the birds as they crowded around us to get their share. Sometimes Natasa would hold a small quantity of the seeds in her tiny hand and giggle as the chickens plucked them from her palm. She offered some grain to me and, to her delight, I let the greedy birds peck at my hand as well.

After we had finished feeding the chickens, our next job was to milk the goats. There were several goats kept near the house just for the purpose of milking. Natasa tied a she-goat to a post and sat down on a small milking stool which seemed the perfect size for the little girl. Natasa began to squeeze milk into her pail with even, rhythmic strokes. The first goat was quickly done, another was tied to the post, and the process repeated. After the second goat was milked, Natasa must have decided that I had had enough instruction and it was time for me to be put to work. She pointed out the next goat to be milked and waited while I tied it to the post. I looked at the tiny stool and decided that it probably wouldn't hold me. Instead, I knelt on the ground, took the teats in my hands and began trying to emulate the girl's movements. At first, the results were not good. Natasa giggled. Then she took my hands in hers and led me through the process. Soon, the milk was coming out into the pail in long, even streams like the girl had produced. Natasa clapped her hands with delight and patted me on the back.

By the time we finished milking the goats, the late summer sun was high in its arc across the hazy blue sky. Natasa spoke to me almost constantly by that time, although I could only pick out a word now and then that I understood. I suppose that she thought I would gradually absorb the language if I heard it often enough. I gathered by her words and gestures that she wanted to take a walk and beckoned me to follow her. We walked down the hill away from the house and followed a copse that divided the path from a deep ravine. Near the bottom of the hill was a large meadow of long waving grasses. Here and there were clumps of wildflowers that added reds, blues, and yellows to the pale green hues of the grass. The edges of the meadow were particularly abundant with flowers, and Natasa set out to pick some. When she waded into the higher grass, the stalks came nearly to her waist, and in those moments she joined with the meadow as completely as one of the flowers. Her movements from one patch of flowers to the next were as smooth and natural as a bee gathering pollen. The warm sunlight cast a soft glow over the scene, and the luster of the girl's brown curls and rosy skin blended perfectly with her surroundings. She came back to me with a brilliant red poppy and put it in my hand. She skipped away like a hare and returned to her browsing. I studied the flower in a way that I had never done before. Its delicate petals unfolded intricately, infused with so much life that it almost seemed to have a pulse. I looked up from the blossom, and Natasa had merged seamlessly with the meadow again.

A few days later, in my attempt to immerse myself in the family activities and be more useful, I went with old Georgios as he took his flock of goats out to graze in a distant pasture. Most of the time they grazed in the fields nearby, but as the dry months wore on it, was necessary to move them to lesser-used areas to avoid ruining fields by over-grazing. The animals seemed accustomed to the routine, for once the old man began moving toward them with his stick, they moved in orderly fashion ahead of him. Without having to make any large or sudden movements, he steered the herd in the direction that he wanted, and the goats moved with a unity that made them appear to be tied together with an unseen tether.

The pace of the herd was unhurried, yet neither were various individuals allowed to impede the group's progress. The old man's calm purposefulness seemed to be indistinguishable from that of the animals that he led. Whether he led from in front, beside, within, or behind the herd did not matter. I tried to copy his movements to contribute assistance, but usually I only succeeded in being a disruption. At these efforts the old shepherd just smiled and, without rancor, restored order with the slightest of actions.

The day was of that kind when it is difficult to feel that anything could possibly justify complaint. It was warm without being too hot, and a gentle breeze wafted over the rolling countryside. The pale blue sky was streaked with wisps of thin clouds. The very air that we breathed, infused with the scent of the sea, seemed to cleanse my soul. Finally, we reached the place where the herd was to graze. It was so secluded that it was possible to imagine that no one else existed in the world. The pasture drifted off in gentle contours in all directions, although in the distance there could be seen higher and more severe acclivities. Here and there the continuity of the field was interspersed with gatherings of trees that cast cool shadows over the vibrant green grasses that covered the hills. A small meandering stream trickled lazily through the pasture and wandered off through a wood.

Being used to riding wherever I went and unaccustomed to walking great distances, by the time we reached the pasture, I felt the effects of my exertions. The old man, however, showed no signs of fatigue. His vigor, despite his advanced years, impressed me greatly. He sat down on a rock that somewhat resembled the seat of a chair, having a wide flat surface that curved upward slightly at the edges. The goats browsed peacefully on the gentle, grassy, slopes.

I sat down underneath a large tree with spreading branches and leaned back against the trunk. The leaves above my head rustled slightly in the soft breeze.

Fragments of thought passed in succession through my mind although I can't recall them. Perhaps I was thinking of home and wondering when I would again see the mountains and the lakes and the forests of Swabia. A young kid bleated at one of his companions and woke me out of a shallow sleep. The tranquil scene before me of the old shepherd and his flock remained unchanged. I stretched my arms and legs and adjusted the position of my back against the tree. I didn't resist the next wave of blissful sleep that came upon me. I dreamed of Verena. She was tending her goats in pastures familiar to me, much like the first day that I saw her when we were children. Only in my dream she was as I had last seen her.

When I awoke, I passed through that half-conscious state where dream and reality merge and imagined that the flock was being tended by an aged, weathered tree stump that vaguely resembled a man. So perfectly it blended into the setting! As I continued to emerge from my sleep, the stump gradually took on more human shape and finally, as my mind reached near full clarity, I realized that it was Georgios, still sitting on his rock. I looked around me and found that the goats had joined me in the cooling shade under the tree. They lay peacefully scattered about in the grass, many with their eyes closed in perfect tranquility. One kid was so close to me that I put out my hand and stroked the stiff brown hair of his bony head.

As the sun dropped lower in the sky and the shadows from the hills and trees grew longer, the goats got up one by one and started grazing again. I walked down to the stream and watched the water move rapidly along its course. It gurgled and splashed as it cascaded over the smooth rocks that had seen the passing of centuries without changing. I knelt down and drank the cool, sweet water from my cupped hands. I would have liked to follow the channel of that stream to find the spring that was its source, but at that moment the old goatherd got up and began to round up his flock. Like before, it took only the slightest of action by him to get the goats moving in the right direction. Soon we were walking back toward the farm along familiar paths. The sun by that time was almost touching the treetops on distant hills, and a pale orange glow was spreading across the sky. Although another day was coming to a close, there was a timelessness to that moment. It could have been happening a thousand years before, or two thousand for that matter.

Early fall was the time for the grape harvest on the island. The vineyards were shared areas since not all parts of the island were suitable for growing grapes. Several families came together for the harvest, all contributing the labor necessary to harvest the grapes quickly when they were at their best. Both men and women participated in the harvest with the women and girls doing the picking of the fruit and the men carrying the heavy baskets. Walther was staying with a family nearby, and one of the few times that we saw each other was during the harvest.

The first day of picking dawned brilliantly, with clear skies and a slight chill in the air. The females, some young and pretty, others middle aged and heavy, still others old and ugly, all set out picking the ripe fruit with their careful fingers. I moved my basket from place to place until it was full and then carried it to a wagon or cart drawn by horse or donkey. The work was accomplished at an efficient, but unhurried pace, and the mood was light with much playful banter between the neighbors who seemed happy to be together. I was so busy with my labors and trying to catch pieces of the conversations going on around me that I was not even aware of the passing time. When the sun was high, Fillipos called a stop to the activity and we all, man and woman, young and old found places to sit under the spreading trees of a nearby grove. A wagon rolled up close by, and the children too young to participate in the work of the harvest walked around handing out loaves of fresh bread and shallow bowls, which were filled with wine from clay pitchers.

The wine that we drank from the bowls was sour and weak, but the work was hot and I was grateful to be able to quench my thirst. I looked around at all the healthy, sun-reddened faces, laughing and talking with each other. I thought about their simple life here on the island, with no masters to oppress them, no yoke of servitude, no covetous ambition. Their labors were for themselves and their families and neighbors, with the cycle of their lives tied to the land they inhabited.

By the time the last of the grapes were picked and loaded, the sun had descended below the hills to the southwest and each family started off toward their homes. We followed the last of the wagons back to the house in the cool, clear air of the evening. By the time we reached the farm on the hillside, a few bright stars had decided to reveal themselves to us in the blue-black sky. A stew, made beforehand, was warmed over the fire, and better fare I had never tasted. After the meal, I walked out into the yard under a canopy resplendent with a thousand-thousand stars. I stood gazing at the wondrous heavens and mused that Verena was looking at the same stars over our home in Zurich. As I stood there, wishing that there was a way for me to let her know that I was safe, a star plunged from the sky in the west, momentarily leaving a brilliant streak of light in its wake. I smiled and thought, 'that will just have to do.' When I went back into the house, everyone had gone to their beds and there was only a single candle casting is wavering light over the room. I blew it out and eased myself quietly into my bed in the corner. I lay there for a while, not quite ready for sleep, thinking of Verena, trying, as I did every day, to recall every detail about her. It was as though I felt, deep inside, that if I didn't keep her image fresh in my mind she might cease to exist.

The next day the families came back together to crush the grapes. Fillipos had a large vat for this purpose, and the grapes from the baskets were emptied into it. The making of the wine was a festive occasion, and music and song accompanied the stomping of the grapes. The vat was big enough for four or five people at a time, and their energetic steps were made in time with the music. The women tied up their skirts to mid-thigh, and the men rolled up their pants. The first group contained a pretty young girl with dark eyes, and thick, raven hair which bounced upon her shoulders with each step. She danced with unbridled enthusiasm, a sly smile gracing her red lips. I couldn't take my eyes off of her, although it was with feelings of both delight and embarrassment that I watched her. She thrust her shoulders forward and back with each high step of her knees. She tossed her hair from side to side as she twirled merrily, and she let her loose dress fall in careless disarray off one shoulder. In her movements there was uninhibited innocence tinged with a slightly aware hint of seduction. As I watched her eyes, I noticed that they always seemed to fall back in one particular direction. I followed them and discovered their object. It was young Nickolaos, Fillipos' son. The boy's gaze was fixed on the girl, and his self-conscious look said that he knew the seduction was for him. I felt like an intruder watching the intimate game that they played, and I pulled my attention away from it. Fortunately, I was able to find work to distract me.

The juice from the grapes was collected in barrels, and the barrels were divided up between the families. By the time the last of the grapes was crushed, Nickolaos and the dark-haired girl were nowhere to be seen. When the other families had taken their share of the juice and returned home, I felt a little sad that such a festive occasion had come to an end and wouldn't be repeated again for another year. I also went to my bed that night with a disturbing sensation of restlessness within me that couldn't be quelled.

Fall faded into winter, temperatures dropped, and rain came often. It was nothing like a Swabian winter, but the cold rains and wind did cause us to spend more time inside by the fire. Natasa continued her crusade to teach me their language, and having little else to do, I applied myself to the task. Farm work did not cease, of course. It simply took on new forms. The animals still needed care, firewood had to be gathered, tools and harnesses were mended. We went down to the sea to catch fish, some of which we ate, others we salted for later use. We made cheese from the goat's milk.

Gradually, the storms coming across the sea began to subside, and the days grew warmer. One day word came that a ship had arrived and would be able to provide passage for us back to Italy. When it came time to leave I felt a bit somber. I had thought all along that I would be elated to be going home, but my feeling was different than I thought it would be. I wondered if Walther and the others felt the same slight sadness at leaving the island. We never talked about it.

I had grown to love the family. The kindness that they had shown me as a stranger in their house was, at first, nearly incomprehensible to me. I came to realize, however, that their way of life, so closely tied to the land and the elements, nourished virtues like compassion, honesty, and cooperation. I would miss them long afterward.

Saying good-bye was hardest with Natasa. She hugged me and tears rolled down her little cheeks when we had to part for the last time. I kissed her forehead and thanked her for all that I had learned from her. I told her I would never forget her. My last words of good-bye and thanks to all the members of the family were spoken in Greek.

22

It was well into May by the time we got back to Swabia, and spring had pushed out all but a few remnants of winter. The hillsides were growing lush in grass and wheat, and the swollen rivers rushed blue-green from out of the mountains. Flowers bloomed in profusion in the meadows and along the roadsides, and buds swelled on the tips of tree branches. We arrived at *der Ludwigsburg* late in the afternoon after many hard days of overland travel. It had been a fine day, with cool temperatures that made it easier on the horses. In spite of that, we had pushed hard to avoid spending another night on the road, and we were all, horse and man, very tired. By the time we had unloaded the horses and seen after their care, Mother and Verena were aware of our arrival and were waiting in the great hall. Their joy and relief at seeing us again after such a long absence was clear, but for Verena and I, the complete and uninhibited feelings of our reunion remained suppressed until we were alone.

It had been a very long time since we had eaten at our own table, but it wasn't long before it seemed like we had never been away. Like a fox returning to its den, there is comfort and tranquility in the place we call home.

After the meal, Verena and I retired to our chamber. We were barely out of my parents' sight when Verena was in my arms. We held each other for a long time, finally convinced that we were no longer separated by towering mountains and vast oceans. Together, that night, we were able to chase away the loneliness and longing.

Our fine weather continued the next morning, and the day dawned clear and cool. I went to see Diomedes and found that he had wintered well. He was fat from lack of exercise, and his eye was soft and contented. He still bore remnants of his winter hair, and I spent a long time grooming him. I then climbed aboard his broad back and rode out down the old Roman road toward the horse farm. The old horse was lazy at first, balking at anything faster than a walk, and I indulged him for a while, letting him plod slowly along. It was a beautiful day, in any case, and I had spent a lot of time on horseback lately. I took in all the familiar sights along the way and realized how much I had missed home. All the excitement and anticipation and pleasant memories of going to the horse farm as a young boy came flooding back to me whenever I rode along that road. The only thing that had changed was that Verena was missing from the chestnut grove when I passed. But the memories of our meetings were still there and revived thoughts of those happy times. Those old memories mingled with all the wonderful new memories that we created together every day.

Diomedes could always sense when we were nearing the horse farm and, after a while, began to show more energy. He broke into a trot, then I urged him into a gallop. The last mile of road swept by in minutes, and soon we came to a stop on the rise that overlooks the farm. I always stop there to take in the beauty of the valley. The vibrant green of the spring grass in the pastures stretched before us, bordered in the distance by the darker evergreens. Many of the pastures had foals alongside their mothers, occasionally scampering away with bursts of energy, then returning quickly.

I rode down the hill in the best of spirits. Several of the men greeted me with smiles and nods, but many of the young boys didn't know me. I sought out Helmut and found him with the yearlings. When the old man looked up and saw me, he didn't smile or speak. He continued what he was doing, which was looking over one of the young horses with another trainer. He ran his hand over the animal's back and down its hind legs. Apparently satisfied, he allowed the horse to be led off. He then turned to me and said, "Are you just going to stand there? We have plenty of horses to train."

I smiled. "Which one would you like me to start with?"

He led me to a pen where several two-year-olds had been turned out together. He pointed to a black colt with three white feet and a white star on his forehead. "What's been done with him?" I asked.

"Haltered and led. That's it."

"Good," I replied. "Then he doesn't have any bad habits."

I separated the colt from his friends and turned him loose in an empty pen. I let him watch me warily for a few minutes, then used my rope to get him to move around the pen. After about three turns, I stepped in front of him and made him turn back the other way. I repeated that pattern one more time and then let my body relax. The colt immediately stopped and stood still. I thought to myself, 'He seems like a sensible colt.' I worked my way closer to him without approaching in a direct line. He didn't move. When I was beside him, I reached out and put my hand on his neck. His muscles twitched a little, but his feet stayed in place. I ran my hand over his shoulders and back and hips. After a few minutes, he let out a big sigh. He was getting used to me. I moved away and circled around behind him. He followed me with one eye. I flicked the rope out at his flank, and he took a step away. I did it again, and he didn't move. After the fourth time, he turned around and faced me. I walked up to his head and petted him.

I attached the rope to his halter and worked with him on turns, moving his hips, moving his forequarters, bending his neck, bringing his head toward me, and backing up. He was a smart little colt, and we got along well. When I left the farm that day, I couldn't have been happier. I was back doing what I loved most in the world.

That same year, Otto led an army to regain control of North Saxony, which had been seized by an alliance of Wends and Danes. At around the same time, there was trouble in the south. The Italian King, Lothair, had died and Barengar ll, Margrave of Ivrea, had taken the throne and made his son, Adalbert co-ruler. Barengar tried to force Adelaide, Lothair's nineteen year-old widow, to marry Adalbert, and thus further secure his hold on the crown. Adelaide refused the marriage and was imprisoned. Word of her plight reached my father who had connections with the Italian nobility. He was busy trying to secure her release, so it fell to me to take the Swabian knights to join Otto in Saxony.

I was unhappy to leave home at that time, since I had so recently returned from Constantinople after nearly ten month's absence. Verena and I had just begun to settle back into a comfortable life with each other, and I was training a number of very good horses. But I had no choice, so I rode north with one hundred knights to meet the King at his camp outside of Magdeburg. The journey, made the last time in mid-winter for Eadgyth's funeral, wasn't difficult in summer. But throughout the long days on the road, I was troubled by the persistent images of Verena at the time of our parting. She did her best to remain in control of her emotions, but there was an odd aspect to her countenance that left me with an unsettled feeling. Her sadness and concern over what was to be an uncertain period of absence was there, but I had seen that before. There was something else that I would not understand until much later.

It had been four years since I had seen Otto, by then in his late thirties. He seemed to me only slightly altered in that time. Of course he was a little less youthful-looking; that was to be expected, having gained some weight and a few grey hairs, but he was still robust and handsome. When I had first seen him, he was still grieving for Eadgyth. His eyes had borne the look of sadness. This time, his look was clear and resolute. His presence inspired confidence. Since taking the throne, he had brought all the German dukes under his control and shown that he could keep the kingdom safe from outside threats.

One such threat was the Danes from the Jutland, ruled by King Gorm the Old. The Slavs in North Saxony had rebelled against Otto's rule years earlier but had been driven back across the Elbe by Otto's forces under the command of Margrave Herman of the Billung March. But the region was vast and marshy, and resistance among the Wends was strong. When the Danes joined the fight, all the territory that Herman had gained was lost, and the Margrave was taken prisoner.

The Slav-Dane alliance was commanded by Gorm's son, Harald Bluetooth. Harald was using the captured town of Hamburg as his base, and the bulk of his army was camped there. We encountered our first resistance about twenty miles out from the town when small bands of Slav fighters launched hit and run raids on our right flank. The attackers would let loose a hail of arrows from the cover of the trees near the riverbank. These resulted in a few minor injuries to our knights, their armor helping to prevent serious harm in most cases. Some horses were hurt, and two servants that were with the baggage at the rear of the column were killed. When pursued, the Slavs rode away to the south, staying behind us. The Slavs lacked the strength to attack a column of fully-armed knights, so those raids were of little consequence. I suppose they hoped to draw away some of our knights to weaken the column, but Otto ordered us just to chase them off and then return to our ranks.

When we reached Hamburg, we faced Harald's main army, which consisted of fierce Dane warriors and the best fighters from the rugged Wend Slavs. They had positioned themselves along a relatively high bar of land situated in the marshland outside of town. There was a wide bog between us and the defenders. It was obvious that they had chosen their position hoping that they could lure us into attacking across the bog and getting our horses mired in it. At the least it would have slowed us down and prevented us from overrunning their line. Worse, our horses might not have been able to maneuver at all in the marsh. Being trapped in the bog, not able to go forward or back, would have put our cavalry at a serious disadvantage against the axe-wielding Danes.

It appeared that the only way to attack Harald's army was at its flanks, but a crossing with visible solid footing for the horses was miles away to the east and easily twice as far to the west. As leader of the knights from Zurich, I attended the meeting of Otto's lieutenants as they discussed ways for mounting an attack. The concern was that it would take many days to move the entire army into a flanking position, and that a smaller, more mobile force wouldn't be strong enough to face the full enemy army. The meeting reached an impasse, and finally, I suggested that I test different locations for crossing the bog to see if there was a place that we could get across safely to attack the enemy's flank. I convinced the others to give me a day to explore.

That afternoon, I took off all my armor and all the armor from my horse to make us as light as possible. The horse that I had chosen for the campaign was a large chestnut with two white stockings and a wide white blaze. I had spent many hours working with him at the farm, and he was brave and willing. I rode east until I was out of sight of the Slavs and then started seeking entry points into the bog.

The first place that I tried looked shallow, but we had only gone about twenty-five feet in when the horse sunk up to his belly. His feet got stuck and we came to a standstill. Being the good horse that I knew him to be, he didn't panic, but instead stood calmly. I slid off his back into the waist deep water. I got him turned around and led him back to solid footing. Again and again we tried promising-looking places, but all ended up having unstable footing. This went on throughout the afternoon. It was getting late, and I was about to give up for the day when, scanning the marsh, my eye caught a slight irregularity as the wind blew ripples across the water's surface. My willing horse, who had bravely gone into the bog over and over again stepped carefully off the bank and, to my surprise, found firm footing. With only his hooves sinking into the soggy soil, we ventured farther and farther out. We made it all the way over to the narrow peninsula that harbored the enemy forces.

Next I had to confirm the width of the path across the bog. I crossed at several places and each time rode to the other side. The bar was wide enough for four horses abreast. I marked the passage with two piles of stones that could only be seen from the south bank. I rode back to camp at a gallop, anxious to report what I had learned.

A plan was put into place. Three thousand knights, nearly two-thirds of our army, would form a column four lines wide and ride across the bog and attack the left flank of the enemy. The remainder of our forces would stay to the south of the bog, maintaining a visible presence.

In the morning, the sun came up across the marsh under a low line of clouds creating brilliant streaks of orange light shooting up into the sky. By that time, we were already on our horses and moving toward the crossing. I was at the head of the flanking force with the commander, Baron Gebhard. Once we reached the place that I had marked with the stones, Gebhard sent me back into the ranks with my knights. I joined Walther and the others about fifty yards back. I looked at the faces of my comrades and saw a full range of emotions, from fear on some of the younger knights to steely determination on the older ones. For many of the men, myself included, that battle was the largest, and most significant one of our lives. We didn't have long to think about it that morning. The order was given to move, and the first horsemen plunged forward along the bar that crossed the bog. In minutes, our part of the column had reached the water as well. The horses, seeing their herd-mates entering the marsh ahead of them, didn't hesitate. At a gallop, we were on the other side quickly and fanning out into a broader attacking front.

By the time the enemy force came into view, all of our knights had crossed the bog, and we were gaining full attack speed. The leading corps of knights, the Saxons, formed a wedge and lowered their lances. We were close on their heels and did the same. I was on the right side of the wedge and, with many riders ahead of me, could barely see the enemy that we were to face. The first wave of arrows from behind the Danish lines came hurdling down on the men ahead of us, and many found their mark. Horses screamed and men fell, but still the momentum of our charge could not be slowed.

I heard the crash of initial contact as the Saxons slammed into the enemy lines. The sound of savage yells and the clash of weapons hung on the air like the raging of a storm. The second wave of arrows rained down on us. An arrow glanced off my helmet and another struck the rump of my horse. One of my men fell from his mount, and I couldn't see what happened to him after that. The line ahead of us slowed as the Saxons plowed through the mass of warriors ahead of them. Some of the Danes broke through and came running at us with swords and axes. We had lost the momentum of our attack. I spurred my horse forward and aimed my lance at a man whose arm was raised to throw an axe. The point hit him in the side, and I could feel it sink deep as the forward surge of my horse drove it into him. As he spun around, the lance was twisted from my hand and fell to the ground. I drew my sword and brought it crashing down on another fighter who was attacking the knight next to me. He crumpled sickeningly and was trampled under the hooves of iron-shod horses. Our wedge was pinched in by the fighting on both sides, and our horses became forced together. At that point, we were nearly shoulder-to-shoulder with each other. Maneuvering became impossible as the melee filled the narrow peninsula.

Gradually, spaces opened up on the right side of the wedge, and we started moving forward again. The enemy lines were broken, and the men were trying to escape across the marsh. We had been told not to pursue their forces into the bog but only to drive them off of the rise. We didn't want to get the horses mired in an area where the enemy could turn on us. Once the retreat was started, all resistance on the peninsula ceased. Slav and Dane alike showed us their backs as their unity dissolved into disorganized flight.

We split into two divisions. One to stay behind the fleeing enemy to ensure that they were unable to re-group, the other to tend to the dead and wounded. The second division was to then follow in support. I was in the first division as we carefully picked our route through the marshes, always heading north behind the fleeing Danes. The Wend Slavs seemed to be absorbed into the countryside. North Saxony was their home, and we didn't wish to destroy them as long as they were willing to yield to Otto's rule.

The Danes were another matter. Otto was determined to punish them for their incursion upon Saxon soil. We were to drive them back into the Jutland

and force Harald and his father to accept terms. On and on we pressed north on the heels of Harald's retreating army. The order came from Otto that we were to burn the farms in our path and confiscate the animals. We were to leave nothing that could be used by our enemies.

I despised that kind of warfare. The peasant farmers unlucky enough to be in our swath of destruction were left with nothing. When the harsh Danish winter came, their families would starve. Yet on and on we moved, leaving a blackened and desolate land behind us. In order to cover more area, we divided up into smaller squads to reach more isolated farms. There was no resistance from Harald's army which was pushed farther and farther north.

One day I was leading a squad of twenty knights as we came upon a small farm situated east of a large fjord that the Danes called Aabenraa. There the fields still contained wheat ripe for harvest, and a small herd of goats grazed on the hillsides nearby. We rode up to the tiny house and were met by a little girl with a basket of eggs. She stood firmly in place before us, a look of determination upon her dirty little face. The memory of Natasa, the little girl on the island in the Aegean, came vividly back into my mind. Walther, still my constant companion, asked if we were going to burn the house and the crops. I looked at the little girl and her chickens. "When we were in training to be knights, we were told that we should always protect the helpless. Does that not apply here?"

"We were ordered to destroy all farms," he replied.

"This farm is far to the east of the route that Harald's army has taken. It is of no use to them. Perhaps we could by-pass this one as if we never came upon it."

Walther shrugged. "I have no taste for waging war on farmers. I will follow your orders."

I turned my horse around and rode back to my men. As I led them away from the farm I said, "Innocent children are not the foes of Swabian knights." None of my men ever mentioned the incident again.

Two weeks later, King Gorm accepted Otto's terms of surrender. Margrave Herman was released, and the Danish King acknowledged Otto as overlord. Harald had lost all of the territory previously claimed in Germany, so Otto's victory was complete.

23

By the time the campaign against the northern Slavs came to an end and I was able to return to Zurich, nearly eight months had passed. When we reached the lake and familiar views of the town, we were close to exhaustion, but I had pushed hard on the last part of our trek because it had been so long since we had seen our families, and we were anxious to be home. I had spent so little time with Verena since our marriage, and every day away from her seemed to stretch into an eternity.

When I arrived at *der Ludwigsburg*, there was no one to greet me in the great hall, and the house was ominously quiet. My footsteps resounded in the hall, and I called out loudly to announce my presence. When I heard no response, I walked back to the quarters that Verena and I shared. Leaving the hall, I was met by mother coming down the corridor the other way. Her tired old face showed so much distress that it struck me in the chest like being kicked by a horse. She smiled weakly at seeing me and held out her hands. They were cold and bony and seemed to tremble slightly. "I'm so glad you're back," she said, her voice cracking with emotion.

"Mother, what's wrong? Where is Verena?"

"She's having the baby, Max."

"The baby? I…I didn't know about it," I stammered.

"I know. She wasn't sure when you left."

"How is she?" I said, beginning to grasp the situation. My mother's look of concern filled me with dread.

"It's not good," she said finally. She started yesterday and has been in labor for almost two days. She has nearly given up because she has no strength to continue pushing. The physician is not hopeful."

A cold rush of fear swept over me. I thought for a moment what my mother's words could mean, and I shuddered. I rushed past her and, not knowing what I would find, hurried into the bed chamber. There, I saw the small, pale, figure of Verena propped up on the bed, her belly greatly distended. At first I thought that life had already left her body, so still and deathly white she appeared. Her eyes were closed and her arms lay limp by her sides. I could see no sign of breathing as I approached in terror. The mid-wife sat beside the bed looking at me with worry in her eyes. "She's resting," came the words from her mouth in a whisper.

I sat down on the edge of the bed and took Verena's cold, tiny hand in mine. She stirred slightly and took in a breath. I started to breathe again myself and realized that I had stopped when I entered the chamber. "Verena. It's me." I said, breaking the heavy silence of the room.

Her eyelids fluttered almost imperceptibly, and then gradually opened part-way. Her gaze, as if looking through a fog, fixed upon me. I expected a smile of recognition, but instead, her mouth grew hard and grim. The eyes, I imagined, had the look of accusation, and I felt their full weight. "Verena," I said in a firm voice, "You have to keeping trying. We'll do it together." I squeezed her hand encouragingly. A moment went by and then I felt the pressure of her hand gripping mine. With great effort, she drew her small, frail body up against the pillows and lifted her head. In a weak, raspy voice she said, "We? I would gladly let you help. But you are of no use. I will have to do it myself."

Her words stung me, but I was happy to see the life return to her eyes. I put my arm around her shoulders and let her squeeze my hand as she pushed with all the effort that she could summon forth. When the contraction passed, she settled back into the bed to await the next one. She looked at me and said softly, "I'm glad you're here."

For a time that was probably much shorter than it seemed to me, the contractions came and went and Verena expended all the energy that she could with each push. At the end of each she let out a shriek, more animal than human, that chilled my blood. I feared that she could not survive such pain as wracked her body and wished that I could take it into mine. Finally, when I thought she could endure no more, the mid-wife, who had been trying to give encouragement, exclaimed, "The baby is coming! Just one more push!"

"Did you hear, Verena?" I said stupidly, as if she was not aware of what was going on. "It's almost over."

Verena held up her hand to me. "Wait," she whispered. Then, as though listening to a voice within her, she lay motionless. Then, she gathered her strength again, and with one more effort, the new life which she had carried for so long was expelled into the world.

For the first time since I had arrived, a feeble smile broke the lines of her face. Then came sobs of joy and relief. Tears rolled down her red cheeks, which stood out against the ghostly white of her face and neck. Ringlets of wet hair clung to her forehead. My attention solely on Verena, I was completely unaware of the actions of the mid-wife. After a time, I do not know how long, there came a weak and fitful cry which gradually grew into a wail. It drew my attention to the pitiful little creature held by the mid-wife. Having cleaned it up and wrapped it in a blanket, she place it in Verena's arms. Although I had no feelings in particular for this small, naked and wrinkled intruder in our midst, my heart felt deeply the love with which my wife looked upon it.

Over the next few days, my concern over Verena's safety grew. She had lost a great deal of blood during the birth. All of her strength expended, she lay motionless in the bed, unable to get up. She refused food and slept all but a couple of hours a day, during which she held the baby. In those moments, I watched the light that flickered in her eyes as she looked upon our son with the serene and unselfish love of a mother for her child. I mused that even the love for God felt by the very devout could not surpass that bond.

For myself, I felt nothing for the child. I had had no time to prepare for the event, being completely unaware of my wife's condition. All of my emotion since arriving back home was spent on the crushing dread that I might lose Verena. I tried to summon up some of the love that I imagined I should be feeling for this new person, which was part of her and part of me. I felt guilty that I couldn't find some love in my heart for my son, which Verena named Christoph. It wasn't as if I felt angry with the child. On the contrary, I felt a degree of pity for the poor creature, so roughly brought into the world with no choice in the matter. When Verena and I were married, I tried to imagine what it would be like to be a parent. At that time, I thought I would be filled with love and pride and a sense of starting out on an exciting adventure. The reality was quite different. I knew nothing about being a parent. I stood by helplessly while others attended to its needs. I felt quite useless. The only time I felt anything toward the baby was when I saw how it brought life into the eyes of Verena when she held him. In those moments, I began to sense a gradual merging of the child's existence with ours.

Verena's condition continued to worsen until the physician could offer no hope for her survival. The priest came and administered the last rights of the Church. When it was thought that she would not live through the night, I refused to leave her bedside. I was terrified at the thought of having to spend the rest of my life without her. In the dark room, with the lone candle flickering its dying light on the walls, I sobbed and begged God to spare her. I had not been a particularly good Christian, relegating God to the background of my life. I had not spent much time thinking about my beliefs. I wasn't even sure that God existed outside the imagination of men. But it hadn't mattered much before. Now, faced with losing the person that I loved more than life itself, my desperation left me only the last hope of a man who can see the vast chasm of death ahead for themselves or a loved one.

I finally lay down on the bed beside her to await the end. I placed my hand upon her body to feel the signs of a life to which she still clung: the slight rise and fall of her breast, the barely perceptible beat of her heart. In the yellow candlelight, her beautiful face looked serene. I shook away the images that came into my mind of seeing that face in a coffin. At some point during the night I fell asleep.

I awoke to the feeling of a hand on my forehead. I opened my eyes in confusion to see Verena's soft, weary eyes looking into mine. She had turned toward me and was stroking my hair. Sunlight was pouring through the window and filling up the room. Somehow, she had survived the night, and her condition seemed less dire. "I thought I had lost you," I said softly, placing my hand on her cheek.

A faint smile creased the corners of her mouth. Her gaze left my face and seemed to search inwardly as if trying to recall a dream. "I was alone," she said after a moment, "and wandering in a strange place. The light was behind me, but I kept walking toward the darkness. Then you came and found me and brought me back."

"We'll always find each other," I replied. "No matter what."

Verena continued to grow stronger and eventually left her bed. She was able to take some food and walk short distances. She spent many hours holding Christoph, and the sight of them together was a great source of pleasure for me. After a time, the physician told me that Verena would not be able to bear more children. At first this was disheartening, mainly because of the great sadness that it would cause her. But I didn't dwell on it for long. Verena was still with me, brightening my days, and I had a son that appeared strong and healthy.

The months passed, and I returned to training horses at the farm. Each week, Christoph seemed to gain a new baby skill, which caused much excitement among us all. Verena, however, remained frail and in poor health, and tired quickly. Her fresh beauty and vitality never fully returned. But my love for her was undiminished, and I treasured the time that God had allowed me to have with her.

24

In 951, Otto mounted an expedition to cross the Alps into Italy. Adelaide, through her emissaries, had proposed marriage to Otto, an alliance that would be beneficial to both. Otto, widowed for five years, accepted the proposal and took his army into the Po River Valley to join his son Liudolf, who had become Duke of Swabia after Herman's death. Liudolf had taken it upon himself to cross the Alps with his own army several months before. Faced with certain defeat by the German army, Barrengar ll fled, leaving Otto to be crowned King of the Lombards in Pavia. There Otto married Adelaide before he returned with her to Magdeberg.

One June day, Verena was feeling a little stronger and asked to go up on the mountain. I was pleased that she wanted to go but, in my own mind, I questioned if she was able. However, I didn't want to discourage her, for she had not ventured far from *der Ludwigsburg* since Christoph's birth.

I brought out old Diomedes, who I still rode to the farm almost daily. He needed regular work to keep his joints limber and to keep from getting fat. It was a fine day, with the air warming rapidly as the sun rose in the clear morning sky. Using a mounting step that I employed at home, Verena got up behind me. I immediately had a rush of old feelings from the times that we rode double on the broad back of Diomedes as fourteen year olds. She put her arms around my waist and squeezed in close to my back.

We rode out to the base of the mountain, passing small houses where women were out working in their gardens. Roses, blood red, were in profusion everywhere. Flowers of other hues were also in full bloom, some scattered about in the meadows and others clustered together on bushes. We came upon a herd of goats crossing the road, going from one pasture to another, and there were several young kids, only a couple of months old. The spring in their little steps seemed so light that at any moment they could have taken flight. The sound of their bleating as they scampered around their mothers echoed against my memories of both home and those far away in the Aegean. "Do you miss it?" I asked Verena.

"A little," she answered, knowing that by "it" I meant life on the farm and carefree summer days spent watching over her goats.

The countryside was cloaked in the new, rich shades of green, from the lush grasses in the meadows to the dark greens of the recently unfurled leaves on the trees. Birds, big and small, flew about, going about the serious business of gathering food for their waiting babies. Their songs, carried on the soft breeze, seemed to surround us.

We reached the little make-shift pen that I had constructed for Diomedes many years before, and it showed obvious signs of neglect. Some of the rails had come down, and clumps of brambles had grown up around the posts. I hadn't been going up on the mountain as much as before, my duties growing as I assumed more responsibilities from my aging father. The trail, always narrow and rocky, was unsuitable for riding and was also overgrown with brush. We left

Diomedes in the pen, happy as always to get to graze after a ride. I had a foreboding that Verena might not be able to climb the steep paths, but I was willing to let her try.

I suggested that we start out slowly to conserve our energy for the steeper climb near the top. Verena simply smiled and said, "all right," and took my hand. We walked at a languid pace in the cool shade of the densely forested slope. Sometimes we had to go singly to negotiate the path, with Verena placing her feet carefully where mine had previously gone. About halfway up the trail, I felt that she was beginning to tire, so from there we took frequent rests.

We were about two hundred yards from the lookout point when Verena's energy finally gave out. I said, "It's all right. We don't have to make it to the top."

A look of disappointment spread over her face. "No, I want to get there," she said with determination and got up from where she was sitting and started walking again. We had only gone a little way when she stopped again. Her shoulders slumped, and she was breathing hard. Coming up behind her, I swept her up in my arms and carried her. She didn't protest. Her arms folded around my neck, and her head settled on my shoulder. She was as light as a child.

When we got to the place where the rock juts out over the precipice, I set her down gently on the ground facing the lake. The familiar view, of which I never tired, spread out before us as for the first time. The colors that time of year are always so vivid on a sun-drenched day. The blue of the water, the greens of the forest, the whites of the snow-capped mountains in the distance all burst forth anew like they had just been created.

We were silent for a time. Eventually, Verena said, "When I die, I want to be buried in a place that has a view of the lake."

I hesitated in making a reply. Finally, I said, "I will be there as well. And we will both have a view of the lake."

She smiled faintly at me and nodded. Tears seemed to gather in her eyes, and she looked back at the distant mountains. "I fear I will not live long enough to see the man that Christoph will become."

That caused me great pain. Not only did the thought of losing her stab me in the chest, but I also felt the full weight of her sorrow at possibly being torn by death from her child. I wanted to reassure her that not only would she live to see Christoph grow up, but that she and I would grow old together. I hesitated. I, myself, had lingering doubts. That hesitation, I fear, conveyed more than words. I hurried to cover up my mistake. "You will get stronger. We will have a long life together. You will be a grandmother." But the damage was done. An uneasiness came between us for a moment.

Finally, as was her way, she broke through it. "What will happen, only God knows. But we will make the most of whatever time we have left. I am so happy that we were able to come here together once more. It is a beautiful day."

Rested, we started back down the mountain path. Going down was easier, and with frequent rests Verena was able to make it back to Diomedes. Once upon his back again, she settled into her familiar position behind me. On the short ride back to *der Ludwigsburg*, Verena said, "Do you remember when we fell asleep in the meadow and were chased by wolves on the way home?"

"Yes," I replied. "We stayed just ahead of them, thanks to Diomedes."

"That was the most exciting experience I have ever had. Something like that makes you feel so alive," said Verena in a wistful voice.

25

In the winter of 952 Adelaide and Otto had a son, who they named Henry, after Otto's father. Liudolf feared that Otto and his new Italian wife would change the line of succession to put the child ahead of him as heir to the throne. Liudolf convinced Duke Conrad of Lorraine (who was Otto's son-in-law) to join him in a rebellion against Otto. Never before had my father and I had to choose between our loyalty to Otto and the Duke of Swabia. When Liudolf and Conrad moved against Otto's brother Henry, Duke of Bavaria, my father and I talked about what we should do. After some discussion, I convinced him that we should stay out the conflict. I felt that there would be plenty of time to get involved if fighting came to Swabia. To me, it was a family matter and would be resolved quickly.

Also that winter, a great sickness spread through the town that claimed many lives. In February, Verena's mother fell ill. Verena went to the house daily to care for her. I was deeply concerned about Verena's health since she was so frail, but what could I do? Her mother was gravely ill. Verena could not have been persuaded to stay away, and I would not have asked her to. Indeed, Verena seemed to gather strength from being needed and actually showed more vitality at that time than I had seen from her in months. The days of her mother's illness turned into weeks, but gradually, the woman's condition seemed to improve, and it appeared that she was out of the worst of it. Verena returned home in good spirits, saying that her mother was sitting up and talking and sipping broth. Verena's eyes were radiant as she talked about her mother and how our prayers had brought her back from the brink of death. She slept more deeply that night than she had since her mother had first fallen ill.

The next day, Verena seemed tired and went back to bed after having a little food. She spent most of the day in bed, but we thought she just needed extra rest after all of her exertions. However, by the next day, she had a fever and could not keep any food down. She was chilled and shook uncontrollably. All of the strength that she could have used to fight off the illness had been expended nursing her mother, and she had none left for herself. The horrible sickness progressed rapidly, and it soon became apparent that death was near.

Christoph, only two years old, would remember nothing about his mother's last days. Near the end, I brought him in to see her. She was too weak to hold him, but her eyes showed a flicker of gladness at having him near. Her fevered cheeks were wet with tears.

I sat by her bed during the final hours, holding her tiny, limp hand. I felt so guilty that I would live on when she would not. I thought of all the times that I was gone from her that could have been spent adding to our memories. Our time together was so short, and the thought of spending the rest of my life without her left me feeling empty and desolate. In her, I saw how good the world could be, and a world without her seemed dark and cold. God had returned her, his angel, to me once, and I knew I had no right to ask for that miracle again. I squeezed her hand and said solemnly, "I will find you once more, someday, and we will be together."

Her eyelids fluttered almost unperceptively, and her pale lips started to move. I put my ear close to her mouth but could not hear what she said. I kissed her softly, and then she was gone.

I had a small chapel built in a clearing about halfway up the mountainside where the priest could consecrate a plot for two graves. Through the trees, the shimmering waters of Lake Zurich could be seen.

26

Liudolf's rebellion was not to be ended quickly. It raged across Germany for two years. Conrad eventually made peace with Otto, but Liudolf continued to fight. His position weakened without Conrad, Liudolf retreated to Swabia just ahead of Otto's pursuing army. Liudolf appealed to the nobles (including my father) to support him, but by then it was obvious that the tide had turned, and his pleas were mostly ignored. Liudolf had no choice but to make peace with his father. After two years of turmoil which threatened Otto's power, the King emerged stronger than ever. Liudolf was replaced by Burchard lll as Duke of Swabia; Otto's younger brother, Bruno, became Duke of Lorraine, and Henry remained as Duke of Bavaria.

During the civil war in Germany, the Magyars had taken advantage of the situation by staging raids in Bavaria and Franconia. By 955, the invasion had reached all the way to the border of Swabia. A large Magyar army, camped by the

Lech River, laid siege to Augsburg. Otto left Saxony with his army in July and travelled south. He was soon joined by a new ally, the Bohemians, led by Duke Boleslaus, who, as recently as 950 had been at war with Otto. Another former foe, Conrad, who had joined Liudolf in the rebellion against the King, brought a large contingent of knights from Franconia. Adding two more divisions to Otto's army were the Swabians, many of whom had also recently fought with Liudolf in the civil war. The threat of the ruthless Magyars, who looted the countryside and burned villages, unified all the German people like nothing else could.

My father and I, leading our knights from Zurich, joined the other Swabians, commanded by Duke Burchard, outside Bregenz on Lake Constance. A rainy summer had given way to a hot, sunny August. The glistening water of the lake seemed to beckon to me. My many layers of clothing and armor were stifling in the sun. I recalled the days of my youth when I swam with my friends in the cool waters of Lake Zurich. Of course, nearly all of my memories of growing up were intertwined with thoughts of Verena and re-opened the wounds that I still bore from her passing. During such moments, the pain of my loss, always lying just below the surface, rose afresh in my consciousness. After she died, I thought there was no way to go on living with the emptiness I felt. And yet I did live. The sun came up each day, the seasons changed, Christoph grew, I worked, I ate, I slept. For a long while, I felt guilty that, for stretches of time, I could forget about the pain. I came to realize that even misery, while leaving scars, can heal.

Once assembled, our army, gathered from all parts of Swabia, crossed over into Bavaria and headed north toward Freising. Three divisions of Bavarians, under the command of Duke Henry, were camped outside the town awaiting the arrival of the Saxons, Franconians, and Bohemians.

In early August, all the components of Otto's army were in place, and we began to move toward Augsburg with about 10,000 men. But, from the accounts that we had heard, we would be facing a much larger Magyar force. Wary of attack on the open steppe before we reached the city, we kept to the forest on our march westward. On August 10, the Magyar horde took a position on the eastern side of the Lech to meet our advance. Otto deployed his divisions in a long line to avoid having smaller units surrounded by the fast-moving Magyar horsemen. The three divisions of Bavarians led, followed by Otto's Saxons and Conrad's Franconians. Our two divisions of Swabians, numbering about a thousand men each, were next, and the Bohemians were at the rear, guarding the baggage wagons.

The Magyars attacked along our front, engaging the Bavarian divisions. From our position at the back, we were still awaiting orders. Not long after the din of battle began to the west, we heard more sounds of fighting behind us. Burchard ordered us to turn, and we could see the Bohemians fleeing toward us, pursued by an enormous number of Magyar cavalry. I had been at the front of one of the divisions on the right side of our line, which put me at the rear of our defense when the attack came. I tried to rally our men to stand and fight, but by the time they reached my position, the flood of men was impossible to stop. Between our retreating soldiers and the mounted bowmen of the Magyars, we were forced to fall back toward the Saxons. My shield stopped at least one arrow, and another glanced off my helmet. I managed to un-horse one warrior, but most others raced by, pursuing the fleeing infantrymen. Finally, we were able to gain fighting formations again when we reached Otto's line.

The Magyar attack lost some momentum as the Saxons came up in support, and we held them back with bloody hand-to-hand fighting. Gradually, we became aware that our enemies were facing an attack at their rear. The

Franconians had flanked the Magyars and forced them to fight in front and behind simultaneously. Suffering heavy casualties, the Magyar cavalry withdrew.

The main Magyar army, infantry and cavalry alike, had abandoned the siege of the city and faced us on the plain. The Bavarians, who held off the initial frontal assault, marched steadily toward the Magyar lines. We gathered our forces behind them. The Magyar archers, positioned behind their infantry, rained arrows down upon our lines. Our armor and shields deflected much of this attack and kept us from losing many men. Otto had cautioned us to maintain ranks and not give chase if the enemy seemed to be retreating. It was a favorite tactic of the Magyars to feign a retreat and then, getting their pursuers to break their formations, turn and attack with their mounted archers.

However, with the Lech at their backs, the Magyars had not left themselves much room to retreat. When their lines broke before the onslaught of our heavily armored knights, many of their soldiers tried to flee back to their camp across the swollen river. The high, muddy banks collapsed and slowed their escape. The battle became a rout. The Magyar camp was located to the east of the Wertach and west of the Lech, and their army became trapped between the two rivers. We were able to capture most of their leaders and force a surrender.

The huge Magyar army, without its leaders, disintegrated into fragments. Many groups tried to escape to the east, but in order to do that they had to first travel south to get around our lines. After years of savage Magyar raids, the full wrath of the locals was turned upon these fleeing men, many of whom were captured and killed.

We began the ordeal of gathering the dead for burial. Among the casualties was Conrad, whose actions helped turn the tide of battle in our favor. It was he that had led the Franconian knights in the flanking maneuver on the Magyars at our rear that caused them to withdraw. He then returned his troops to the front lines where they were part of the frontal assault. During the battle, he was hit by an arrow and died on the field. Eager to make amends to Otto for his participation in the rebellion, he performed valiantly in battle and paid the ultimate price.

Gallows were constructed at the site of the Magyar camp on the plain between the Lech and the Wertach. If the Magyar leaders were expecting mercy from Otto, they were mistaken. All were condemned to die. On a warm August morning, while mist still hung over the river, we assembled to watch the executions. A large number of citizens from Augsburg came out to view the spectacle as well. They had suffered at the hands of the Magyars during the siege, and they were not to be denied their measure of justice.

The men were brought out, I believe there were about twenty in all, and stood in a line awaiting their turn on the gallows. Two at a time they were brought up on the platform to meet their end. The look of men facing their deaths is a terrible thing to see. Some wore grim and hateful expressions which they tried to maintain until the very end. Others could not hide their fear and shook uncontrollably in spite of their efforts at composure. In all, they seemed to me, like brave men, and I wondered if I would have been able to hold up as well if the situation had been reversed.

It is one thing to ride into battle, knowing that injury and death is possible, but trusting your own fighting prowess to get you through. It must be quite another to walk up the gallows steps with your hands tied and knowing for certain that what you see and hear and feel around you is the last thing you will experience in this life. I shuddered as I imagined what that would be like. To avoid the tortured eyes of the condemned, I watched the faces of the people in the crowd. There were some women there, and even some children. I thought to myself, 'why would a parent let a child witness something so horrible that I, myself, would never expunge from the darkest recesses of my mind?' Still, no one looked away. Two by two the prisoners dropped through the platform, snapping the ropes taut. Their bodies twitched and squirmed and then were still. We had usurped the role of God.

27

After the battle of Lechfeld, the Magyar raids on the German territories ceased, bringing about a few years of peace for us in Swabia. Italy, however, remained in turmoil, with Otto's vassal, Berengar II rising in power again. Liudolf, Otto's regent in Italy and at the head of Otto's army, died in 957 leaving Berengar to mount attacks on the Papal States. Pope John XII appealed to Otto for help. In the summer of 961, Otto responded by leading his army into Italy. He reached Rome in January 962 and was crowned as Emperor by Pope John. With Otto's and Eadgyth's son Liudolf dead, the King had his young son by Adelaide crowned successor and co-ruler.

While I was away from Zurich during the Magyar campaign, Helmut had been taken ill and died. On our return from Augsburg, Father appointed me to oversee operations at the farm. He insisted that it was only temporary, since he did not consider the position to be a suitable one for the son of the highest ranking noble in the district. My new responsibilities required me to spend all of every day at the farm. I would leave in the early morning and return home at dark, and the solitude of my rides there and back suited me. Since Verena's death my mood had grown sullen and withdrawn, and I generally resented any interruptions of my thoughts by intrusive conversation with others.

The farm, however, was as it had always been, a world apart for me. It was a world where I was able to experience the continuous cycle of life among the horses, which I considered somehow more innocent and natural and inherently good than humans. Each spring I saw them born and watched as they discovered the joy in their fresh, new lives. Each day I saw them learn and grow and pass through the same stages of development as I had seen with every other horse. I continued to observe how they learned, within the herd, how to communicate with each other. Every movement, every outward appearance of an individual, clearly carried its meaning to another horse. Those silent messages, conveyed so subtly, resonated throughout the herd so as to create a sort of group understanding of their world. Sometimes I thought that they didn't even require an outward, visible sign to convey their messages. Perhaps it was my imagination, but I thought I could see a reaction before a gesture was made, leading me to believe that they could discern each other's thoughts.

I missed Helmut. His gruff and hardened exterior could not completely hide the good man that he was. He let me hang around the farm and be a nuisance when I was a boy because he knew that I loved it there. He had given me an opportunity to train horses when I was still very young. Before anyone else would have, he trusted me to bring the young horses along in my own way. Finally, he brought exquisite happiness into my life with the gift of Diomedes and allowed the old horse a chance to be useful again.

It seems that so much of the direction our lives take depends on the people we meet along the way. Are such meetings providence, or are they just random? How do we know which ones will change our lives and which are insignificant? In any case, I was grateful that Helmut had been a part of my life.

The span of a horse's life, although shorter in most cases, is not altogether different from a man's. The stages of strength and vigor gradually give way to stages of decline. Although a horse does not complain of the various ailments that come with advancing age, the signs are nonetheless there. So it was with Diomedes. I had known for several years that his strength and energy had diminished, but he was still basically sound, and his gait actually improved with riding. One day, however, while riding to the farm, he seemed unable to pick up his feet as well as usual over the rough ground. Suddenly, he stumbled, and went to his knees. He struggled mightily to get his feet back under him and finally was upright again. We stood for a moment, and then went on, but the episode worried me. After thinking about it for a time, I decided that his riding days were over.

As long as he didn't have to carry any weight on his back, he was still quite comfortable in his pasture grazing with our other horses. He would still find the best places to stand, out of the wind and with his side to the sun to soak up its warmth. Often he would lie down in the grass to take the weight off his old, weary legs. Sometimes, when I would see him lying still for so long, I would get concerned and call to him. His head would pop up, and I would breathe a sigh of relief.

One day, he didn't come in at feeding time with the other horses. He stood by himself with his head down. He didn't come to me when I called. I walked up to him and spoke softly. His head came up a little, but his eyes were dull. I stroked his great head and neck and then put his halter on. I led him to a small pile of hay on the ground, and he took a few mouthfuls. "That's a good boy," I said.

But the next morning when I went out, he was lying by the uneaten pile of hay and I knew, somehow, that he would not get up again. I walked over to him and knelt by his side. His eyes, half open, were clouded over and saw nothing. I placed my hand on his neck which was stiff and unfeeling to my touch. A knot rose in my throat, and I fought back tears. He was the horse of my childhood and lived to see me into manhood. I was grateful that we had had so many years together. But everything dies, I told myself, and it was his time. I was glad that he didn't suffer long, and that I didn't have to bring about his end by my own hand.

28

The farm took up so much of my time that I had little left for Christoph. When he was very young, he was cared for by his nurses and my mother, and truthfully, I didn't know what to do with a child. I was very young when he was born, and I had no idea how to be a father. As time passed, I was scarcely aware of the changes that were taking place in him as he went from small child to young man.

During his early years, my dark and gloomy mood was incompatible with his childish whimsy. He didn't grieve for his mother the way I did, since he really didn't remember her. He wasn't a robust child. Instead, he was pale and thin, and stayed indoors most of the time. By contrast, I spent my days outdoors, even in the winter, only coming in at night when it was time for Christoph to go to sleep. Therefore, we spent very little time together. I'm sure that the child felt the great distance between us, but my coldness kept him from drawing closer. I could have shown more affection, but I was selfish and stubborn and had built an impenetrable barrier around my feelings that I would let no one breech. It is to my great regret that I let those years slip away without making the most of them.

When he was nine years old, Christoph was taken seriously ill. This was of grave concern since, even at the best of times, he always seemed frail. Suddenly, I was seized with the same sense of dread that I had felt when I realized that I was going to lose Verena. The strong, proud, arrogant wall that I had built around my feelings crumbled to dust. As I watched the illness stealing the life and the light from my son's small body, I felt helpless and desolate.

I sat at his bedside day and night, pleading with God to spare his life. I swore that if he could be returned to health, I would become the father that I should have been all along. I recalled the time that my father spent with me when I was young and how much those moments meant to me. How could I have been so blind not to see the needs of my own child?

During those lonely hours of prayer and contemplation, I began to see clearly the things that should have been so obvious to me. Christoph had none of the greed, and hatred, and envy of an adult. His world was one of discovery, and wonder, and imagination. Even when I had shown him the worst of my nature, he didn't show any resentment. Children seem to be born with the quality of forgiveness that is so often missing in adults. He seemed to need only for me to love him and share my life with him.

If he survived, I thought, and grew beyond childhood, how would he become a good man if I wasn't the one to show him the way? Perhaps, came the thought, I myself had avoided the specter of death by illness and survived the carnage of the battlefield for a reason. And that reason was to guide my son's progress into the world much as the mare guides the foal to its place in the herd.

Three awful days and nights went by. I hardly ate or slept. When I did sleep, I was tortured by dreams of suffering and death. Each time I awoke, my son's condition remained unchanged. He was so weak that he was unable to lift his arms to feed himself, so I tried to spoon a thin gruel into his mouth during his waking moments. At the worst of the fever, he grew delirious and thrashed pitifully and babbled incoherent words until he fell exhausted into sleep once more.

Sometime during the fourth night, a change took place that I cannot explain except by the intervention of God. When I touched Christoph's forehead, it was cool and wet where it had formerly been hot and dry. His covers were also wet with sweat, and on every part of his body his skin was cooler than before. The fever had left him, and by morning he was much more comfortable and able to sit up in his bed.

"I was very worried about you," I said. "You seemed so far away."

Christoph was able to squeeze my hand and give me a slight smile. "But you were with me all the time."

In the following weeks, Christoph began to regain his strength. To get him out of the dark, smoky burg, I insisted that he spend a part of everyday outdoors in the fresh air and sun. He had the pale skin of his mother and needed an infusion of sunlight to bring the color of life to his cheeks. Soon he was able to walk greater distances without tiring as much as before, and we ventured out into the meadows north of the lake. It was spring, when the new grasses hold so much vibrant green color and are intermingled with tiny wildflowers of white and pink and purple. Every sign of the changes of season, which I had begun to take for granted, sprang forth anew in my consciousness as I saw it all through the eyes of my son. The gentle south breezes carrying busy birdsongs swayed the tree limbs with their fat buds ready to burst open. Bees streaked across the tops of the grass in search of pollen for their hives. Small animals made fleeting paths through the grass that disappeared instantly. Everywhere there was brightness and life, such a change for someone who only weeks before was slipping away toward the abyss of oblivion.

I asked Christoph if he would like to go to the farm and see the new foals. And after a moment of wide-eyed astonishment, of course he said yes. We made plans to go the next day, and Christoph asked if we would ride double to the farm or if he would ride by himself. He had ridden within a small enclosure before but had never been allowed to ride away from home. I said that I thought it was time for him to go on his first real ride and that we would take two horses. Until that moment, I never realized how much he wanted to ride, so mindlessly I had lived my life apart from his. Equally surprising was that, until then, he had not been to the farm.

Once it was determined that we would go to the farm, Christoph bubbled over with excitement and could talk of nothing else. We left shortly after the sun came up, as was my usual practice. Summer was still at least another month away, so it was chilly as we started out down the road out of town. The surface of the road was soft under the horses' hooves, the freezing and thawing of the ground not long past. Christoph rode a bay mare which had somehow reached about age thirteen in spite of my still thinking of her as a young horse. She had calmed down a lot since the early days of her training and was a reliable mount. I rode the chestnut with the three white stockings that had been on the Slavic and Magyar campaigns with me. He had become my favorite when I stopped riding Diomedes, and I had grown fond of him. In spite of my attachment to this horse, I had resisted giving him a name. Perhaps it was a way of protecting my feelings from further pain, in the event that misfortune should befall him.

It is strange how a place that you see all the time becomes slightly different in so many ways when you see it with someone else. It was that way with everything I did with my son. The ride to the farm, always pleasant, became a new venture of discovery on that first day with Christoph. Of course the memories of Verena came flooding back since she was the only one that I had let accompany me before. But I somehow wanted Christoph to see in that countryside what I had always seen. And at the same time, I wanted to see it anew through his eyes. As we approached the chestnut grove, I said, "Up that hill is the farm where your mother grew up. She used to wait for me in that grove and then we would ride out to see the horses together."

He looked up the hill and then watched the passing trees. Although he was silent, I guessed that he was envisioning the image of his mother waiting there beside the road and seeing the pieces of the scene fit together in his mind.

We passed the trail up into the hills where Verena and I fell asleep in the meadow and then escaped from the wolf pack on Diomedes. 'Like being carried on the wind' she had called it. There were so many places, so many memories. 'Someday,' I thought, 'I might take Christoph to the places of my memories. Someday. Not yet. And one or two I may keep to myself.'

Up and down the winding road we rode as the beautiful countryside open up before our eyes – the forests and the streams, the hillside meadows and the deep ravines. Occasionally I would glance at Christoph riding beside me and see the wonder in his young eyes. Then I would look wherever his gaze took me and discover something that I might otherwise have overlooked—a patch of wildflowers, the pattern of bark on a tree, a tiny waterfall bubbling and splashing down a rocky slope.

I rediscovered what it is like to have a child's imagination. Christoph would sometimes point out to me a tree, or a rock, or a cloud that was shaped like something conjured up in his whimsical mind. 'How many more things were created in his fertile thoughts that he didn't even mention,' I wondered?

When we reached the place in the trail that overlooks the farm, I stopped as I always did to take the whole scene into view. I glanced over at Christoph as he stared wide-eyed at the gently rolling pastures before us. He turned to me and a smile filled his face.

As we approached from the south side of the farm, Christoph suddenly stood in his stirrups and pointed excitedly. "Look!" He said.

A group of yearlings were racing each other across their fenced pasture. One would lead and the others would chase. The leader would suddenly slow down, allowing the others to catch him, and then he would rapidly change directions, and off they would all go again. It was a thrilling sight and one that I never tired of watching, no matter how many times I saw it. But that time it was a little different. Christoph helped me see it with all the wonder of the first time.

We passed a pasture with new foals and their mothers. Some of the babies lounged sleepily in the lush grass, others suckled under the mares, while still others boldly explored a small area around their mothers. "I think there was a foal born yesterday. Let's see if we can find her," I said.

Near the barns, we found what we were looking for. A large bay mare was grazing peacefully in a small enclosure with a day-old foal at her side. The foal's new soft hair was reddish and buff-colored, and her large brown eyes were wide and bright on her tiny face. Her stubby tail swept back and forth as we approached. The mare eyed us warily but not with alarm, and I gently placed a rope around her neck and petted her between the eyes. Christoph followed close by my side. Gaining trust from the mare, the foal curiously approached Christoph and let him extend his hand and stroke her neck and shoulder.

As we were leaving the pen, I said, "It's good for the foals to be handled by people early in their lives. The Arabs raise their foals in the tents where they live to create a bond between the horses and their families."

"I would like that!" He quickly replied.

Christoph followed me around that day and watched with interest everything I did. As we rode away from the farm after a long and satisfying day he asked, "Can I come back with you tomorrow?"

"You can come with me whenever you want," I replied.

And so began Christoph's education about horses.

29

After the death of Verena, following a year of mourning, Father had insisted that I consider marrying again. He said that I would soon succeed him in Zurich and that I needed more heirs. I had no interest in finding a wife at that time and fortunately for me, the daughters of nobles nearby were either still children or already married. This allowed me to avoid the question altogether for several years.

However, the issue arose anew one day when father said that he had news from Raimund of Arnstadt. The name seemed familiar to me but, at first, I had difficulty recalling where I had heard it. Father could see that I needed more information so he said, "We stayed at his burg on our way to Magdeburg for the Queen's funeral."

The memories crept out of their hiding places in my mind. "Oh yes, and on the way back there was a big snowstorm, and we stayed an extra day," I replied.

"That's right. You may recall that Raimund had two daughters."

The images of two young girls playing in the snow emerged in my mind. A pleasant feeling stirred within me as I began to unravel long-forgotten memories of those two days. I seemed to recall thinking that the two sisters possessed great beauty, but when I tried to picture their faces I couldn't.

Father's voice interrupted my thoughts. "One of the girls, Svenja, recently lost her husband, and Raimund wishes her to re-marry. She is still of child-bearing age, and he thought that she would be a good match for you. Will you at least consider the possibility before rejecting it?"

In some faint recess of my mind there lay a small, sweet, memory of a fleeting, youthful, infatuated moment with Svenja, the fair-haired older sister. I suddenly had a curious desire to find out what she looked like now that she was no longer a child. "I'll think about it," I said.

For several days afterwards, that discussion with Father kept intruding into my thoughts. I was strangely intrigued with the idea of meeting the beguiling

Svenja once again. Of course, I kept reminding myself, she could have grown fat and hideous in the ensuing years. But my curiosity about her had been aroused, and I finally decided to go to Arnstadt and see her.

The journey to Arnstadt was a long one, requiring nearly a full week in the saddle. I asked Walther to accompany me, and he readily agreed. Walther was first and foremost a knight. Without battles to fight, he grew bored and quarrelsome. Many years before, when father first assigned him to me, it was primarily for my protection. The relationship became one of mentor and then companion. Finally, as I got older and my responsibilities grew, Walther was my closest friend and advisor. That summer he was in his forties and had, for some time, begun to show signs of age and the effects of many battles fought. Each year he moved a little slower and with less ease. At first, I kidded him about the little groans and grimaces that he made doing routine things, but I could see that it bothered him so I eventually stopped. He had fathered six children, four of which survived childhood, and the youngest, a boy, was sixteen and in knight's training.

It was late summer, and the ride was pleasant. I have always enjoyed travelling the countryside at that time of year. The trees were in full foliage and the fields were filled with crops. Fat cows, goats, and horses grazed happily in the pastures. Everywhere we went, the labor of the peasants was in evidence. One day, when the sun was high, we stopped to rest the horses in the shade of a small wood that was located between two hayfields. We watched as a line of men moved toward us, cutting the ripe second-growth hay. In perfect unison, they swung their blades across their bodies from right to left, together producing a clean cut. When they reached the edge of the field, the foreman called a halt to the work. Not far from where we were, wagons had been brought out by the wives of the hay-cutters, and they bore bread and beer. The men sat in the shade of the trees as the women and some of the older children passed among them with the food and drink. All in the group had seen us, and we got an occasional glance from some of them but nothing more.

After a short time, a stout woman and a girl of about twelve came timidly over to us with two chunks of bread and two bowls of beer. They wore heavily soiled, ragged dresses, and the woman's forehead was dripping with sweat. She had probably spent the morning next to an oven baking bread. Both had sun-reddened cheeks, which was more becoming on the twelve-year old's fresh skin than on the wrinkled and weather-worn face of the woman. The bread was soft and warm, and the strong beer helped satisfy our thirst. I offered the woman a silver coin. She shook her head and said, "It is not necessary to pay for something that we would share with any traveler." With that they turned and walked back to the others. The girl looked back over her shoulder at us and smiled.

The scene with the hay-cutters was one repeated similarly countless times across the countryside. Everywhere the bounty of the land, brought forth by the labor of the peasants, provided for all, noble and serf alike. I thought how good it would be if those men, in harmony with the cycles of nature, could live their lives in peace, and never have to go fight in a distant land, or see their villages and fields burned by raiders.

We arrived in Arnstadt in the late afternoon and were shown into the great hall of Raimund's burg. He had just returned from hunting with his dogs and seemed happy to see us. "Your arrival could not have come at a better time," he said. "I have had a successful hunt, and we will prepare a fine meal tonight in your honor."

The meal was indeed a fine one, with several kinds of roasted meat served, along with fresh bread, cheese, and even apples. Before the food was brought to us, however, I had a vague sense of apprehension about the evening. Although not expressly stated, the purpose of our visit was for me to meet Raimund's daughter and consider her for marriage. Walther commented that I seemed distracted, and I assuredly was, with my mind imagining so many possibilities resulting from the whole affair. At one point I even regretted going at all. I longed to be back home with my son and my horses and without the weight of such a decision hanging over me.

When Svenja finally appeared in the great hall, at least some of my apprehensions disappeared. The woman that displaced the pretty young girl in my mind was, in fact, lovely. As the slender, tightly furled bud becomes a full, brilliant flower, so had Svenja blossomed. The fair skin and billows of blonde hair remained. Her shape, although fuller, was still pleasing. She walked with more dignity and grace than she did as a fourteen-year old, but her complete form was similar enough to stir a youthful excitement in distant memories.

My fears about Svenja's appearance were set aside, but new ones arose. I had spent no time in the presence of women, other than my mother, since Verena's death. I wasn't sure how I would act, or how I would be viewed. We were not permitted any contact that first evening, which was probably a good thing, since I needed time to process my thoughts. Svenja was seated next to her mother at a table on the other side of the hall from where Walther and I were positioned. When it did happen that we came eye to eye, a slight, shy smile graced her lips, and I felt somewhat relieved and happy after that. What a strong tonic – the smile of a beautiful woman!

After the women had retired from the hall that night, Raimund came up to me and said, "I would like for you to spend some time tomorrow getting to know my daughter. And then we can talk."

"It would be my pleasure, sir," I replied.

I feared I would not be able to sleep that night, so occupied were my thoughts of this affair which seemed to have taken on the force of a boulder rolling down a hillside. Fortunately, our day had been a long one and sleep came on rapidly. Just before I drifted off Walther asked, "What do you think of her now that you've seen her?"

"She is pleasing to the eye," I replied.

"That she is. What do you think you will do?"

"I don't know yet."

"If you don't marry her, then I will."

"You're already married."

"Elke doesn't have to know," he answered.

A brilliant sunrise ushered in a warm summer day. In mid-morning, I was told by Svenja's attendant that the lady awaited me in the small rose garden between the entrance to the house and the chapel. On entering the garden, the warm fragrances of the rose blossoms still in bloom filled the air. My eyes fell upon the small figure sitting on a stone bench set between rows of the thorny bushes. She was turned slightly toward the entry arch, but as I approached she rose from her seat and faced me. Almost immediately, her eyes dropped shyly as

I walked forward to meet her. I extended my hand and said, "*Guten Morgen*, Svenja. It has been a long time since we last met."

She raised her head, and I immediately fell under the enchantment of her beautiful blue-green eyes. She smiled demurely and placed her small, delicate hand in mine. "I was but a child then," she replied.

"A lovely child, and you have grown into a beautiful woman."

Her cheeks colored slightly and her eyelids dropped self-consciously. "You made quite an impression on two young girls on that visit."

"How is Nadja?"

"She is well. She is married and living in Erfurt. She has two daughters."

"And you have a son?" I asked, having already learned of it.

"Yes. His name is Georg."

"How old is he?"

"Six. And your son?"

"Christoph is ten…or perhaps eleven," I answered a little uncertainly.

Svenja looked amused. "Tell me about him."

I thought for a moment. "He's a good boy," I started slowly. "A better son than I am a father, I'm afraid. I haven't been around much. But we have begun to spend more time together. He has started to help me train horses. He's good at it. His manner is quiet and gentle, like his mother's…" I trailed off.

A silent moment hung over us. "How long has it been since…?" Svenja hesitated, "how long have you been without a wife?"

"Almost eight years."

"It must have been very hard on you."

I felt uncomfortable. But I found myself saying, "We had known each other since we were children. I didn't know how life could go on without her. But it has."

Another heavy moment filled the air around us. Finally I said, "How long have you been widowed?"

"My husband died in Italy about a year ago. I don't know much about the circumstances. It seems that there is always a war somewhere."

"Yes, and sometimes it seems so senseless. And so little changes in the outcome." I suddenly thought how insensitive that sounded and regretted saying it. "I'm sorry, I'm sure he was a good and brave man."

A slightly melancholy smile graced her lips. "We didn't know each other before we were married. He was older and had seen a lot of fighting. He had earned quite a bit of land, and I think he wanted to finally take some time off from being on campaign. He didn't really get to. We weren't together very much, but when we were, he was kind to me."

Despite the colorful blossoms in the garden and warm rays of sunlight that had begun to creep over the courtyard wall to create patterns of light on the bright green bushes, a veil of gloom settled upon us. "Would you like to walk?" I suggested.

"Yes," she answered quickly.

We walked through the arched gate of the garden and out onto the grassy hillside overlooking the village. The pale blue summer sky was fringed with a thin line of white clouds over the distant, dark mountains. A warm breeze carried the aroma of bread baking in the outdoor ovens on the other side of the burg. "I remember a snowman on this spot. Wherever could he have gone?" I mused.

"He vanished about the same time that you did," Svenja put in.

"He's probably with our lost youth," I suggested.

"I remember you hitting my sister in the face with a snowball."

I laughed. "I felt really bad!"

Svenja smiled broadly, and the light from that smile made me feel happier than I had in years. Then I said, "I remember being in a very small closet with you."

Svenja blushed and looked down. I reached out and gently lifted her chin so I could see her eyes. She tried to hide her crimson cheeks by turning away, but I took her shoulders and brought her back so she was facing me. "In the closet, we stood very close," I said softly. I brought her nearer and lightly enfolded her in my arms. Slowly, she lifted her arms and placed them on my back. "Does this seem about right to you or am I remembering it wrong?" I asked.

"This feels right," she whispered.

After an all-too-brief moment, we separated and both looked around to see if anyone was watching. If there was, they didn't reveal themselves. She looked up at me with the guilty, but pleased, smile of a child caught stealing sweets. "Perhaps we should keep walking," I said.

We walked down the hillside to the village below growing more relaxed in each other's presence. We talked about things so trivial that I would not have considered them significant enough for a thought, but with her, conversation came so easily that I found myself talking more than I had in years. Her smile, so shy at first, became more open and less guarded. Its warmth melted away the tension between us and the time passed quickly.

Neither of us mentioned our families' intention to have us wed. We both had the option of refusing the proposition, and regardless how appealing the union seemed to one, there was the possibility that it could be rejected by the other. When we parted after our walk, my mind was in turmoil. Under any circumstances Svenja was charming, and as soon as I left her I was counting the hours until I could see her again. But until that day I had had no intentions of ever marrying again. I asked myself how one morning could change a conviction held for eight years. There were moments when I felt that I should never have come to Arnstadt at all. I felt that I had trapped myself. By meeting Svenja again after so many years, I had perhaps raised in her an expectation that I could not fulfill. A rejection of marriage would be regarded as a rejection of her and that I could not bear. But perhaps, I thought, she would reject a proposal by me, and I could return to Zurich and resume my life the way it was. That, I almost convinced myself, might be the best conclusion.

Almost. The thought of never seeing her again caused, in me, a distressing ache. How could I have regretted a void only imagined? A void left by someone I had only known, as an adult, for a few hours? Once I had acknowledged that feeling, I recognized the loneliness that had been a part of my existence for so many years.

Someone would marry Svenja soon. That was assured. Perhaps, I thought, I could make both of us happy by being the one. But if I didn't make the attempt, surely, at least one of us would regret it forever.

That evening, any doubts that I still held about the course that I was about to embark upon disappeared as soon as I was again in Svenja's presence. Her beauty was unquestionable, but unlike most beautiful women, she seemed unaware of it. Her quiet, unassuming manner sought not to draw attention to herself for the sake of vanity, but rather from the warmth of her smile, and the kindness in her eyes emanated the sweetness of a flower that attracts the bee.

As I sat watching her during dinner but trying not to be conspicuous in doing so, apparently Walther was studying me. "Have you reached the obvious conclusion that even the slowest-witted man would eventually come to?" He asked.

I smiled a little and nodded. "Only I am unsure how she will answer."

"I'm sure you have nothing to worry about, Max. Be bold."

After everyone had finished with dinner, the drinking and talking continued deep into the evening. Raimund had a large number of guests at dinner that evening, such a gathering being a good way for the nobles of the district to share news with each other. While people were moving about the great hall to converse in different groups, I took the opportunity to rise from the table where I was seated and move toward the door on the opposite side. Svenja was still seated at the long table on that side of the hall, and she happened to look up as I was passing. I caught her eye and made a quick toss of my head toward the door. When I was sure that she saw me I continued out into the side hall where I waited for her to follow. I waited for what seemed like a desperately long time and began to wonder if she would come. Servants passed in and out of the hall as I stood there feeling very awkward. Finally, when I had convinced myself that she wasn't coming, she appeared in the doorway. When she saw that I was there she walked up and said, "Are we to play hide and seek in my father's house like we did on your last visit?"

"No, no hiding this time, although without Nadja in the game I might have a chance to win. I thought we could take a walk outside along the wall."

A questioning looked passed quickly over her face. Then she smiled, and with a little bow said, "I would like that."

I offered her my hand, and she took it without hesitation. We walked together down to the end of the hall and through a door that led to the outside. Once out into the night, we took the staircase up to the walkway between towers along the inner wall. A cloudless sky welcomed us. There was no moon, so the sky displayed a thousand thousand stars against the blackest black imaginable. Only at the horizon was there even the faintest light to silhouette the ragged outline of the mountains. Down below the hill, a few candles still shown as pinpoints of light in the windows of the houses in the village. The air was still warm, and the slightest of breezes ruffled the ringlets of Svenja's blonde hair as she walked along beside me.

I stopped and leaned against the parapet, looking up at the wondrous dome of sparkling stars. "When traveling, I find it comforting to look up at the sky and see familiar constellations and know that it's the same sky as I would be seeing if I were home. The stars are like land-marks. They keep you from feeling lost even when everything around you is strange."

"I've never traveled more than a hundred miles from Arnstadt," Svenja mused, "but I love looking at the night sky. I enjoy the constantly changing patterns of stars. It's like how the land changes its look with each season."

"I see mystery in the depth of the sky like I see mystery in the ocean. For example, what if the smaller, dimmer stars look that way just because they are farther away? And by comparison, the sea could be so deep that there could be creatures in it that no one has ever seen before."

"My father says that it's pagan to imagine shapes in the sky or to think of the forest as anything more than a bunch of trees. He says that we should just accept that the sky above is heaven and the land and animals were put here by God for us to use."

"And that the sea is just a place for men to catch the fish that God has provided," I put in.

"Yes," she answered a little apologetically.

"That's what the church teaches us. But why do we have the ability to think if not to look with wonder on God's creations and try to discover what more He has created that we have not yet discovered?"

Svenja was quiet for a moment. Then she said, as if confiding a secret, "Don't tell Father, but I like mysteries too. I go into the forest and study the trees and the flowers and the birds and the animals and I have so many questions! And I'd like to see the ocean," she concluded.

"Your secret is safe with me. And perhaps we can arrange for you to take a journey to the sea."

Svenja's eyes grew large but then narrowed. "Don't tease me."

"I'm being serious. Of course, it would be easier if we were married."

I watched as the expression on her face changed. I'm not sure what I had hoped for in making such a casual statement, but it wasn't what I saw then. She turned away from me.

I felt I had made a costly error in judgement. I had not given her a chance to prepare for the question by making the formal proposal of which she was entitled. Instead I had made it sound trivial and not worthy of consideration. I had done a beautiful and gracious lady a terrible wrong and I felt ill. My head pounded and my face was burning. "I'm so sorry, Svenja. I am awkward around women and I say stupid things. I didn't mean to offend you. What I said was not intended as lightly as it sounded. I wanted to make a formal proposal of marriage to you tonight and that just slipped out. By no means do I take your answer for granted. On the contrary, if you refused me, I would consider it completely justified."

I could sense that she was crying. Her little shoulders quivered and her hands were at her face. I sought more words to soothe her, but I had probably said too much already. The damage was done. "Can you forgive me?" I asked meekly.

Svenja turned back around. There were tears in her lovely eyes, but instead of the anger and remonstrance that I was expecting, she was smiling. "There is nothing to forgive," she said in a clear voice. "Now, would you like to make a formal proposal?"

It was like a gigantic load had been taken from me. "Yes!" I blurted out. "It is my wish that you would grant me the honor of being my wife."

"I gladly accept your proposal of marriage," she answered, with a little bow.

I placed my hands around her slender waist and drew her to me. Tears still lay like sparkling raindrops on her cheeks. Her lips were parted in a contented smile. I leaned down and kiss her softly, and she returned it with a hint of passion yet to come.

We stayed out on the walkway looking at the stars for a while longer. "From the time that you first visited Arnstadt years ago, I had imagined being married to you," she confided. "It was just a girlish fancy. I don't think I ever really thought it would happen."

We were married in Arnstadt a month later. We travelled back to Zurich with Svenja's young son, Georg, and lived in *der Ludwigsburg* with my father, mother, and Christoph.

30

In the spring of 966 there arose further rebellion in Italy against Otto's rule. It was reported that the leader of the rebels was Berengar's son Adalbert. Otto ordered Burchard into Italy to oppose the rebels, and the Duke quickly raised an army for the campaign. In early summer, my knights from Zurich joined the other Swabians outside the town of Munster, and then we travelled south through the Alps where winter was retreating from the mountain passes. Snow was still deep in the high meadows, but it was melting fast. Full streams coursed down the steep hillsides, and waterfalls plunged hundreds of feet over the rocky cliffs and into the verdant valleys below.

In the best of conditions, a journey through the mountains into Italy is a slow and treacherous process. In winter it is nearly impossible, but even in spring it is difficult. It is still cold, late snowstorms are possible, streams run high, and the trails are often covered with dangerous ice. Warming temperatures can start avalanches in the narrow passes where there is no escape. That year we were fortunate. There were no sudden storms, and our losses were kept minimal.

We rested our animals and replenished our supplies at Milan. There was no rebel presence in the city, and Burchard was able to gain information about the position of Adalbert's army. They were massed outside of Pavia, and had made one unsuccessful attempt to take control of the city.

South of Milan, it was like we had changed seasons. The cold mountain temperatures had given way to much warmer conditions in the low Northern Plain. For almost two days, the bright sun beat down on us from a cloudless sky. That was to change though, as the horizon darkened on the second day. That night, the heavens opened up, and we were deluged in heavy rain.

We made our camp on a plateau overlooking the Po River Valley. Often the spring rains in Northern Italy are heavy and go on for many days, and we didn't want to get bogged down in the floodplain. The days wore on in camp with unrelenting rain and wind making it difficult to even keep cook fires going. We were pinned down, but the heavy rains also prevented Adalbert from mounting another attack on Pavia. The long days and nights in camp with little to do gave me time to think about the enemy that we were to face. We were not fighting invaders from outside our borders, or even lawless raiders from within. The conflict was over the right of Otto, a German king, to govern Italy. Although we called these Italian nobles rebels, I wondered how Swabians would feel about being called rebellious if an Italian king imposed his rule north of the Alps. But it's unwise to think too deeply about such things. I had never known a time in which Otto was not king. The order and stability of the world in which my family and I lived was maintained by the loyalty of knights like me.

After six days, the rains ceased, and the skies finally brightened. We packed up camp and headed down off the plateau. Footing on the road was soft, and everywhere the streams and rivers that flowed into the Po ran high. But we made progress moving south toward the river where we expected to meet Adalbert's army. By the afternoon of the second day, the banners of the Italians were visible on the left bank of the Po.

Perhaps Adalbert had suffered heavy losses in trying to take Pavia, or perhaps when faced with opposing Burchard's forces, some nobles had withdrawn their knights, but the army that he had assembled did not match ours in size. Although there was a large number of infantry, Adalbert's knights were outnumbered nearly two to one.

Burchard rode out to meet Adalbert to negotiate. They met on the flat plain between the opposing armies on a bright morning in late June. I hoped that the Italians would withdraw without a fight and avoid a bloody battle that would cost the lives of so many brave knights. But it was not to be. Adalbert would stand firm, and we would have to try to drive them from the field.

Once the leaders had withdrawn, our two armies advanced toward each other. The Italians moved their infantry to the front to slow our cavalry, probably hoping to offset our superior numbers. We deployed in a wedge formation for the charge, and I was on the right wing of the formation. On command, we couched our lances, and I clamped mine firmly under my arm to brace for impact. My horse, encouraged by the thundering hooves around him, thrust his head forward and strained at the bit. It was all I could do to keep him, with one hand, from surging ahead of the horses around him. The enemy line came up quickly, and the point of my lance landed hard on an infantryman. Bones were crushed and sinews were ripped by the impact, and the weight of the falling body wrenched the lance from my hand. I quickly drew my sword and fended off the point of a spear thrust up at me. My shield deflected another spear. My horse was shoulder to shoulder with Walther's horse to my left. On my right, however, the gap to the next horse grew wider, exposing my flank as more and more soldiers rushed forward. My sword fell again and again upon the men on the ground inflicting terrible wounds. I glanced to my right briefly and saw the next knight in the line dragged from his horse. He had become isolated from the formation and surrounded by the sea of bodies.

Burchard had held back a division of cavalry to send in after the initial attack. When they entered the fray, the infantry lines began to collapse and fall back. Adalbert's cavalry had little distance to gain speed or room to maneuver. Although they fought bravely, they were unable to hold back our charge. Burchard moved our infantry up to attack the decimated Italian foot soldiers. After less than an hour, some of the Italian knights began to surrender, and others broke off and fled. We started taking prisoners as the rebels realized the hopelessness of their resistance.

Two of Adalbert's brothers were killed in the fighting. We captured six more known leaders of the rebellion that day. Others, including Adalbert, escaped. Our sources were able to identify several of them, and Burchard undertook a course of action to apprehend them. I was given two hundred mounted infantry, three hundred knights, and a hundred builders and miners and ordered to pursue a man named Baldassare who escaped with most of his men during the battle.

Baldassare had a two day start on us and was reported heading south toward his homeland in the mountains. Burchard assumed that Baldassare would return to his well-defended *castello* and that we would need a sizable force to extricate him. Thus, our pursuit was slower than it would have been if I had been traveling with just a few men.

The green and fertile Po valley gently gave way to the foothills of the Apennines, and we were fortunate to have favorable weather conditions. We passed through a couple of small villages, and although the inhabitants were not particularly welcoming, we were at least able to replenish our supplies without too much trouble. We arrived at larger town, Bobbio, on the third day, and crossed the Trebbia by way of a remarkable old bridge with eleven arches. From there, we headed east for another day, and at the end of a rough, winding road there came clearly into view the mountain summit where Baldassare made his residence. A small village surrounded the base of the hill, and vineyards propagated the nearby slopes.

On our approach, we were wary of attack, but since none came, we assumed that Baldassare didn't have enough soldiers to take the offensive. The forward observers that had been sent on ahead of us confirmed that the *Cavalieri* was inside the *castello* with all of the men who had fought for him in the Po Valley. We set up camp just above the village and immediately cut off all entrances to the fortifications so that no supplies could get in. Their water was supplied by wells, but we blocked the latrine trench that took wastes out of the compound. We were prepared for a long siege, if necessary, and we had to create as many hardships inside as possible.

I sent my herald to the *castello* with a message for Baldassare so that he knew our intentions were to stay until he surrendered to us. It simply stated that it was only he that we wanted but that everyone inside the residence would necessarily suffer while it was under siege. Briefly, I received a reply from him that said, in essence, that we had no jurisdiction in the region and I had no right to arrest him.

The fortress home of Baldassare was undergoing a change in its defenses. The older, wooden wall and tower were being converted to stone, but the construction was only partially done. This provided us with the opportunity to concentrate our efforts on the part that was still susceptible to fire.

At first, I wanted Baldassare to think that we planned to take no action but to wait him out, so we showed no overt activities during the day. I did, however, send my miners to the walls at night to dig deep trenches at their base. These were concealed with brush before daylight. After about a week, my builders began constructing a battering ram within sight of the walls to indicate that we were growing impatient and would soon attempt an attack on the main gate. By the time of their completion, our trenches had become deep pits exposing the underground portion of the wooden posts of the palisade. The pits had been filled with dry wood and brush, and each was set aflame during the night. The system of towers and walkways along the walls was inadequate to have access to all the vulnerable points. Our archers further impeded the defenders from extinguishing the fires from above. Fires were set in six separate locations around the wooden section of wall to compound the defenders' problems with fighting the flames.

By early morning of the next day, many of the posts were charred, but still standing. It would take many nights and many fires to breech the walls.

At the beginning of the third week, we had sufficiently weakened the base of the wall that I sent the miners with axes to finish fracturing the wooden posts. This process took an extended period of time, and Baldassare sent soldiers to prevent it. But we defended each position with a corps of knights, and the Italians were forced to fall back within their walls.

By mid-July, we were ready for a coordinated attack on the *castello*. We felt that Baldassare lacked the numbers to defend seven positions at once, so as the miners worked on toppling the posts of the palisade, the battering ram was brought up to begin its assault on the main gate. Patiently we awaited the first breech of the wall. When it came, a cry went up among the men. It was followed by another and then another. The ram fell heavily against the gate, and the sound it made echoed through the hills. Our men poured through each cataract like water through a mill run. Baldassare massed his infantry behind the gate, and in the courtyard stood his cavalry. The ram did its job, and the gate was smashed to splinters. Our horseman charged through, scattering the foot soldiers, and engaging the mounted force behind them. The Italian position was a strong one, and the fight to control the yard was fierce. However, by that time, the number of our infantry coming through the wall had begun to overwhelm the defenders.

Walther and I entered the *castello* through the main gate just behind the cavalry. The clash of weapons and armor rang out on the side of the mountain, and the bodies of men and horses lay strewn about the field. Baldassare fought at the center of the fray, in full armor and mounted on a large black warhorse. I was momentarily struck with a sense of admiration for his courage and fighting skills. His corps of knights was dwindling, and the circle of his defense was collapsing around him. Finally, with his cause lost, and his loyal knights in tight formation around him, I called off the attack. For a moment, the two sides faced each other with only the slightest of spaces separating their positions. The silence, in contrast to the awful cacophony of battle just a few minutes before, was strange. Everyone was waiting to see if the fighting was truly over and they had escaped death this time, or if the horror would resume. I rode forward and said, "*Cavalieri*, you and your knights have defended bravely, but to avoid more needless deaths, I urge you to surrender your sword. Your men will be spared."

Baldassare walked his horse up to me with his sword lowered on his right side and his battered shield by his left. "To whom do I surrender?" He asked.

"Maximillian, Knight of Swabia, serving Emperor Otto," I answered.

"My family and my men will be left unharmed?"

"You have my word."

Baldassare bowed his head slightly and handed over his sword, pommel first. I took it and handed it to Walther. Baldassare took off his helmet, and I had my first opportunity to see the man with whose apprehension I was charged. He was still young, with black hair and beard unmarked with grey. His long hair was curly and wet with sweat on the hot summer day. His dark eyes were tired and sad. I felt a tinge of regret that I had to be the one to take him in to answer for the insurrection. It would have been far easier to see him brought in by someone else. He had risked everything for Adalbert's cause. Or perhaps it was just as much his cause. I didn't know. But the siege was over, and we began the process of burying the dead and caring for the wounded. Life in the mountain village returned to a nearly normal state, and we prepared for our return to Pavia.

Baldassare asked that he be allowed to say goodbye to his wife and children, and I agreed to his request. I had them brought to the small house on the edge of the village where we were holding him. The dark-haired woman was dignified, but the strain of the siege and her husband's imprisonment showed its effects in her still youthful face. The children, a boy about seven and a girl around five, who did not really understand what was happening, just looked confused and apprehensive. I let them go in and see Baldassare alone inside the house. When they came out, the little girl was softly sobbing and had tears rolling down her cheeks. The boy's eyes were red and swollen, and he was angrily wiping his face with his sleeve. The woman's face, so contorted in anguish, was terrible to see. A tightness rose in my throat, and I had to look away. The three were escorted back up to their home in the *castello*. Baldassare would never see them again.

31

The unrest in Italy was not confined to the north. In Rome, Pope John, whose election had been approved by Otto, was removed and imprisoned by a group of Roman citizens. John appealed to Otto to come to his assistance, and Otto led his army to Rome to restore order. Otto's presence in Rome brought the insurrection to an end, and John was soon back on the papal throne. The rebellious citizens responsible for the actions against the Pope were hanged. The leaders of the revolt in the north, including Baldassare, were also sentenced to die. On the day of the executions in Pavia, I was taken ill and confined to my bed. I did not witness the hangings. I was told that Baldassare and the other leaders of the revolt faced their deaths bravely. Only Adalbert escaped execution. I heard later that he had fled to Burgundy with his family.

I saw Otto briefly as he passed through Lombardy on his way to Rome. We lined the road to salute him where he was to pass. It was a bright, warm, fall morning as we waited the Emperor's arrival. Over the nearby line of hills rose a cloud of dust that signaled the approach of his army. When it reached the crest of the hill, the sun reflecting off armor and weapons sent off brilliant streaks of light. Soon colorful wind-whipped battle flags came into view. Otto was astride a magnificent grey warhorse, helmetless, at the head of the procession. Then in his mid-fifties, he showed notable signs of aging since I had last seen him during the war against the Slavs. Although mostly grey and with more lines marking his handsome face, he still projected a quality of indomitable leadership. Indeed, the Emperor was at the height of his power. For the next five years he would rule the empire from Rome with Empress Adelaide by his side. Expansion pressed his rule further and further south into regions held by the Byzantines.

My service in Lombardy lasted almost two years. The time passed slowly for me. There was little for us to do there other than to keep order. Otto's fist had crushed the most recent rebellion and the two that had preceded it. The Emperor had learned that he needed to maintain a strong army in Italy to keep the peace. But peace translates into idle time for a knight. I, at least, was able to amuse myself by training my horse. Even that, however, grew dull when he started giving me the correct answers to my requests almost before I made them. So, I purchased another young horse to help pass the time. He was a black stallion with a narrow blaze and a little white on one forefoot. He progressed nicely, and by the time he turned three, we were taking long rides in the country outside Pavia.

While I was in Italy, Svenja gave birth to a daughter which she named Ilse. The information that reached me from the other side of the Alps indicated that neither Svenja, nor her child, were having any difficulties. That news was a relief to me but did nothing to help the frustration that I felt at being so far away and not being able to be with them. By the time I would see Ilse for the first time, she was nearly two years old.

In the spring of 968, I received word that my father had died. With a state of calm prevailing in Northern Italy and replacements arriving weekly, Burchard allowed me to take half the Swabian knights and return home. It was with a mixture of feelings that I left Pavia and began the long trek over the mountains. The news about my father was extremely difficult to receive. He was old, of course, and had a number of infirmities that had limited his activity and travel in those later years, but there was nothing in my memory to indicate that his end was near. It was particularly hard to accept since I had been absent for so long and could not be with him before he passed on. I had always had the feeling that I hadn't lived up to my father's expectations, and I felt that I would never have the chance to make him proud of me. We had seldom been in conflict with each other, and I felt that that was because my father let me follow my own path, even when he didn't approve. I always appreciated that, because it kept us from arguing, but deep inside, I felt guilty because I wasn't always sure what he wanted me to do, and I wanted to please him.

I had always fulfilled my duties as a knight but by the barest means possible. My father knew I didn't like fighting, but he never criticized me for it. I devoted most of my time to training horses, something in which he had no interest. He never watched me work with a horse that I was training, so I doubt that he really understood what I did. We had had very few conversations in recent years, even when I still lived in Zurich, since I had my own family to fill my time. I longed to talk to him one more time before death had parted us forever.

In spite of the sorrow and guilt I felt during the long ride back, I was glad to be going home. It had caused me great pain to be separated from Svenja, who made me feel happier than I thought was possible when we were together. I regretted deeply having been away during the birth of our daughter. I was anxious to see Christoph too. I had missed two years of his life. Two years of growing, learning, and discovering. When I left, he was just beginning to work with horses while I watched. Up until then, training horses had always been a solitary practice for me. I was surprised at how much I had started to enjoy sharing it with my son.

Whenever I would start to feel a sense of elation over being re-united with my family, I would be stabbed with the pain of reality. I was going home because my father was dead.

When I finally arrived back at *der Ludwigsburg*, a sense of dread came over me as I made my way up to the gate. It was only during the last hundred yards that the situation hit me with true clarity. There was a feeling of emptiness in me, knowing that my father wouldn't be there as usual. But my mother would be, and I feared the pain that I would see in her. However, the first person I saw, much to my relief, was Svenja. While I was still outside, she came rushing up to me, a radiant smile on her face, and wrapped her arms around me. We held each for a long time before either of us spoke. Finally, in a choked voice she said, "I'm so sorry about your father, Max, but I'm happy you're back."

She raised her head, and there were tears in her lovely eyes. They held little sorrow, for it was long past that, only a poignant mixture of joy and sympathy. "Come, we can talk later," she said. "Your mother is waiting in the hall."

After walking through the door with me, Svenja retreated into the background. She soon vanished from the hall altogether. Mother seemed as composed as ever. Her voice was steady and calm as she asked about my journey, the state of affairs in Italy, and if I had seen Cristoph yet. I said that I had not yet seen him, that I had come straight there and had only seen Svenja.

Her eyes, which seemed weary and sad, brightened a little at the mention of my wife. "Svenja is an angel. She has been a great comfort to me," she said with feeling.

"I am glad," I answered.

We were silent for a while, and then I asked, "How did it happen?"

"Oh, they found him by the creek in the little wood that runs between the wheat fields. We're not sure what he was doing there exactly, but it was a hot day, and he might have gone into the shade to cool off. He had his dogs with him so they might have chased something in there. They were still with him when old Josef and his son found him."

Mother's eyes began to glisten with tears as she spoke. "I suppose it's the way he would have wanted it, out walking the fields with his dogs, but it would have been nice if I could have said good-bye."

"I know," I said and put my arm around her shoulders. She cried a little, then quickly recovered herself. "You haven't seen your daughter yet!" She exclaimed suddenly. "Go. Svenja is probably with her in the courtyard."

As I was walking out of the great hall to look for Svenja, I felt a little relieved. Seeing Mother was not the painful experience that I had expected; it was actually somewhat comforting. And finding out that Father had died suddenly while out walking made me feel much better than when I had imagined him lying helpless in his bed awaiting death.

When I came out into the warm sunlight of the small courtyard, I quickly spied a tiny creature with blonde curls running about in the grass. Her mother was sitting a few feet away watching. It was the first time I saw Ilse, and from that moment on, she held my heart in her little hands. When she saw me, she stopped suddenly and stared with bright blue eyes at the large, dusty apparition that had invaded her peaceful world. She quickly scurried over to Svenja but not letting me out of her sight. I approached slowly and knelt down beside them. Ilse shyly buried her head in her mother's skirt. "Ilse," Svenja said in a reassuring voice, "this is your father."

Ilse finally looked up, and after studying my eyes for a long minute, let a small smile come over her face. "She looks like you, thank God," I said.

"Do you think so?" Asked Svenja. "I thought she might have your chin."

"No. She's beautiful. Just like you."

Late that day, Christoph returned from the horse farm where, apparently, he went every day. The change that had come over him in two years was remarkable. No longer the unsure sixteen year-old, finding his awkward way in the shadow of his father and grandfather. He appeared so much older and more confident-looking as he rode up the hill toward home, like I had done countless times in the past. I waited until he had dismounted and taken care of unsaddling his horse and getting it fed and watered and settled down for the night. Unseen, I watched from a distance as though I was observing my younger self. I had turned out my horse in the small pasture behind the stables along with the black colt that I had brought from Italy. Christoph stood at the fence for a long time watching them. When finally, walking from the stables, he saw me, a broad smile came over his handsome face and a little chill went down my back as I thought it looked eerily like Verena's. After greeting me with a strong handshake and a hardy embrace, he said, "I saw your horse, so I knew you were back, but you seem to have brought another one with you."

"Yes," I replied casually, "do you like him?"

"He's a fine animal. A three or four year old?"

"Three. I've worked with him a little. He's smart and eager."

"I will be anxious to see you work him."

"Actually, I thought I would turn him over to you."

"Really?"

"Yes, he's yours if you want him."

Christoph's eyes widened, and his mother's smile spread across his youthful face. "Thank you, Father!"

We had much to talk about that night and it was long after everyone else had gone to bed that we finally succumbed to our own happy weariness.

The next day we took the horses to the farm, and Christoph had a chance to work with the black colt. My son had a quiet, gentle way of working that made it seem like he was doing nothing at all. But the horse responded to him with smooth transitions between energy and calmness. Like watching two butterflies in an intricate dance between earth and sky, Christoph and the black colt moved around each other with the silent language of horses. Once in a while, I would start to make a suggestion, and then stop myself. My son was doing quite well on his own – much better than my clumsy efforts at the same age.

Svenja's son, Georg, was about eleven years old and being away for so long, I had had very little time to get to know him. He hadn't been old enough to remember much about Svenja's husband, so he was raised to regard me as his father. I had taken Christoph up on the mountain at a similar age, just as my father had taken me. I decided that it was time for Georg to make the small journey too.

As we started out on the trail, Georg was quiet for the most part, only speaking when I would ask him questions. The trail had narrowed a bit over the years, a result of my less-frequent trips there. As we moved a large tree branch that had fallen across the path, I said, "We need to come her more often and work on clearing this trail. Would you be willing to help me do that?"

Georg nodded thoughtfully. "I would be able to help you more if I had a sword."

I smiled. "Yes, you definitely need a sword. And probably an ax." Then Georg smiled.

Georg then decided to let me in on his observations, which turned out to be quite extensive. Hardly a tree, a rock, a nut, an insect, or a spider web was passed without examination. And each was accompanied by a lengthy discourse. As we moved at a plodding pace up the trail, the cool shadows falling on the soft cushion of leaves and pine needles under our feet, I thought about how different life seems for a man after his father dies. No longer the son, he moves to the top rung of the ladder, looking down at his own children scrambling up through the years in such a hurry. He assumes the role he always assigned to someone else, someone wiser, someone more experienced, and someone always closer to death.

At last we reached the summit, and there was the rapt silence that always accompanied the view over the lake, and the valley, and the mountains. I remembered what it was like to see the Alps from that vantage point for the first time, when I dreamed of travelling across them to lands then only imagined. Finally, Georg turned to me and said, "I love it here. I think this is my favorite place in the world."

"Mine too," I answered.

32

The last time I saw Otto, he was returning to Saxony after having spent nearly six years ruling the empire from Rome. There had arisen over the years, some discontent over the Emperor having been so long absent from Germany. I think that he wanted to make his return as highly visible as possible to the German dukes to re-assert his sovereignty, and that of his son, who had been crowned Co-Emperor by the Pope in Rome. At each of the stops in his journey, there were feasts and celebrations as the nobles paid tribute to the most powerful ruler in the world. Otto had brought nearly all of Italy under his control, and all of his former rivals, the Magyars, the Bohemians, the Danes, the Slavs, and the Byzantines acquiesced to his title as Emperor. He also had strong, peaceful relations with the Kingdom of France, Saxon Britain, and Muslim Spain.

Otto's route took him to Konstantz where he would be able to cross the Rhine, and the Bishop there invited all the Swabian nobles to a feast held to honor the Emperor. When I saw Otto that night, it took me a moment recognize the man that I had seen infrequently over the years since the Queen's funeral in Magdeburg. Even those individuals most favored by God with ability and power succumb eventually to the passage of time. His stature, always so imposing, seemed much smaller than before. His clear, penetrating eyes seemed more sunken and moist under iron grey brows. His face was deeply lined, and his skin was sallow and marked with blotches.

He received all the nobles in turn, and when I came before him he hesitated a moment as if searching his mind amidst clouded memories. "You were with us when we fought the Danes, were you not?" He finally said, as if coming out of the night.

"Yes, my King," I answered, pleased that he remembered me.

"And you were in Italy with Burchard."

I nodded and said, "And I was with you at Lechfeld in 955."

"Lechfeld," he answered faintly, his eyes no longer fixed on me, but on some distant image of the past. "That was a long time ago."

Otto's sixteen-year-old son, Otto ll, the only surviving child of Otto and Adelaide, was with the Emperor that night. He had recently been married in Rome. His wife, thirteen-year old Byzantine Princess Theophanu, was beside him. She was slender and dark-skinned with black hair and eyes. Although it was easy to see the beautiful woman that she would become, I never saw her smile, and I thought there was a slight look of sadness in her dusky eyes. Perhaps she was not completely pleased at being wrenched from her childhood to seal, by marriage, the alliance between two kingdoms.

I returned home to Zurich with a vague feeling that I might have seen Otto for the last time. The feeling passed soon after I got home and settled back into my life with Svenja and the children. But less than a year later, just after Easter, we received word that the Emperor was dead. Otto ll, just seventeen, had ascended the imperial throne. The young ruler declared a thirty-day funeral for his father. I travelled north to Saxony to pay my respects. Christoph accompanied me, as I had gone with my father for the Queen's funeral twenty-five years earlier. Otto's funeral was a magnificent celebration attended by the leaders or representatives of every land touched by the German Kingdom in some way, no matter whether they were allies or rivals. Young Otto ll, with his wife Theophanu, presided over the official functions, while Otto's widow, the still-young Adelaide, seemed strangely relegated to the background. When I studied her noble face, I thought a troubled look mingled with her sorrow. Fleetingly, I wondered if it caused her distress to have her influence diminished and perhaps see that influence shift to her son's young wife.

Finally, Otto was laid to rest in Magdeburg Cathedral next to Eadgyth. Personally, I felt a profound sense of sorrow. I had never known a world in which there was no King Otto. He had led us in battle against all threats against the German people, cultivated alliances with other powerful leaders, and forged a unified empire from all its disjointed parts. I remember thinking as they closed his coffin, "What was to become of us now?"

In 974, Christoph completed his knight's training. He had not yet been required to go on campaign and was not particularly interested in doing so. His interest lay in training horses, and he spent almost every day at the farm. In the past year, the young Emperor Otto ll had been constantly embroiled in family discord, dissention among the nobles, struggles within the Church, and foreign strife. But those troubles were far from our minds on a fine spring day as Christoph and I rode out along the familiar road to the green pastures of the horse farm. It was the type of day in which God seems at peace with mankind and gives us respite from the struggles against the world he created for us. On those days, He sends no floods, no snowstorms, no winds, no drought, and no plague.

We rode by the hillside fields where there were flocks of sheep being watched by children who, in their youthful innocence seemed, in their harmony with the world, to be more like the animals they tended than they would ever be as adults. Indeed, it seemed that among all God's creatures, it is man who has the most trouble adapting to the world in which he lives. The squirrels, the hares, the birds, and the deer feel no need to start wars over arbitrary borders, murder for political gain, or argue over who has the better right to govern God's Church.

Although I said that I trained horses, I have learned much more from them than they have from me. Horses not only adapt well to their place in the world, but they also learn, at a very young age, to live at peace with each other. From the herd, a capable leader emerges, and that leader makes each horse feel safe and at ease. Each individual knows its place in the group, and their mutual safety depends on their cooperation. Any success that I have in working with horses depends not on conquering the horse, but on learning to understand what makes it feel safe. Only then does the horse become my willing partner.

I felt certain that Christoph understood this, for it was in his nature. He had begun to see a girl from the village named Adele. She was a pretty girl, sweet and shy, and he was kind and gentle with her. On that morning ride past the

251

pastures, the millpond, the chestnut grove, and the hill where Verena once lived, Christoph said, "Adele asked me why I love horses. I had a difficult time explaining it."

I said to him, "I have asked myself the same question many times, and I never have an answer. Perhaps the truest love is one that you can't explain."

Editor's note: This was the last entry by the knight of Swabia which we know as Max. No other information has been uncovered about him or his family.

Tom Nelson lives in Central Ohio with his wife, Carolyn, and his horses. Carried on the Wind is his fourth novel, following Warrior of the Dusk (2012), The Paladin of Callendro (2010), and The Winds of Wharhalen (2008).

You can visit him at www.wharhalen.com

Made in United States
North Haven, CT
21 August 2023

40587096R00143